W9-BTD-590

life without summer

ALSO BY LYNNE GRIFFIN

Negotiation Generation:
Take Back Your Parental Authority
Without Punishment

life

LYNNE

without

GRIFFIN

summer

ST. MARTIN'S PRESS
NEW YORK

This is a work of fiction. All of the characters, organizations, and events portrayed in this novel are either products of the author's imagination or are used fictitiously.

www.stmartins.com

Library of Congress Cataloging-in-Publication Data

Griffin, Lynne Reeves.
    Life without summer / Lynne Griffin.—1st ed.
        p. cm.
    ISBN-13: 978-0-312-38388-6
    ISBN-10: 0-312-38388-6
    1. Mothers and daughters—Fiction.   2. Children—Death—Fiction.
3. Bereavement—psychological aspects—Fiction.   4. Grief therapy—
Fiction.   5. Psychological fiction.   I. Title.
    PS3607.R5484L54 2009
    813'.6—dc22

                                                          2008035891

First Edition: April 2009

10   9   8   7   6   5   4   3   2   1

For the children of my heart,

Caitlin Mary and Stephen Reeves

O summer day beside the joyous sea!
O summer day so wonderful and white,
So full of gladness and so full of pain!
Forever and forever shalt thou be
To some the gravestone of a dead delight,
To some the landmark of a new domain.

—HENRY WADSWORTH LONGFELLOW,
"A Summer Day by the Sea"

the

PART ONE

fall

day 18 *without Abby*

There's a thud as her little body collides with the steel fender. No scream. Just a soft sigh, a surprised breath inhaled as she's lifted from the ground only to be returned there. I hear it happen. I see it happen. And I wasn't even there.

Like the other twelve mornings I'd driven Abby to preschool, she skipped out to the minivan. Her backpack slung over her shoulders. It was so wide her little head of curls stuck up like a turtle's out of its shell. The only sound I heard that sun-drenched morning was her chirpy voice telling me to hurry. It was too early in the season to hear discarded leaves under her feet, though I wouldn't have heard them anyway. She was wearing her new ballet slippers, the ones she'd worn every day since I'd bought them for back-to-school. The ride to Bright Futures Preschool was only seven minutes, and she talked the whole way, wondering whether they'd start the day indoors or out. Neither of us could've known that the light kiss and fleeting hug she gave me outside the gate of the playground would be our last.

I've gone over and over every detail of that morning, thinking if only I'd kept her home because of those sniffles, or if only it was my day to volunteer. Maybe if I had changed one single thing about that morning, life would be different now.

I can't see how writing about it will help, but Celia says it will. My first therapy appointment was yesterday. I gripped the railing as I made my way down the steps of my farmer's porch; it was my first time out in two weeks. In seconds, I realized my capri pants and flip-flops were geared to the weather before—not to the crisp fall air that hit me in the shins as I walked to my van. I didn't have the energy to change.

I hoisted all 110 pounds of me into the driver's seat, which was positioned too far back for my legs. The van was cleaner on the inside than it had been in months. Ethan must have been the last to drive my Voyager, which no longer has a car seat. I reached under the seat to pull it forward, and my hand felt the stiff body of a plastic ballerina, the one Abby had been looking for weeks ago.

I held the tiny dancer to my chest and drove one town over to talk to a stranger about my life without Abby. Ethan wants me to see Celia. He says it isn't normal to sleep in Abby's bed, to surround myself with her baby blanket and stuffed bunny. I don't care what's normal. It isn't normal to lose the only child you have or ever will have. It isn't normal for someone to run down a four-year-old outside her preschool and not stop to help her, or tell her mother why this had to happen.

My life won't ever be normal again.

day 20 *without Abby*

Last night I slept more than two hours; I set a new record, three and a half. I wish I hadn't slept that long because when I woke up in Abby's bed, clutching Tootsie Rabbit, it took me a few seconds to remember. I wasn't in her bed because I'd fallen asleep reading "Wynken, Blynken and Nod," or because I'd comforted her back to sleep after a bad dream. No, this was my nightmare.

I hate myself for forgetting for a single second. I'm afraid if I could forget for a few seconds, maybe someday I'll forget for a few minutes, or even a few hours. I don't want to forget.

I slipped out of her bed and smoothed the wrinkles I'd made. I tucked the sheets, blanket, and spread under the mattress, instead of letting them hang to the rug. The new way I made her bed didn't look right. I was willing to make one small change in her room in hopes I could trap Abby's smell between the covers.

At the second-floor landing, there was no need to peek into my bedroom. The hallway was filled with visible dust motes, and the smell of coffee brewing told me Ethan was already up. My choices were limited. I could creep back into Abby's warm bed. There I could concentrate on the ache in my gut that came in waves every time I looked at the clouds I'd painted on her walls while pregnant. Or I could brave the frigid weather downstairs. I chose to drag myself down the uneven steps, trying to think of something to say to Ethan. In a matter of weeks, our conversations had gone from breezy to bleak.

He sat staring out the kitchen window, all expression washed from his face. He looked like a different person without the smile that reaches his eyes. After pouring myself a cup, I lightly brushed his dark curls with my hand to let him know I was there, and sat across from him.

"Do you ever forget, even for a minute?" I asked.

Now his eyes were deep in the bottom of his cup. "Not yet." He took a sip and put it down.

I didn't ask him if he wants to. I think he does. I'll never forget. I'd rather be pierced by the sword at the sound of her name than forget. Abigail Anna Gray.

"Did you sleep?" he asked. He reached one hand over to my side of the table. "I missed you in bed."

I brought my cup to my lips, desperate to avoid his touch. "A little. Aren't you going to work?" Dressed in navy pinstripes, I knew he was. I thought I could sidestep our new sleeping arrangement by changing the subject.

"I'm going to the police station first," he said. "Do you want to come with me? I could drop you back here before I head to work." His irresistible blue eyes begged me.

I sat up. "Did Caulfield call? I didn't hear the phone ring." Ethan leaned back hard against his chair. His shoulder slump told me what I was sick to death of hearing.

"No, *Detective* Caulfield didn't call," he said. "The last time I talked to him he said he was going to finish the interviews with the people on Beach Rose and the teachers, and then call us. That was four days ago."

I didn't miss Ethan correcting me for leaving out the word *detective*—as if I considered the one we got assigned anything but another stroke of unlucky.

I'd met Detective Hollis Caulfield only once, but once was enough to know I didn't like him. His junior officers beat him to our house to tell us an investigation into Abby's death was under way. Caulfield's arrogance beat him to my kitchen on his one-and-only visit. One that had to be protocol, since he had nothing to add to what we already knew before he got here.

No one saw what happened.

Three days after Abby died, Caulfield, in a blazer that didn't cover even a third of his bulk, hauled himself through my antique Cape. My house that had once been a home was filled with the sights, sounds, and smells of tragedy. Teary neighbors holding apple squares and crumpled tissues crowded our family room and kitchen. He gave them sideways glances, right and then left, over a pair of half-moon glasses parked low on his nose, as if he'd expected them to clear a path for him without even the hint of a polite *excuse me.* The din fell to a hush as everyone realized he wasn't a prince of a guy. Caulfield was police. I knew right then that he was a royal pain.

Ethan topped off my coffee, still waiting for my answer about going with him to the station.

"No, you go without me. I didn't sleep so much that I have the energy to shower, get dressed, and deal with him. If it's okay with you, I'll stay here. He doesn't tick you off like he does me, and he'll probably tell you more. He strikes me as a lady hater."

"I hate when you do that." Ethan turned his back on me, putting the pot back on the burner.

"What?" I asked. "Come on, you can tell inside of five seconds he's a man's man. He doesn't look me in the eyes when he's talking, and he directed all the answers to my questions to you. He called me *the wife,* for God's sake."

"So he's tough, you don't have to assume the worst. You're not going to help this thing one bit if you alienate him." Back when we finished each other's sentences, one of us would've rounded out the conversation with a joke. Some kind of *you know how Tessa can be* remark. Instead Ethan, the diplomat, finished it with, "Okay?"

I didn't like Caulfield. I wasn't going to promise not to provoke him. I would if I had to. All I was willing to agree to was a cease-fire with Ethan. "That's why it's better if I stay home. You go. Come back here and tell me what he says—if you want." It was the best I had to offer.

Our eyes were drawn to the movement outside the kitchen window. A squirrel pranced along the long limb of our maple tree. When he got to the rope that held Abby's tire swing, he jumped to avoid its knot.

Ethan leaned over to kiss my cheek. "I will."

Two hours later, he found me in the same place he'd left me. I was drinking cold coffee.

"You really should eat something, you're going to get an ulcer." He opened one of the four bakery boxes on the counter and handed me a day-old muffin with a paper napkin covered with smiley faces.

"Caulfield pushed me off again. I can't believe this is taking so long. He said the interviews aren't done. He's waiting for the crime scene evidence to be processed." Ethan swallowed. "And the autopsy results."

The one-two punch made by the three words *crime scene evidence* paled in comparison to the single blow that came with the word *autopsy*.

"I know. Wenonah Falls is hardly Boston." I started talking because thinking about a monster in a sedan was preferable to seeing Abby on a cold metal table.

"He should've solved this in a couple of days, whether someone saw something or not." I was pulling at a thread hanging from the oversize pajama top of Ethan's I was wearing.

"There wouldn't be anything to solve if it weren't for Abby's teacher," he said. "I still can't wrap my mind around the fact that she didn't count the kids on the way back from the playground." He tried to beat the wrinkles out of his suit coat with his hand.

I pictured Miss Janie with her perfect posture and her indoor voice saying it was only a matter of minutes between the time she came inside Bright Futures and the time she went back out and found Abby in the street.

Abby must have been dawdling, getting farther from the rest of the kids. She was probably humming and didn't hear her teacher say it was time to go back in. She must've seen a flower she wanted, or maybe she found a blue jay's feather. She always collected things, and she treated each thing like treasure. It's hard to believe it only took a few minutes to destroy my family. Abby doesn't have a bright future. I don't have a bright future.

"Tessa, honey, are you okay?" Ethan removed my fingers one

by one from the muffin I crumbled into smaller and smaller pieces. He brought me back to the kitchen, where we hadn't had an uninterrupted cup of coffee in four years.

"So what else did Caulfield say? Don't tell me that's it."

"He said he'll call us when all the evidence is processed, and he'll respond to anything new that comes in, but for now this is where things stand. He told me we have to be patient. We just have to wait."

Even as I did it, I knew I shouldn't be yelling at Ethan. He should've known the words *patient* and *wait* are sticks of chalk squealing down the length of a blackboard.

"That's easy for him to say, she's not his child. What good is waiting going to do? I want him to check every car in town. I want him to get out there and find who drove a three-thousand-pound weapon over my thirty-two-pound daughter."

In two staccato beats, Ethan put his elbows up on the table and rested his head in his hands.

day 22 *without Abby*

Rosemary and Matthew came over this morning. She knows Wednesdays are the hardest day of the week. It's been three weeks since Abby took her last breath.

I was in Abby's room replaying different scenarios in my mind, still trying to figure out how the accident really happened. I hate the word, *accident*. An accident is when you drop a plate or glass, not kill a child. I spend most of every day sitting in the rocking chair by her window. From there, just about everything is the same. When I get tired of sitting, I walk around and touch her things, and hold them. I smell her sweet little girl scent. Part No More Tangles, part Country Apple body lotion. Her dresses hang in her closet ready to wear. Today, I would've chosen the indigo jersey dress with the little daisies because the three-quarter-length sleeves keep her warm on cool days. I picture myself slipping it over her curly head, and then down over her bony shoulders and slim waist. I'd insist on tights. She'd fuss over the seams. Then we'd head down to the kitchen where she'd eat her Rice Krispies with three blackberries, while I'd drink my coffee and read *The Runaway Bunny*.

Rosemary tried to pull me out of my trance with her cheery mood and fresh blueberry bread. She wore pencil thin slacks, without a single wrinkle, and an electric blue V-neck, off the rack at Lord & Taylor. Rosemary is slightly taller than me, as dark as I am light. Her neat outfit the opposite of my stained sweatpants and sweatshirt. We've been compared for our contrasting looks all our lives. A comparison this morning would have been cruel. Rosemary looked just right, like always, and I looked like something was dreadfully wrong.

I never used to mind her dropping by. Now I'm sick of her pushing me to eat and get dressed, two of a million things I don't feel like doing.

"Come on, Snow. You'll feel better if you take a tub and change. I'll run your bath, and lay out some clean clothes. Okay?"

Really reaching, she dug up my childhood nickname. The only thing Daddy left behind. He called me Snow White and her Rose Red, his way of identifying his daughters born two years apart.

Rosemary looked around, her eyes settled on the miniature stroller that held Dolly. "I don't think you should spend so much time in here." The still life of my daughter's room pulled tears from her lids. "Why don't we go for a walk?" She wiped one eye with an index finger. "It would do you good to get out in the fresh air."

"Stop it," I said. "A bath and a walk aren't going to make everything all better. It doesn't matter what I eat, or what I wear." I wanted to shout, *she's dead,* but I saw Matthew playing on the floor with one of Abby's horses.

I love Rosemary, but when she's over I'm always on the verge of screaming. She treats me like a fragile heirloom. Doesn't she know I am the delicate vase that has already fallen off the mantel into a million pieces on the floor? I can't break any more. I hate the look on her face that says, *thank God this didn't happen to me.* She doesn't know I see it. She keeps it hard to find. I've seen it so blatantly on every other mother's face that I could recognize it through any mask a mother chooses to wear.

On the subject of things I hate: I hate when she brings Matthew, and I hate when she leaves him at home. When he's here, I'm mad because her baby's alive. When she doesn't bring him, I'm angry because she doesn't think I can handle seeing a mother with her child. Perfect Rosemary with her perfect Matthew.

Matthew didn't mind spending time with me in Abby's room. He patted the mane of one of her horses, as he crawled into my lap. "Auntie Tessa, where's Abby? I want her to come home."

Rosemary sat down on the end of Abby's bed, still holding her stupid bread. I buried my face in Matthew's neck. My skin tingled all over from the pressure of holding on to a real child. I was proud of Matthew for asking about his cousin, for saying how he felt, right out loud. He wasn't tiptoeing around it. He misses her and wants her back. Like me.

FRIDAY, OCTOBER 28   4:30 P.M.

I dug my journal out of the bottom of my briefcase and pivoted my chair to face the window. My office was overdue for a change, and the view of the park will be inspiring. It's good to be writing again. I love the feel of my pen gliding over parchment. With the turmoil of last year behind me, I'm optimistic I can be more consistent with my entries.

A new client reminded me how therapeutic keeping a journal can be. After only one session, she took my suggestion to write down her thoughts and feelings. I admit I was surprised. She's a freelance writer for magazines, but I didn't think she'd find the energy it takes to write from the heart.

Tessa's four-year-old daughter died in a hit-and-run accident outside her preschool. I knew when I read about the accident in the *Globe* and heard everyone from the bank teller to the mailman talking about it, that the mother of the little girl would need counseling. It's ironic she chose me.

She's so petite, it's hard to imagine her carrying such a heavy burden. Maybe it's her delicate complexion, or the way she wears her silky white hair caught up in that messy ponytail, but at thirty-three she looks closer to Ian's age than mine. Though she's certainly more confident than any teenager I know.

She walked through the door, shook my hand, and took the seat I reserve for clients. Within seconds, she kicked off her sandals, tucked her legs up under her, and began to tell me about her daughter. At first, it bothered me she had her feet on my chair. A minute later, I was more interested in her story than my upholstery.

Tessa's loss is affecting me more than I'm used to. A little child taken away from her family is the biggest fear for most every mother. Thank God only a few have to endure it. It wouldn't help to tell Tessa the pain eases with time, or that at least she had her daughter at all. Those are tired—some would say heartless— expressions.

They won't help.

I'm thinking of her all the time now. Driving home from here yesterday, her small picture-perfect face appeared out of nowhere. I forced the image back into its proper place, and concentrated on the winding road that leads away from that ocean and toward my home, in the shelter of tall pines and my new husband. It's best to keep sad stories confined to the office.

Then Ian's face took her place. I shook my head, as if I could toss the nagging worry from my mind. I can't let the fear of losing my boy lodge inside my mind, not even for a minute.

At fifteen, Ian's perfect. His wavy hair, sharp features, and height fit together in a way they didn't when he was a little boy. His lanky frame has him towering over me, and no one has ever said I was short. I think he's taller than Alden, too, but who's ever seen a stepfather and stepson put their backs together to compare? Though I've seen Harry a handful of times since the divorce was final, it's been weeks and by now Ian's got to be taller than his father.

Ian and I don't talk much about Harry. I try to be one mother who actually keeps her promise not to criticize her child's father in front of him. Since I can't talk about Harry without putting him down, it's best I leave the subject of Harry off limits.

Try not to put your child in the middle of your marital issues. Respect your child enough to respect his father. Sitting in my ivory chair, watching the rain pluck the colorful leaves from their branches, I hear the advice I gave with confidence to not one but two divorced mothers today. Like so many therapists, I find it easier to give advice than to take it.

day 24 *without Abby*

I saw Celia today. I didn't notice her icy eyes the first time I met her. Rosemary asked me the other day what she looked like, and I couldn't describe her. That first visit is pretty much a blur—like everything else I've done in the last month. All I could remember was how stiff she was, though her voice was kind of calming.

Today I looked at Celia and her office more closely. The first thing I noticed was how neat the waiting room was; two chairs were angled just right in front of a broad coffee table. Does someone line up those magazines, one on top of the other, or doesn't anyone read while they wait for her? No pictures askew on the walls. No plant leaves dry or dusty. The plaque outside her door that reads CELIA M. REED, PSYD, MFT looks brand new, or maybe someone polishes it along with the furniture. Vacuum cleaner tracks were still obvious on the rug. I had the sudden impulse to mess them up with my cross trainers.

Celia was surprised I took her suggestion to write in a journal. She must toss that idea out to every mother grieving a dead child.

"I'm a writer, so it seemed like something I could do. What else am I supposed to do while I wait for the police to find who murdered my child?"

"You sound angry, Tessa." Celia folded her hands on top of her lap. She made eye contact with ease. "*Murder* is a very strong word."

I almost said *am I paying you for this?* You don't need a degree in psychology to call that one. "Yes, I'm angry."

"Anger is an important first step in grief work. It's much healthier to express your feelings, especially the difficult ones. It helps you fend off a deeper depression."

It sounded canned and got me wondering how many times a day she had to say the same things to people sitting in my seat.

"Oh, I know how to do depressed. It's just that if I stand by and let a killer go free to hurt another child, what kind of person would I be?" I uncrossed my legs and recrossed them in the opposite direction. Her rigid pose made me move more, to overcompensate for her lack of it.

"Does the person who killed Abby even know he did it, or was the bastard drunk on a Wednesday morning in October?"

Celia leaned toward me, no more than a few inches. This must be Celia interested. "What makes the police think it was a drunk driver?"

"I don't know what the police are thinking, or doing. The lead guy never calls us to tell us anything."

Celia didn't rush to fill the silence. Her office had grown dark from a mass of storm clouds that gathered outside her window. Without saying anything she got up to turn on twin lamps strategically placed to the right and left of me. She waited for me to finish. I guess she's already pegged me as someone who has a lot to say.

"I can't think of any other reason a person would hit a child, and keep on driving. Who does that?" I asked.

She didn't have the answer either.

I'm not sure Celia can help me. She's caring in that clipped, *I know how to get close, but not too close* sort of way. She's nice enough; she even insisted I take her only umbrella, because of the unexpected burst of rain that let go right when I was leaving. But there's a lot about her that bugs me. She wore the same pearls and sweater she wore last Friday. She's a little too Mr. Rogers for me. Maybe I don't want to be helped. Maybe I don't want someone caring about me because my insurance company pays her to. Still, I go.

The house, once full of happy noise, television characters solving little problems, high-pitched voices singing contagious jingles—Abby laughing—is so dead quiet now. There's nothing else to do.

I'm not going back to work. I can't see myself interviewing experts about bratty children, or writing answers to questions about fashion emergencies. Imagine not really knowing the definition of the word *emergency*. How insensitive were we to title a column that? I wonder how many people have been disgusted by our thoughtlessness. I would probably tell someone off by saying, *If the only problem you have is whether or not to wear your leather jacket with your linen pants, lucky you, you son of a bitch.*

"I don't recommend making any big decisions at a time like this," Celia said. "Maybe you could push off some of your deadlines."

"Too late. I already backed out of all my assignments. I know I'll never ever want to do that again. Work is the least of my problems."

"You're right, in time your work life will sort itself out. I'm only suggesting you keep the door to your magazine work open." She smoothed out the hem of her skirt, even though it hadn't shifted since she sat back down. I covered a stain on my sweatpants with my hand.

"Ethan went back after only two weeks. I don't know how he did that. I told him we could afford it—at least for a little while—if he wanted to take a leave of absence. He said the first two days would be the worst."

I stayed away from him those first few evenings after he'd gone back to work. I hid out in my study, pretending to read sympathy cards, because I knew I wouldn't be able to stop myself from telling him how pissed off I was that he got on with everything so soon. Then one night, I looked out the front window and saw him in silhouette. He was getting his things out of the back of his car. Burberry raincoat. Laptop shoulder bag. Even in shadow, he looked worn-out.

It reminded me of the way he came home from work after Abby was born. He was more sleep deprived than I was back then. In the middle of the night, he'd be the one to go get her. He'd bring her to me for a feeding, and by the light of a tiny reading lamp, he'd hold her fingers while I patted and rubbed her back. The next morning, he'd be up on time and put in a full day's work. He repeated this five, sometimes six, days in a row.

"And were those first days as rough as you both thought they'd be?" Celia asked, her tone sincere.

"He never told me if they were." I was too listless to care if Celia thought I was a bad wife. As it was, I'd already been a bad mother.

"I don't even go to our old grocery store," I said. "I'm not going to put myself through it. Why should I have to look at the pity on their faces, and listen to more superficial *I'm sorrys?*"

"You might be able to avoid certain things right now," Celia said. "But at some point, you'll have to confront these painful experiences." She folded her arms in front of her. "It's not a good idea to hide from your life, Tessa."

Is Celia for real? These painful experiences. Hide from my life. She doesn't have any idea how painful it is to wake up every morning in my daughter's bed only to be reminded that my life is over.

No light, no joy, no love. No Abby.

day 27 *without Abby*

I'm writing in the dark by candlelight. I don't want it to look like we're home. I can't stand the thought of opening the door to children dressed like ghosts, or to candy-mongering teenagers who go door to door to feed their sugar addiction. Unfortunately, we live on a perfect street for trick-or-treating. The houses are close together. Sidewalks carry parents carrying children. There's no traffic on our tree-lined street.

I thought Bright Futures was on a perfect street, too.

Her first Halloween, we dressed her in a pretty nightgown with a princess crown carefully placed on top of her six-month-old head. She slept while we answered the door. Her second Halloween, she hid behind me, peeking out every so often to catch a glimpse of a fairy.

Last year, Ethan took her out around the neighborhood. She chose her own costume, a Cinderella gown, azure blue with silver sequins. She wore it the entire week leading up to Halloween and to bed that night. Weeks later I threw it away. I don't know what I was thinking. We didn't pick out a costume this year. She couldn't decide what she wanted to be.

On what would have been her fourth Halloween, I'm in the dark with Ethan. He's beside me listening to that ridiculous CD about men's grief. I wonder if Father Mike let him borrow it or if he walked into the Wenonah Falls Public Library and asked what they had on the subject.

Ethan. Abby's Daddy. My best friend. My tender lover. I miss him, but he's ahead of me on the road to the place that is life without Abby. I don't want to take the trip yet, and he's already left me to go there. He keeps turning around reaching his hand out to me. He wants to pull me to where he is. But like Abby used to say about Candy Land, "Mommy, you have to wait until you have the right card to get to the end of the game."

We haven't made love since before. I want him to hold me. I just don't want what goes with it. It's not difficult to avoid Ethan. I spend my nights in Abby's room, and he won't step one foot in there. I could go to him; sex might feel good. I don't want to feel good. After all we've gone through to have a second child— doctor's visits, scheduled sex, endless worrying something might be wrong—now the thought of getting pregnant is unimaginable.

So, alone together we sit, dodging our neighbors. Maybe they had no intention of ringing the bell. Who wants to be the one to remind the Grays they don't get to do this anymore? I thought about the two women I overheard this morning when I stopped to get my coffee. They were complaining about how they hate the cheap costumes, the trick-or-treating in the cold, and the ridiculous amount of candy. I wanted to get in their faces and cry out *You don't know what I'd give to have the chance to take Abby out one more time.* I didn't get in their faces. I did cry. All the way to the police station.

I took my grande black and went to see Caulfield. We still hadn't heard anything. Whether Ethan liked it or not, one of us needed to confront him about the progress of the investigation.

At the station, people were stealing stares at me while Caulfield kept me waiting his requisite twenty minutes. According to Ethan, it's always twenty minutes; not fifteen, not thirty. Just enough to give you the message you can't drop by unannounced, unless you're willing to pay. I know the type. He doesn't want anyone to get the impression he isn't busy. Caulfield didn't know it wasn't wise to keep me waiting. The longer I sat, the madder I got.

With nothing to do, I counted desks and detectives. Two rows of three mismatched desks, dark wood and chipped. With only three occupied, the officers there were drinking soda and leafing through folders like magazines. What I'd wanted to see were police officers running. I wanted to hear phones ringing.

When Caulfield came out of his glassed-in office, he was dripping with excess. His fleshy paw was holding his own oversize coffee. He could've eaten a doughnut off one of his gold rings.

"Hello, *Theresa,* how are you doing?"

He flicked each syllable of my name at me. I don't know what bothered me more, the thick pity that came with his baritone saxophone voice, or the fact that he still couldn't get my name right. I told him again my name is Tessa, not *Theresa.* His eyes, the only small thing about him, told me his inability to get my name right was intentional. He didn't know I'd interviewed enough people to know passive-aggressive when I see it. I knew he was trying to build a road block between those who investigate and those who grieve.

"Come into my office, we'll have more privacy there." He plucked a manila folder off the desk of a detective not much older than Abby, and gestured for me to go in. Then he closed the door and opened the file to the investigation.

His office looked and smelled yellow, a combination of a bad paint job and cigarettes. Before I sat down, I noticed two empty packages in his wastebasket. Nicotine gum and Good & Plenty.

"Let's see, I bet you're wondering how things are moving along." He tipped his head, looking down at me over his glasses. "Sad to say, there isn't much to go on. I do have some forensics I'm waiting on: a bit of glass, some paint chips. But no eyewitnesses. No suspects, either." He sat on the corner of his desk. The only visible movement was the scrunching of his eyes and mouth.

"That's it? It's been almost a month. Why are things taking so long?"

"Like I told your husband, I'm doing everything I can. It's not a good idea to rush the folks at the lab. They get irritated if I try to hurry them along, and I need to be able to call in favors from time to time." He winked. "You understand."

If my arm wasn't so short and his head so far from my seat, I would've smacked him right across his Jay Leno jaw.

"Why can't you ask them for a favor in our case?" I felt a rush of color heat my face. I turned from him, hoping he wouldn't notice he was getting to me.

In the corner of the room, two boxes sat on the floor. I'd heard he was nearing retirement. Though I wished he was drinking a Guinness by some fairway in Florida already, I knew I needed him to find out who'd done this to Abby.

He took off his half-moons, and stuffed them into his breast pocket. "This has got to be the hardest part of my job." He paused. "Sometimes no matter how much we want to know what happened, we just don't have enough evidence. I am so sorry."

"So then what's your plan, detective? You're not telling me you're done investigating the death of my little girl, are you?" I scrunched up my own features to mirror his insincerity.

"I know you'd like me to check out every car in Wenonah," he said. "I can't do that. You understand." He crossed one thick hairy arm over the other, telling me our conversation was almost over.

I moved to the edge of my seat. I clutched my messenger bag and jean jacket to my stomach. "No. I don't understand. I want you to do whatever it takes. Maybe you need some help. Are the state troopers involved yet?"

I was talking loud and fast, thinking maybe I could show him how to be urgent. He stared at me like I was crazy, which made me madder.

"You are planning to get help from people who know how to investigate these kinds of cases, right? After all, you've been a cop in Wenonah your entire career. This might be a little too complicated for you."

He just sat there, so I stood up. "You know, detective, I have contacts at the *Globe* and the *Herald.* If I have to, I can keep this story front and center, along with your inability to solve it. The public loves an unsolved mystery. Especially one about a dead child and her grieving mother."

Caulfield looked beyond me and nodded his head. I saw two shadows move up the rows of desks toward his office door. They reminded me of the suits that had moved up the pews of the church toward Abby's little white casket. Caulfield heaved himself off the desk and opened the glass door.

His voice was low and loud. "Now, now. Of course, we've involved the proper authorities. I'm not saying it's over. You're going to have to be patient. You certainly don't want to sound like you're threatening me, *Theresa.* This must be your grief talking."

"No, detective. This is *me* talking. Find out who killed my daughter. Or turn the case over to someone who can."

Without anyone escorting me out, I tried to leave the place with force. Fighting to get one arm through my jacket, I dropped my bag. The young detective sitting at the desk outside Caulfield's door picked it up. After he helped me with my sleeve, he gave it back to me.

"We're working on it, Mrs. Gray," he whispered. "I swear to you, we're working on it."

They'd better be working real hard, because these men can't possibly know how fierce and long-lasting a mother's need to know can be. I'm not going to let this go. I don't care how much of a pain I have to be. Either they find out who did it or I will.

TUESDAY, NOVEMBER 1 **8:00 A.M.**

I've decided to keep my journal at the office. The only way I'll be able to write freely is to keep it tucked away in the top drawer of my simple desk. Safe from nosy eyes.

I've lost count of the number of clients who've told me how hard it is to resist the urge to read their child's diary or their wife's journal. To me it's taboo. Like opening someone's mail. No matter how curious, I wouldn't do it.

Harry would say I'm being paranoid leaving it here. Which I find amusing, since if I had to pick one man certain to give in to temptation, Harry Hayes would be my one and only. An open book himself, he never could understand my need for privacy. Lucky for me, I no longer worry what he thinks of the things I choose to do.

Alden, on the other hand, would never read my journal. We've been married three months, known each other for ten, still I'd put money on the fact that he wouldn't even be tempted. He shows me in little ways that he respects my need for space. Yesterday, he got home before me, and when I walked into the kitchen I saw he'd set out a china cup, and my favorite tea waited in a pot, resigned to being brewed. He'd piled my mail largest to smallest on the counter, not a single slit made by the letter opener we keep nearby. Next to the stack sat a package, obviously a couple of books. Without a doubt Harry would've opened the box. It's hard to say whether the promise of good fiction or the need to see inside would act as the magnet.

If someone had asked me a few years ago if Ian would read my journal, my answer would've been, absolutely not. Back then, adolescence didn't seem to have its talons into him yet. Now I'm not so sure.

Last night, like all the other nights since Alden moved in, I caught only a glimpse of Ian. Down the back stairs he came, through the kitchen, scrounging for snacks and then into the library to grab a dictionary. Without a word, he took the stairs in twos, back to his sanctuary. His room. His privacy.

I miss my boy who lives with me. Before I went to bed, I knocked on his door. I heard a distracted *come in* and opened the door to rumpled jeans on the rug, a sweatshirt's head hung from an open closet door, and a desk covered in loose-leaf paper.

"I brought you a cocoa. How's the studying coming?"

He had a crazy swirling desktop image blinking like a strobe light on his computer. Three programs were minimized. It didn't take a genius to realize he wasn't doing homework.

"I'm pretty much done for the night."

He leaned back in his desk chair and watched me hesitate to come in deeper.

"You can come in, Mom, you won't catch anything. Sorry, it's a mess."

I put the mug down on his desk and took a seat on his unmade bed.

"I hope you don't stay up here at night because you don't feel you can spend time with us. I know it must be hard for you having Alden here. Especially seeing him come and go from my room."

He put both hands out in front of his body. "Whoa, Mom. Too much information. I don't even want to think about you and Al in there, never mind talk about it." He started closing programs, not making the slightest attempt to hide his MySpace page. The one I still don't like, or have the password for.

"I know you don't like it, Mom, but chill. All I do is read other kids' stuff. I only add a comment once in awhile. Anyway, Dad said it's okay, as long as I only have kids I know on my friend list."

The screen went black, the room reduced to lamplight.

"I'm not overreacting, Ian, and I don't like disagreeing with your father. But he doesn't hear the horror stories I do about kids your age and these sites."

He didn't roll his eyes. He didn't sigh.

"Do I get any points for not hiding it from you?" His smile was halfhearted. It made me wonder when it was that I'd last seen one of his broad open ones.

"Yes. You know you're always earning points with me." I wanted to ask about Lacey. She hadn't been over to the house in weeks. A record for the soft-spoken girl who spent most of July and August curled up on my couch, strumming her guitar and singing. Ian insisted they were just friends, but the way she flipped her hair off her shoulders and laughed at everything he said told me otherwise. Instead, I stood up and leaned over him putting my hands on both sides of his head. I kissed his mane, the way I'd done every night of his life. "Promise me you'll be careful."

I went to the door, opening it all the way. Alden startled me. He stood there, his dress shirt and slacks looking freshly ironed despite his having worn them for the past twelve hours.

He didn't say anything and neither did we. Words weren't necessary for him to be the concrete reminder of Ian's parents' failed marriage. Without intending to hurt Ian, I'd finally managed to shatter his childish fantasy that Harry and I could ever repair the last ten years of damage that claimed our twenty-year marriage.

Ian's mute with Alden. This night was no exception. He didn't throw out an angry remark, or cast a hateful look in his direction. Instead, he simply pretended Alden didn't exist.

After I passed him, Alden reached to close the door to my son's bedroom, as if he'd arrived for the sole purpose of retrieving me. I wondered what Ian was thinking behind his heavy oak door as I walked to the room I once shared with his father, holding another man's hand.

WEDNESDAY, NOVEMBER 2 3:00 P.M.

I stopped at Harbor Liquors on my lunch break to pick up a bottle of cabernet to complement tonight's dinner. I put it down on the counter and pulled a twenty from my wallet.

"Hey Mrs.—you and your better half having a party tonight?" The man behind the counter, whose face I recognized but whose name escaped me, put my wine in a brown paper bag with a whoosh.

"Excuse me?" I wondered what Alden was doing buying wine at lunchtime.

"Your husband," he said. "He was just in here, grabbed a couple bottles of Cutty Sark."

Harry was not my husband. Harry was still drinking.

All I could picture was Harry holding a glass. In fact, it's hard to come up with a memory of Harry *not* holding a glass. Unless I dig all the way back to the beginning when Harry's hands held other things, like the sail of his boat or my hand when we walked the beach.

The first time I saw Harry, he was sitting on the dock at the pier, his legs swinging back and forth, one and then the other.

Before I knew he sailed, I could've guessed he did. When I first looked at Harry, I thought summer.

Always tan, with sunglasses around his neck on colorful strings, he favored soft cotton sweaters and shoes without socks. Our first date, arranged by a girl I barely knew in grad school, I met him in the harbor. Living in a seaside town, I thought it was nothing more than a convenient place to meet. I had no idea he planned to bring me on board. *As You Like It* was a twenty-four-foot sloop stem to stern, though at the time it was merely a pretty boat to me.

Harry showed me the art of guiding the boat under power, not sail. Then he let me steer it, once we were a safe distance from the harbor and other boaters. At first I hesitated, not sure I could handle the expanse of the open ocean. By the end of the day, I was in love. I'd fallen fast for the ocean—and though I didn't admit it for some months—for Harry, too. Wrapped in mismatched fleece blankets, we talked about Shakespeare and Paley. The boat swayed to the rhythm of our conversation. He made me laugh like no one ever had before. Or since. What began as self-conscious, first-date laughter went out to sea and stayed there. Sitting on that boat looking back at the harbor, everything looked different and felt possible.

Now Harry's complexion's ruddy and his trim waist has given way to empty calories and empty bottles. I don't know why I hung on so long. It might've been better if I'd started my new life when Ian was younger, less aware of the destructiveness left in the wake of alcohol.

I left my memories of Harry in the liquor store and headed home with my groceries.

Juggling three bags, I opened the door to Puccini and caramelized onions.

"Alden, I didn't expect anyone to be here," I said. "I didn't see your car in the driveway." I dropped the bags on the counter in the nick of time. Only a roll of paper towels slipped out of one bag.

"It's in the shop. Nothing wrong, needed new tires. What are you doing home in the middle of the day? You ruined my surprise."

With his hands over the cutting board and the squint that comes from onions on his face, he leaned his balding head back for me to kiss it. "I'm making you something nice for dinner."

I put a box of granola and jar of almonds in the cupboard. Cottage cheese and skim milk in the refrigerator. He continued to chop.

"I didn't have anyone scheduled for noon, so I thought I'd pick up some things for dinner. I'm sure yours will be better."

"Why, because you don't have to make it?" He laughed. "My mother used to say everything tastes better when someone else does the cooking."

I didn't want to go back to the office. It was fun to play house with Alden. He'd tried to surprise me. He'd made dinner. Even Ian would have to admit that was nice. All I want is for Ian to respect him, like Alden respects Ian.

From the beginning, everything we've done has been aimed at being considerate to Ian. Our simple July wedding was our effort not to flaunt our happiness. Everyday clothes and an ordinary meal marked our union. No public displays of affection, no champagne toasts, no outward promises of undying love. Alden's move into our home was as gradual as Harry's departure was abrupt.

For a man who likes fine things, Alden's concession to keep most of his things in storage was a generous gesture. The plan to gradually introduce his things was an attempt at not changing the landscape of the house too much. All he brought from his home was a leather armchair, his impeccable clothes, and boxes that held his treasured history books. It seemed only fair to let him have some space to call his own. I hesitated to offer Alden anything that had once belonged to Harry. But Harry and I have moved on. Alden has moved in.

I packed up some of Harry's old books and let Alden take over half of the shelves in the library. He was grateful for the gesture and discreet about shelving his books. Neither one of us wanted to give Ian another opportunity to deal out the cold shoulder.

Alden started off strong trying to connect with Ian. The first time we included him on an outing, we took him to the Museum of Fine Arts. Alden suggested I sneak off to take in the Millet paintings, while he walked through the contemporary wing with Ian. It would give them a chance to get to know each other, he'd said. Later he told me it's hard to get to know someone who refuses to talk to you.

In the kitchen watching Alden cook for me, I wished Ian could see that Alden is a good man. He's not Harry, but I don't expect Ian to love Alden the way he loves his father. We have to be patient. Ian will come around.

With all the groceries put away, I put my arms around Alden from behind. "You didn't happen to stop at the liquor store earlier, did you?"

"I didn't," Alden said. "I think we have at least one Pinot in the wine rack that will go perfectly with this."

I pressed my cheek against his sweater. No, the store clerk hadn't confused my impossible-to-confuse husbands.

"So, are you going to tell me what we're having?"

"A scrumptious version of coquilles St. Jacques," Alden said.

I didn't think before I spoke. I should have.

"Ian doesn't like scallops."

FRIDAY, NOVEMBER 4   3:00 P.M.

Every client today has commented on the view from my office window. The predictable rows of ornamental cabbage and multicolored mums in the Verity Park garden are thriving, despite the brisk weather. Vibrant leaves are deposited on the ground in haphazard patterns. This typical New England scene, laid out over these windowpanes, would make a gorgeous watercolor. If I still did that.

It's not easy to forget the last time I plunged a brush into paint.

I'm always thankful for the view, even more so on the days I have a no-show. It keeps me from feeling confined. It's irritating to be in the office with a free hour and little to do to fill it. There's always billing, or client notes to take care of, but once I'm into those things, seeing another client is a different kind of annoying.

While I wait for my next client, I'll write about my last. Tessa's session was easier than I'd anticipated. At the outset, we'd agreed she'd be a weekly client. Every Friday.

I like Tessa's spirit, I do. She's direct and independent and passionate. It makes me wonder what type of little girl she was. I'd guess Tessa was a staircase of emotion, one minute up, the next minute down.

Her powerful personality doesn't frighten me. I've known the joy intensity brings to family life. Bright chatter. Infectious laughter. Light. It would be nice to spend time with an enthusiastic Tessa. One who smiles. One who's happy. She won't be that girl for a while, if ever again.

It's Tessa's dark emotions I fear. She'll go deep into the tunnel of mourning, and whether I like it or not, I'm a passenger on the trip. From our very first phone call, I knew what I was getting into taking her on as a client. I thought I was ready to ride.

Looking down on the parking lot that abuts the park, I saw her walk toward my office building. Like most clients, she was in no hurry to get to me. I wondered if we'd keep talking about the investigation. I hope she didn't see me cringe during her last session when she'd used the words *murder* and *drunk driving* in the same sentence. From the time of Harry's first arrest until the last night of our marriage I feared he'd hurt someone. Her theory unearthed my old fears.

I wouldn't mind if Tessa told me more about her husband, Ethan. Helping her navigate the gouge in her marriage is something I could do. I know a little something about fractured marriages.

After only two sessions, I knew she'd choose to focus on the agony of not knowing what happened to Abby. What she hasn't realized yet is that knowing what happened won't answer the question: why me? It's too bad she doesn't have another child forcing her to wake up every day, demanding to be fed and played with. Loved.

I don't think it was a good idea, her giving up her job. I tried to persuade her to slow things down, take it one day at a time. I've always been thankful for my work, this office, and my needy clients. It's my safety zone, the one I need to keep me from getting too attached to being a mother. Over the years, I've seen that it's the wiser thing to do. Far less dangerous than being swallowed up by motherhood.

When I first became one, I waited for the magical moment when I'd feel different. If it hadn't been for the horizontal scar running across my abdomen, and my protective posture at day's end, I would never have believed I'd had a child. I knew not to expect pixie dust, or shimmering light, or angelic music. I wanted the fairy tale nonetheless.

It took five years for me to realize I already had the charmed life I'd longed for. I had a healthy, happy family. Like every beautiful dream, I woke. Harry said that overnight I became overprotective. He promised me everything would be fine. I stood in grocery aisles scrutinizing labels looking for carcinogens. I bought multivitamins in bulk. I even tried single-handedly to instill a water purifier on the tap in the kitchen.

Parenting became a job to be done; a series of tasks to be completed, all aimed, like my work, at caring for someone other than me. Parts of those middle years are lost to me. I'm not interested in examining the kind of mother I was then. It serves no purpose to go back over it. My focus now is on how to be the best mother I can be to Ian.

Push, but don't push too much. Be involved but nurture inde-pendence. All these messages tossed out by parenting experts, simple to say, not easy to do.

Ian, my boy in a man's body, needs little physical tending any-more. Still, I make sure he goes to the doctor. Even working full-time, I manage to juggle the grocery shopping with doing his laundry, and we have a family meal most nights. I've accepted the reality that motherhood is sometimes a thankless job. You can spend your whole day doing everything with your child in mind, and he'll still find some small thing to complain about. Last night Ian took issue with the snacks I buy.

He stood with one hand holding open the cabinet door, as if staring into it would refill it with more appealing food. "Mom, can't you go a little crazy and buy some chips and soda? I get so tired of all this healthy shit."

I gave him my look, the one I use to remind him how much I hate it when he swears. I reached into a bowl on the counter and handed him an apple while I pulled a bag of pretzels from the cabinet. He took them from me and sighed on his way up to his room.

I try not to take his outbursts personally, because Ian never stays irritated for long. Later, while I sat in the library reading, he came to me; it was nice. I'd given up asking him to join Alden and me. He sat down on my ottoman, and awkwardly tried to make conversation, his signature way of apologizing.

"Hey, how was your day?" he asked. He looked at me but didn't hold my gaze.

"It was fine. I have a new case that's challenging. Nothing I can go into." I closed my book and placed it on the table beside me.

"How are things with you?"

Ian's hair, longer than I would've liked it, fell down his forehead. I could still see his eyes, almond shaped and outlined in lush lashes.

"I have something I need to tell you," he said. He picked at the ruby red cord of the ottoman where it meets the fabric.

"Is something wrong? You look so serious." I covered his hand with my own, and he started to relax his shoulders.

"Dad—"

"Well, look who's here." Alden's tone was a mix of pleased and put out. Along with his book and the glass of port he carried, came an onshore breeze so powerful it slammed the door shut on our mother-son chat.

Ian stood up and backed away from me. "Hi, Al," he said. "I'll let you guys get to your reading."

"No, Ian, you had something to tell me. Is something wrong with your father?"

"Yeah, no. Dad's fine. It's nothing," he said. "I'm having trouble in chemistry, that's all. Dad said I should warn you I might not do so good on the test tomorrow."

"Well," Alden corrected. "Shall I leave you two to keep talking?"

I couldn't tell if this was a generous gesture or a subtle one telling us to keep quiet.

Ian didn't wait for Alden to answer. He leaned down, so I could kiss the top of his head.

"No, I'm good. Love ya, Mom. Night, Alden." Then he took the stairs two at a time back to his room.

He came to me. He tried to talk. He spoke to Alden. It was progress, and I'll take it. It's too bad about the chemistry, though.

day 31 *without Abby*

Tomorrow is November 5. It's hard to believe I've lived through one month without her. I had my third session with Celia this afternoon. This time I didn't mind being there. It wasn't just that it gave me something to do. I like how her tidy office gives the impression that she's got everything under control. I like sitting in my navy-and-rose plaid chair looking out her picture window, talking without explaining the details. And even though she had on that damn sweater, at least she wasn't wearing her pearls. She asked me to describe a typical day to her. Before and after.

Before. I used to get up earlier than Abby and make coffee. When I put my feet on the floor each morning, I looked forward to the smell of the brew and the twenty minutes of solitude. It gave me a chance to collect my thoughts and plan our day together, when I would work on my articles and when I would get the essential housework done. Everything revolved around Abby. If it was a preschool day, I would write while she was at Bright

Futures. I would write again when she took her nap. On the days she didn't have preschool, we'd walk to Wenonah center to get a doughnut or go to the library. Abby loved her books. She was on a *Madeline* kick lately. We read those books so many times that even now I could recite them without looking at the pages. She'd always stop to count out the twelve little girls in two straight lines.

On those nonpreschool days, I would work while she napped and then again when she went to bed at night. She always helped me make dinner, even though a meal at our house usually consisted of scrambled eggs or English muffin pizzas. She loved to crack the eggs, and I never cared if she made a mess. Most nights, we ate without Ethan. Abby asked for him every night. I got tired of telling her, *Daddy's working.*

Abby never gave me the typical struggles I've heard other mothers complain about. She ate what I served. She slept when she was supposed to. Abby was an angel. Before. And now after, too, I guess.

After.

"What do you do all day now?" Celia asked.

I didn't tell her that I still get up early, but now I drink old coffee left in the pot from the day before. Instead of reading stories to Abby, I look for stories about her in newspapers. There hasn't been a story in the *Globe* for over three weeks. It's pitiful that I keep searching for details because I'm getting nothing from Caulfield.

Impatient—needing some information about anything—I dusted off my laptop and started reading online articles about how police use paint chip evidence to solve crimes. I didn't know there was a national database where samples are matched to thousands of undercoats, which helps to narrow down car make. If they have a big enough sample, they can compare it to the shape of a chip missing from a specific car. If I found this out by reading forensics 101, I hope to hell Caulfield knows it. He didn't tell me any of this when I met with him, and I haven't heard from him since. My scattered attention span and interruptions from Rosemary and Pam keep me from deciding whether I should call Caulfield to ask or go back to the station to find out in person.

Pam, the ideal neighbor, seems to be the only person who can bear seeing me disheveled and depressed, wandering room to room lost in thought. Tall, stocky Pam feels comfortable taking charge. She throws out the latest lasagna. She folds a basket of laundry. She talks about Abby. Pam doesn't think twice when she asks me about the investigation; she says whatever's on her mind.

Every day I spend a few hours in Abby's room surrounded by her things. I told Celia that Rosemary thinks I'm spending too much time in there. Ethan wants to put her things away.

"Ethan said he can't walk by her room without seeing her in there playing with her castle, or reading to Dolly. He said keeping her room that way is killing him. I need it to stay exactly the way she left it. Is it wrong to want to leave my baby's room alone for a while?"

Celia wasn't going to take sides. She glanced out the window, then turned her eyes on me. "Speaking of rooms, do you mind if I open the door a crack? It's getting rather warm in here. My next client is running late; there won't be anyone in the waiting room to overhear us."

I thought the temperature of her office was fine but nodded a go-ahead. She took off her sweater on the way back to her seat, and got right back to business.

"How do you feel about Ethan wanting to change Abby's room?"

"I'm mad, and kind of hurt. How can he be ready? I begged him not to make me put away her toys. Her clothes. I made him promise me he wouldn't take away what I have left of her."

"Did he agree to wait?" She picked at her thumb. Nail picking was very un-Celia.

"Ethan promised. But he said we couldn't leave it this way forever." She handed me a tissue even before I knew I'd cry.

"Some parents think it will be easier if they put away the physical reminders. They hope it will ease the pain that comes from constantly running into something that belonged to their child." Celia words were measured, her tone robotic, but she wasn't unemotional. "Other parents, like you Tessa, want each toy and trinket to stay exactly where she left them."

I dabbed my eyes. They kept filling and refilling with tears.

"Perhaps it would be better not to rush this decision. Some parents look for closure by putting things away. Literally and figuratively. It seems to me you're looking for a different kind of resolution," she said.

Celia closed my folder, signaling me that our time was almost up. She opened her appointment book. Her routine was to check to see if our next appointment was still okay by me. I nodded my head in agreement.

"Why don't you start to add some activities to your day? Ones you think you can manage. Maybe you could go shopping with Rosemary, or meet Ethan for lunch."

I guess that meant she wasn't thrilled with the report of what my days look like. Most of the time, we scrutinized my life before and after. The best thing I got from today's session was ammunition to keep Ethan off my back about Abby's room.

day 34 *without Abby*

I woke up in my own bed to water running in the shower. I can't remember if I chose to sleep there, or if Ethan moved me in the night. I decided to be ticked at him. Though I must admit it wasn't as painful to open my eyes to rich tapestry draperies and silver-colored walls. Our room doesn't hold enough cotton candy blue to make your teeth hurt.

My bare feet on the cold hardwood reminded me the weather's changing. It's raw and dreary, so I don't walk anymore. We used to love to walk the loop around the harbor, her little hand in mine. We would try to decide what color we'd use to describe the blue of the water. Sky or sapphire. Whether I'm inside or out, when I feel a chill, all I can think about is Abby in the frozen ground.

At breakfast this morning I mentioned it to Ethan. He rattled off platitudes about heaven and her being at peace, about how we're the ones suffering, not her. After yesterday's fight, I can't believe he dared to spit his religion out on me.

I was in a fugue state, lying deep under the covers in her bed. He called to me from the other side of the upstairs hallway. He wouldn't even walk to Abby's doorway to talk to me.

"Tessa, you up? I'm going to Mass."

I pushed myself to get up, taking my time with my bed-making ritual. He called my name again before I met him in the hallway. Minus the guns, we looked like we were about to start a duel. He in a cotton shirt and Dockers. Me in thrice-worn pajamas.

"I'd really like you to come with me," he said.

"I can't. I'm not in the mood for all those peace-be-with-yous or to be protected from all anxiety. And you know as well as I do, there's no point in waiting in joyful hope."

"Don't mock church. If you don't want to go, just say so."

"Surprise," I said. "I don't want to go." I brushed by him to head down the back stairs. My religion these days was my morning coffee.

I wish I didn't care that he still goes to church, reads those books, and goes to talk to Father Mike about loss. I know I shouldn't begrudge him his way, but we didn't lose Abby. She was taken from us. Ethan's trying to accept the cross God asked us to carry. Well, I don't want to pick it up. I won't ever understand why He asked me to carry this one. I would've been content with one child. If God had told me to give up on having another, I would have canceled every last infertility appointment and tossed my Pergonal in the trash. I swear I could've done anything else He asked me to do.

After Ethan left for church, I decided to start to look into things myself. I can't live with not knowing. Or waiting on Caulfield. Didn't Celia suggest I add some activities to my day?

On the family room couch, I wore the newspapers like a blanket. Instead of looking for new articles, I pored over the old ones, recording specific details in a notebook. I reread the articles from the beginning. Even now, it's impossible to believe those stories are about my beautiful daughter.

As I read, I tried to pretend she and Ethan stopped to get her a blueberry muffin after Mass. Or maybe they went to Rosemary's, so Abby and Matthew could play. Any minute she'd come skipping through the back door saying, *Hi, Mommy, I missed you.* And I would hold her so tight in my arms. Tighter and harder than I ever dared hold her skinny body when she was here. This time I'd refuse to let go.

It was hard to get past the descriptions of her lying on the side of the street and of doctors pronouncing her dead on arrival at the hospital. I realized how little information there is about what happened. In the paper, anyway.

Caulfield has to know more than he's telling me. The only information I can get out of the papers is that the car was going fast, and that it had to be a big vehicle, but not an SUV. Some detective was quoted as saying they could tell all of this from the skid marks. Caulfield hadn't told me there were skid marks. Just glass and paint chips. It couldn't have been a noisy car, because the old lady who lives in the house right there was home and didn't hear anything. My luck, she's as deaf as a post.

I wonder if the police have interviewed her once, or if they've gone back to see if she remembers anything else. Maybe she could be made to remember.

Then there's Abby's teacher. I haven't wanted to see Janie, never mind talk to her. She didn't come to the wake or the funeral, because I'd been adamant. I didn't want her there. Now I want to see her. I want to talk to her. I want to know what she knows. She was the last person to touch Abby's warm, soft body. I need to hear the very beginning of the story of my life without Abby.

There's friction in the house, again. Forever friction. Ian and I had words yesterday about him not going to church. In the last few weeks, he's either had to work or he begged for more time for schoolwork. His valid excuses allowed me to look the other way. Yesterday it became clear; he's taking a stand. As close as I ever come to raising my voice, I told him he needed to come to Saint James's with Alden and me. He took the classic child-of-divorce position.

"Dad doesn't go, so why should I?" His flannel pants and wrinkled T-shirt strengthened his case.

His thin body barely took up space in the library, his deep voice begged to be heard as an adult. While he spoke, I locked my eyes on the double picture frame behind him on the bookshelf. On one side was my little boy of eight, showing off his suit. Wearing white pants and a matching jacket, he posed for his first communion photo. On the other side was Ian last spring, in his red confirmation gown. I could almost hear him telling me his new name, Ian Francis John Hayes. He took the name to honor my father. I remember we laughed that day as he struggled to get the gown over his head. A smile emerged from the waves of fabric. When I looked at the real boy standing in front of me, his face was anything but sweet.

"Alden feels strongly we should go to Mass as a family." I lowered my voice and moved closer to Ian. I didn't want Alden to see me losing control. "You always go with us," I said. "You haven't said anything lately about not wanting to go to church."

"You've been a little preoccupied." His eyes darted to the hallway, where Alden was collecting coats. "Anyway, I can't handle it anymore. I look around that holy place and realize I'm sitting next to a bunch of hypocrites. I'm not going. You can't make me." He crossed his arms for emphasis.

He sounded like a toddler putting his foot down over bedtime. He was immovable, and his barb was well placed. Maybe I was the hypocrite he found himself sitting next to. I couldn't make him go, and I wouldn't argue. I went with Alden. Ian stayed home.

When we returned from Saint James's, Ian was in his room, presumably doing schoolwork. He ventured out only to have Sunday supper with Alden and me. A painful meal of lamb chops, roasted potatoes, and silence. It was easier to cut the lamb than the tension. After dinner, Alden took his sherry into the library.

"Ian, are you upset with me?" I asked.

He threw an arm over my shoulder and kissed my cheek. "Never was."

That was the last I saw of him for the day.

Alden said nothing about Ian's line in the sand over church. He has little, if anything, to say about family lately. When we met at the Faith and Reason lecture series, I told him right away I have a son. Over the seven months we dated, we talked about all things Ian. Alden was optimistic he could become a second father to him, or at the very least they'd be good friends. It didn't take long for him to settle into the more comfortable *he's your son not mine* approach. Most stepfathers eventually do. Or maybe he hates conflict more than I do.

I finished the dishes and brought a tray of oolong and shortbread into the library. "I made our favorite. Can we talk?"

Alden looked up from his latest tome on the Civil War, and the briefest look of annoyance crossed his face. He made no move to sit up but took off his reading glasses and put the tip of one earpiece to his lips.

"Sure," he said. "What about?"

"I really want us to be a family. You don't need to be shy when it comes to sharing your opinions about Ian. I'd welcome your support."

That part of the conversation went well. My mistake came later when I asked him to drink less.

"Ian's been through a lot with Harry. His drinking, the arrests." Apparently this feedback, along with my replacement cup of tea, declared the honeymoon officially over.

"Harry's behavior and mine have nothing in common. Just because one man fails to use self-control doesn't mean another isn't perfectly capable of using his. While you may not be able to draw a distinction, Ian, I'm certain, can."

Alden put his reading glasses back on and banged his belt buckle as he placed his book back in the reading position.

I can't think of one way in which Alden resembles Harry, and yet, there I sat on the furniture of both marriages feeling as diminished in one man's company as I had in the other's.

day 36 *without Abby*

I went to see Abby's teacher. I didn't want to meet Janie at my house or at the preschool, so I asked her if I could come to her house. Of course she said *yes.* She wasn't in a position to say *no* to me. I didn't tell Ethan or Rosemary I was going to see her. I didn't want them to talk me out of it, or come with me, or tell me not to bully her. I had no idea what I wanted to say. I didn't know if I'd be able to stand the sight of her. But it was time.

I drove to Janie's the long way; I couldn't bring myself to go by Bright Futures. The harbor looked lonely, most of the boats pulled out for the season. No tourists strolling, few fishermen working. As I got closer to her house my hands shook, I gripped the wheel. At one point I almost turned the Voyager around. I'll never understand why minivans have names that suggest you'll be traveling to the ends of the earth in them. Voyager, Quest, Odyssey. For God's sake, the mothers who drive them spend most of their time driving the same ten-mile radius, going to the same places day after day, week after week.

Janie's Cape, charcoal with white trim, looked so much like mine I thought maybe I had turned around to go home. The festive harvest decorations of pumpkins and mums on her front porch assured me I hadn't. She was waiting right inside the front door. I didn't have to knock. All my anxious feelings disappeared like the butterflies do when you finally step onstage. Her face looked like mine did on the mornings I dared to look in the mirror.

At first, there were no words. Just the awkward silence that I'm sure we both expected. Though we'd met three times before, each time Abby had been there between us. The times before had been filled with little chairs, sticky hands, and the music of children's laughter. Abby was between us still. This time there was heartache so tangible it hung in the air like fog. Until she spoke.

"I held her until the paramedics came. I stroked her little head and sang her that lullaby you told me she loved to hear when she was feeling scared."

She sang her our lullaby. At the beginning of preschool, I told Janie "All the Pretty Little Horses" made Abby feel better when she was sad. I thought if she missed me, they could sing it. I never imagined the reason she'd need to.

"Was she alive, even for a minute?"

"No, she—"

Janie's voice trailed off as her sobs took over. We held each other and cried for what seemed like an hour. However long it was, neither of us rushed it. When we finally composed ourselves, we moved out of the hallway and into her kitchen.

The table was set. Everything matched her bright blue-and-white beach house decor. There were too many seashell accent pieces for my taste. Maybe it was the teacher in her or maybe it's because she has young children of her own, but the kitchen had so many fall decorations it looked like the preschool. Cling cornucopias and Pilgrims on the windows, colored corn and gourds on the table. I could tell she spent nervous energy on making things look nice for me. She'd cut up fruit and made bread, knowing full well we wouldn't eat a thing. When she finally sat down, once again silence fell on us. Once again, she was the one to break it.

"I have a gift for you, Tessa." She folded and refolded her hands. "It might be too soon for me to give it to you. Or maybe you'll be angry I waited. I didn't know what to do. I needed to give it to you in person. I knew you'd want it."

I stopped her rambling. "Janie, what is it?"

She reached down into one of the chairs we weren't sitting in and lifted up a small basket made of twigs. It was pretty and looked handmade, though even as I looked at it, I knew this wasn't the gift. Inside the basket, lying on some store-bought straw was a tiny cracked robin's egg. Blue, speckled, and delicate. I looked at her, and though I couldn't believe there were more, tears ran down my face. I already knew what Janie would say next.

"She was holding the egg in her hand."

FRIDAY, NOVEMBER 11   **8:30 A.M.**

Harry showed up unexpectedly last night; at least, it was a surprise to me. He came to pick up Ian for the long weekend. It's been over a month since Ian slept at Harry's, and he didn't even tell me he was going. I was putting the final touches on dinner for three, when the doorbell rang. Alden offered to see who it was. I poked my head out into the hallway, only to be hit by Harry's unmistakable Boston accent.

"Hey, Al. How do you like my house?" Harry asked.

As Alden struggled to think of a response, I hurried down the hallway toward the door, pulling off my apron as I went. I wasn't able to stop Harry from pushing his way into the foyer.

"What are you doing here?" I asked.

"Well, hello to you, too, C. I'm here to get Ian for the weekend. Didn't he—"

Harry looked up the stairs when he heard feet dancing over our heads. Ian sprinted down by twos with his backpack hooked over one shoulder.

"Dad, I said I'd meet you at Birch Street." Ian shot Harry a look and sniffed. The child of a drinker is quick to assess.

"Birch Street Tavern?" I asked. "But I made dinner."

"Shoot, Mom, did I forget to tell you? I'm staying at Dad's for a couple of days." He kissed me on the cheek and breezed by Alden. "You won't even miss me."

Ian was out the door. Harry lingered. He elbowed Alden in the ribs. This time Harry sniffed.

"The meat loaf's great, but wait 'til you taste the scalloped potatoes that go with it. You're going to love dinner, Al," Harry said.

"Dad." Ian banged the door with his hand.

Before I even thought to offer them a ride, they were walking down the street. Harry, with six more months before he was legal to drive, had his arm around Ian's shoulder.

I could've gone after them, but I was livid with Harry for insulting Alden, and furious with Ian for not telling me he was going. The twenty-minute walk to Harry's rented ranch wouldn't hurt either one of them. The only good thing about the situation: Harry was sober.

While I watched them walk away from me, I tried to decide which deception surprised me more, Harry getting their meeting place wrong, or Ian not telling me he was going to Harry's. Since Harry's motives are always hidden in plain view, I'd have to say it was Ian not telling me about his plans that bothered me most.

Alden's hand on my shoulder reminded me I wasn't alone.

"Are you all right?" he asked.

"I'm sorry Harry offended you. I'm afraid he'll always love this house."

Alden adjusted his glasses; his eyes bore a hole in Harry's back as the pair of them got farther down the street. "He doesn't bother me in the least."

He fixed his eyes on me. "Is something wrong, Celia?"

I put my apron back on and started walking toward the

kitchen, annoyed that Alden needed to be told why I might be worried. He followed.

"I lose sleep every time Ian goes there. Harry doesn't discriminate between days of the week for a date with drinking. I might as well have shoved a bottle of whiskey into Ian's backpack for all the likelihood Harry will drink with Ian there."

Alden put one plate back in the cabinet, the hint of a grin on his face. I took the meat loaf out of the oven to sit. It cuts better when it has a chance to cool.

"Maybe you're worried for no reason. Ian's old enough to know right from wrong. One could argue you've done all you can. Your job is pretty well done at this point."

Wishful thinking, coming from a man without children. A newly married man sharing his wife with her distant teenager.

One by one, he put the three tumblers that sat on the counter back into the cabinet. He took down two red wineglasses. He made no eye contact as he opened a bottle of shiraz.

"None for me," I said. The pang of being dismissed by Ian was replaced with disapproval of Alden.

"A parent's job is never done. I don't think Ian has started drinking, and I don't want him to. The adults in his life have to set the best possible example. Especially in light of the one a certain someone is setting."

With the corkscrew wings horizontal, Alden stopped opening the bottle.

"Are you talking about Harry's drinking, or have you moved on to mine?" One hand gripped the neck of the bottle, the other struck the counter. "For goodness sake, Celia. I drink wine."

"I've shared with you how hard it was to be married to a man who tried to drown his family in alcohol. It's part of who I am."

"It may well be part of a previous chapter of your life. It's not part of our story." Alden's tone was lighter, but he made no move to come to me. He finished opening his wine.

I didn't want to be having this conversation. I knew if we continued to talk about it, he'd say I was being overly sensitive. It was a hot button issue for me. Of course, Alden would've been right.

I waited until he had poured two full glasses.

"Ian's not here." He held out a glass to me. "You can indulge without the least bit of parental angst."

"No, thank you," I said.

I turned back to the food and started plating it. I found it easy to serve.

day 38 *without Abby*

The man from the cemetery maintenance center called late Wednesday to say it was ready. I didn't dare go to see it without Ethan after he got so mad about my Janie visit. I'd tried one of Celia's keep-the-lines-of-communication-open techniques. I called him at work to tell him I'd seen her. It backfired.

"Janie? You went to see Janie," he said. "I can't believe you went there without me. You could have at least told me you were going. How can we get through this if you won't talk to me?"

I was trying to talk about things; that wasn't working out so well. Bone tired, I let him get mad at me. On some level, I didn't mind hearing him sigh and talk loud. Good, he was angry. Welcome to my world.

Then yesterday, the project manager of Netco came in to prep Ethan's team for next week's New York trip. When he pulled in last night, it was too dark to go to the cemetery.

This morning, he took time off, and we went together.

We walked slowly through the rows of flat stone, being careful not to step on anybody. Part of me hoped it wouldn't be there. It took my breath away to see her name on the smooth concrete grave marker.

ABIGAIL ANNA GRAY
BELOVED DAUGHTER

Another surreal image to get stuck in my head, my daughter's grave site. I'd brought the required decorations: flowers, balloons. I always thought children's grave sites looked stupid decorated like that. When Rosemary and I would bring flowers to Mom's grave, I'd see grave sites decked out with stuffed animals and other childish memorabilia and think to myself, why do they do that? Their child isn't going to enjoy or appreciate those gifts. Then there Ethan and I were, making her grave the prettiest darn plot in the cemetery. For her? No. Because of what other people will think? No. We did it for us. You have to do something to make the time you spend there purposeful. What else is there to do?

There were two reasons why I was glad Celia agreed to see me today, even though it was Veteran's Day. It gave me the chance to get away from Ethan, and it gave me an excuse to talk to someone about how horrible it is to go to a grave to make sure your child's name is spelled correctly.

When I told Celia this, she gave me her puzzled look.

"I wonder why it was easier to come here to talk about it, when you were standing right there with Ethan," she said.

Here we go, I thought, the session about the marriage. I wanted to talk about my visit with Janie. I wanted to talk about the investigation, or lack thereof. I ended up talking about Ethan.

"Yes, I'm angry with him. I didn't want her to go to that school. Who says every four-year-old has to go to preschool? She was happy home with me. I know he misses her, but I miss her more. I was her mother. Can I still say I'm a mother?"

Celia sat even more upright—the way she does when she has an important point to make. "Each parent-child bond is unique and complicated. I'm sure Ethan is grappling with losing Abby in his own way."

"Is that what the books tell you to tell me, Celia, or are you speaking from personal experience? Do you even have kids?"

"I do have children, my teenage son lives with me," she said. "I'd rather not talk about my family. It's important we stay focused on yours."

I didn't feel like calling her on one minor detail. I don't really have a family anymore. Still, I got her message loud and clear: don't pry.

"You don't need to worry about me and my anger. I was really mad at Rosemary when Mom died last year. She and I got through it." I pulled my hair out of the elastic and redid my ponytail. The elastic snapped, leaving a tangle of hair in my way.

"I see a pattern here. You get angry with others when you're trying to manage your strong feelings." She cocked her head and wrinkled her brow. "Is that an accurate observation?"

I wanted to punch her right in the nose, but perhaps that would've been perceived as anger.

"I'm intense, what's wrong with that? Ethan knows to give me my space, and things will work out fine." I looked at my watch. I liked it better when I came in and decided what we'd talk about.

"Men and women often take different roads toward healing after a loss. Any kind of loss. It's important to work through your grief in your own time, and in your own way. Be careful not to get so far from each other that you can't find your way back together." She put her hand under her chin and waited for me to say something.

I wanted to strangle her with those damn pearls. Instead I sat in my chair reserved for people traveling the wrong road and said nothing.

MONDAY, NOVEMBER 14   **8:30 A.M.**

Ian made it safely through the weekend and arrived home in time for Sunday dinner. As far as I could tell, he seemed no worse for wear. I didn't ask him about Harry because I didn't want to upset him, in case things had gone badly. Or maybe I didn't ask because I didn't want to know. I don't think Ian talked for the first hour he was home, except to ask about the desk.

I thought about him all weekend, though I kept my feelings to myself. I didn't want to ruin what Alden had planned for our Saturday. The poor man deserved a break from trying to win over my son. It was a perfect day for walking, so we left our cars in the driveway, and took the back roads to Corcoran Village.

"There are two antiques stores I'd like to check out," Alden said. "I'm hoping one will have a piece that could serve as a small writing table. If you don't object, I thought I'd put it in the extra room upstairs. That would be a great place to grade papers. Away from the hubbub downstairs."

Alden held my hand at the beginning of our walk. In time, his taller body and my shorter arms made it awkward. I let his hand go and hesitated, trying to think of something to keep him out of that room.

"I don't mind, I'll just run it by Ian. Even if we find what you're looking for, we'd have to drive back later to get it."

Our walk had an understated companionship about it until I brought Ian in step with us.

"Celia, please don't tell me you're planning on asking your teenager for permission to use a room in your own house." He raised a bushy eyebrow, and his smile contradicted what sounded like an accusation of poor parenting.

"I didn't plan on presenting it to him for a decision. I merely want to respect how hard it is for him to handle all these changes." I picked up the pace of my walking.

"That's fine. If we don't put the writing table in that room, we'll find some other quiet spot for it, yes?"

"Absolutely. I've been meaning to clean out the downstairs studio. I don't work in there anymore, and you could have a place to call your own."

For the rest of our walk, we were content to be still as we moved toward the Village. I didn't feel the need to fill each minute with idle chatter, neither did he.

Alden-silence doesn't begin to compare to Harry-silence. It might sometimes be the quiet that comes from not having anything meaningful to say, but it's never the kind that comes from having said too much.

We walked into the first shop and immediately I wanted to leave. It was dank and crammed with merchandise. The musty smell was heavy; the shop had no windows.

"Alden, I think I'll wait outside," I said.

His voice was calm, his actions measured and precise. "Look, this is the type of piece I'm interested in."

He walked through the crowded shop without getting a lick of dust on his corduroy jacket. I stood where I was and admired the piece from the door. I liked the way his commanding posture and neatly trimmed beard made the store owner take him seriously.

"That's a one-of-a-kind you're looking at, sir," the dealer said.

"Are we looking at the same piece? I'm interested in this fairly common nineteenth-century writing desk." He pointed to the writing desk and away from a nightstand, allowing the dealer to regain his credibility.

"This is in impeccable shape," Alden said.

The dealer quickly realized Alden could tell the difference between antique furniture and garage sale junk. He offered to show him more pieces he kept at the back of the shop. I slipped out the door and back into the sunshine. My eyes took a minute to adjust.

I closed them, not to protect them from the contrast in lighting, but because I wanted to soak in the warmth of a sun much stronger than a typical November Saturday. Alden's hand on my shoulder and his *there you are* startled my eyes back open.

"I'd like your opinion about the desk before I buy it. After all, it's going to be in *our* house." He kissed me on the cheek. "This will be the first piece of furniture we buy together. Come on, you'll love it."

He took my hand and dragged me back into a claustrophobic's nightmare. His confidence and excitement were contagious. We bought the desk.

After a quick lunch and our walk home, Alden went back to pick it up. He hadn't brought it upstairs before Ian came home. It wasn't until I saw Ian's face that I regretted getting swept away by Alden's impulse to buy.

"What's that?" Ian pointed to the desk, parked out of place in the foyer.

"It's a writing desk." I didn't know what else to say, so to buy time I stated the obvious.

"I know that. What's it doing here?" Ian stared at it as Alden decided to try his hand at parenting.

"Your mother and I bought it. We're putting it in the spare room upstairs so I can retreat there to grade my students' writing." He stood a bit taller, proud of our collusion.

Ian turned his head in slow motion and his eyes locked onto mine. "Did my mom say you could use that room?"

day 41 *without Abby*

Celia's kindness is rubbing off on me. After she dropped the brick on me about my marriage in our session on Friday, I cooked Ethan a meal. If breakfast can be called a meal, when I'm the one who's cooking. The scrambled eggs were dry, the toast a little on the dark side; I will not be winning chef of the year.

Ethan walked through the family room, dragging his luggage behind him. He poked his head into the kitchen, as if checking to see if he woke up in the wrong house.

"I thought I smelled something good. Is all this for me?"

All this consisted of paper plates and napkins, real mugs, and instead of a carton of milk plunked on the table, I'd poured it into our ceramic creamer.

"No big deal, I know how you hate breakfast at the airport."

He'd be gone a week. I knew the trip was important for the company, still I didn't really listen to the details. I heard every fifth word—merger, shareholders—nodding my head, faking interest. He finished eating, and I walked him to the door.

He cupped my face in his hands, stroking me cheek to chin to neck. His kiss was coaxing; his lips were pressure on mine. Tears slipped from his eyes. It was strange to know he felt so much for me when I felt only a hint of the love I'd once had for him. If this good-bye had happened only two short—no long—months ago, I would've been crying, too.

This week will be hard for me, not for the reasons other people think. Tessa alone without Abby *and* Ethan won't be why I struggle. It'll be because Ethan's probably arranged for the entire county to check in on me. I'm not suicidal for God's sake. Not yet anyway. I'll put money on the fact that he's set things up so that other people will be his eyes and ears while he's gone.

I can't believe I felt relieved when he left. Me, the one who's loved Ethan from the minute I saw him at Rosemary's Christmas party, eight years ago. I picked Ethan out of the crowd that filled her living room that night. The first thing I noticed was the untamed dark wave of hair that fell on his forehead and his skin, smooth and closely shaven. Those eyes, and his single dimpled smile, reminded me of Clark Kent without the secrets.

We started a conversation that had no ending. After that first night, we never stopped talking. Until the day we lost Abby. Even when my mother died, we talked. Even through the stupid process of trying to get pregnant again—the doctor's visits, the shots—we talked.

Now I'm glad he's gone? I never thought I would feel this way about Ethan. I wonder if he's relieved to be away from me. His wife who rarely leaves the house or his daughter's bed. He has to sense that almost everything he does bugs me. It'll be good to take a break from trying to coexist together without Abby.

Since Ethan's not here to object, I officially started my own investigation. I met with old Mrs. Dwyer this afternoon. I called her to set up our meeting. I didn't want to knock fifty times before she realized I was standing at her door.

"I really don't know anything, dear," she said. "I'd be happy to make you a cup of tea, and tell you what I saw after the accident. If you don't think it will upset you to come over."

At the time, I thought she was being polite. I knew coming face-to-face with the place Abby died would be hard. I wasn't prepared for the shrine that had been erected on Mrs. Dwyer's front lawn. Among the makeshift memorial to Abby was a cross with drooping balloons attached at the top. There were faded cards, rain-stained posters, and scruffy-looking stuffed animals. All of these marked by the hands of other children missing their friend and my daughter.

I don't know if I took a breath from the time I turned onto Beach Rose Lane, parked my minivan in her driveway, and found myself staring at this aging tribute to Abby. How long I stood there is anybody's guess. I'd start to read a card or poster but was stopped either by the childish scrawl, the inventive spelling, or the stick that was taking shape in my throat. *Abby, I miss u. Is it pritty in heavin?*

When I could barely swallow, I pulled myself away from the scene of the crime and into the portico of Mrs. Dwyer's house. She came to the door after my third knock, a tangible reminder of why she doesn't know much of what happened that bright sunny morning. When she opened the door, I realized I must look awful.

"Oh, dear, come in, come in. I knew this might be harder for you than you thought. Come in."

She didn't know *anything*.

"It wasn't until I heard the fire truck that I looked out the front window and saw all the commotion. The ambulance was already here. When the crowd parted to make way for the paramedics, it was only then that I realized a little one from the school had been hurt," she said.

She patted my hand, knowing I couldn't speak.

"I didn't realize she'd passed until the next day when that

detective—you know, the heavyset fellow—came to my door to ask if I saw what happened. He stepped right on my mums. He knew I saw him, and he didn't even apologize. Oh, but that's neither here nor there, is it?"

I shook my head. I could see Caulfield, either too lazy to walk around her garden, or trying to intimidate an old woman.

"I told him I didn't see a thing, I was watching my programs." She kept talking, like lonely ladies do.

"It's very sad to see all the little children coming here, their gifts to remember your daughter so sweet. You saw all those cards? I'll save them for you when you're ready. It's such a tragedy. Who could hit a child and leave her there?"

day 43 *without Abby*

Rosemary called first thing this morning and gave it to me about not calling her back.

"Didn't you get my messages?" she asked. "I was worried about you. I think I called three times. I even drove over to see if you were okay. Where were you?"

I let her get her frustration off her chest, then I told her about my visit to Mrs. Dwyer and the memorial. I'd known some parents and children had put things there, I had no idea how much it had grown since the day of the accident.

"Did you know the kids from the school had done that?" I asked. I lodged the phone between my ear and shoulder while I cut a section of grapefruit, popping a bitter wedge in my mouth.

"Ethan and I thought it would be better if you didn't read the cards. He and I couldn't get through more than a few. They're heartbreaking."

Rosemary's my best friend. I couldn't believe I needed to remind her that nothing breaks a heart already broken. I parked the knife in the center of the grapefruit.

"How often do you and Ethan talk about me behind my back?"

"You make it sound like we hold secret, *talk about Tessa,* meetings," she said. "I call him once in a while. He needs someone to talk to."

My conversation with Ethan on the phone last night was superficial; he didn't mention Abby and neither did I. I didn't tell him about Mrs. Dwyer's front lawn, or that I'm through waiting on Caulfield. I don't even remember what we talked about. I know it wasn't what was on his mind, or in my heart.

"And I suppose he can't talk to me because I'm what? A shrew?"

"No, it's—"

"Look, Rosemary. You can't orchestrate things like you did after Mom died. This is happening to me. Don't talk about me to Ethan. And don't you dare hide anything from me. I'm your sister, not a little kid." When I looked down I was stabbing the fruit with my knife.

"Don't keep anything about Abby from me. Do you understand?"

She was quiet. I would've hung up on anyone who talked to me like that. Rosemary never hangs up when she's mad. I halfheartedly asked her about Kevin. He was trying to convince her to go away for the weekend. She thought it was too close to the holidays. I spent about five minutes asking all the right questions, saying all the right things.

"How's Mattie doing? Does he still talk about Abby?" This was the question I really wanted to know the answer to.

"All the time. I put some pictures of the two of them in a little photo album, and he goes through it every night instead of asking for a bedtime story."

"Okay, well, I'll let you go," I said. The image of a three-year-old wanting to look at pictures of his now dead cousin was more than I could handle.

"I'm going for a walk in a few minutes, want to come?" she asked. "It can be as short or long as you feel up to."

"Not today. Ask me another time, okay?" I didn't have enough energy to walk, or talk, and definitely not enough to do both.

"Tessa, are you mad at me? The harder I try not to upset you, the more I seem to." Her voice was trembling. I could tell she was crying.

"I'm not mad. I'll be okay." I ended the call knowing I'd lied to my sister.

day 44 *without Abby*

I spent two days in a row at the library. I could've done my research at home, but I never knew when someone would interrupt me. The phone calls, the unannounced visits, the instant messages. I've lost my privacy along with my child.

The library was quiet during the daytime hours, though it annoyed the hell out of me when someone started talking really loud. They act as if they've bumped into a long-lost relative on a street corner. Whatever happened to being quiet in the library?

The first time I came, I packed up around three. I had to leave because I suddenly felt like I'd been cast in a rerun of *Boy Meets World*. It was practically a child care center for the kids of working parents. The poor frazzled librarians were outnumbered fifteen to one. The kids didn't seem that happy to be parked in the library to hang until dinner either.

In the two days I'd spent there, I'd been able to find out a lot about hit-and-run accidents, though I didn't know much more about Abby's. I found a psychologist online who profiles people who hit and run. Her own son was killed on his way home from work one Saturday afternoon, and she's been helping other families cope ever since. I didn't realize there were so many reasons a person leaves the scene. I assumed it was a drunk driver. That's still most likely what happened. It's the most common reason someone takes off.

I bet the excuse for that one goes something like, *I was drunk and I didn't even realize I hit the kid.* Well, then maybe you shouldn't have been smashed at nine in the morning, you ass. The lovely psychologist didn't word it quite that way on her Web site. Neither would Celia, I suppose.

Then there was the person who enjoys a little road rage. That person's excuse is probably that they get *stressed.* And there's the person who leaves the scene because she's afraid. Maybe a repeat offender who happened to be sober at the time, or an unlicensed driver. None of these excuses help me understand how someone's fear could take precedence over the lifeless body of a little girl lying by the side of the road.

The more I read the more disgusted I got. I kept reading. As if learning more about who could do this could get me closer to knowing who did.

Ethan and I talked about it tonight. The 230 miles between us made it safer to bring it up. He didn't need to know I sat in Abby's rocking chair holding a doll while we talked.

"Do you ever think about who did it?" I placed the doll on Abby's bed and went over to her bureau. Opening her top drawer, I ran my hand over her favorite nightgown.

"All the time," he said. "I wonder if he lives in Wenonah. Have I walked right by the creep and not known it? Maybe I've ridden by him and he's driving the car that hit my baby. Then I stop myself, because if I go there I'll go crazy."

"I go there," I said.

It was the longest, deepest conversation we've had about it yet. Then he changed the subject.

"I'm not coming home."

I closed the drawer as if he caught me wallowing. I don't think I breathed until a minute later when I knew what he really meant.

"There are a lot of details to go over about the merger, and since next week's Thanksgiving, no one wants to delay it going through. I'm here till Tuesday."

"That's fine." I didn't realize the way he'd take it.

"Well, okay then." His voice was thick with disappointment. "I'll finish this up and get there when I can."

I was disappointed, too, because it was the second time in as many days that I'd lied. For some reason I couldn't say I wanted him home.

"I'll be fine. I know you need to get it done. I'm not alone, anyway." I picked up Dolly and went back to rocking her. "Rosemary's checking up on me every day."

After the bit about Rosemary, I felt bad again. I didn't want him to think I was blaming him for her. She'd be checking up on me whether he asked her to or not.

"Okay, so Tuesday night?"

He didn't say anything for a second, neither did I. "Tessa, you know you can call me anytime, right? I don't care what I'm doing, I'll take your call. About anything."

Ethan, sweet Ethan. No matter what I did to push him away, or how fired up I got, he could find a way to melt me.

It was only six-thirty when I filled three mugs and arranged them in a triangle around a plate of cranberry muffins. Ian walked into the kitchen one way, Alden in the other. Both were drawn to me by the smell of orange zest and coffee beans.

"I love these. You haven't made them in a while." Ian threw his backpack in the corner and plunked himself into a chair. He ripped the paper liner from a piping muffin.

"Something smells heavenly." Alden kissed my neck, letting his arm linger around my shoulders. Ian tensed and I squirmed away to take my seat. Alden leaned his nose in close to the plate to take a whiff before he took his own. "What's the occasion?"

"I have a proposition for you two and I'm trying to bribe you into agreeing to it. It's about Thanksgiving."

Neither one looked at the other. They both kept their focus on eating.

"I'd like to celebrate our first Thanksgiving together at an inn.

Maybe New Hampshire or Vermont. I think a trip would do us good." I'd rehearsed a more convincing argument; it escaped me in the moment.

Surprisingly, neither Alden nor Ian said no.

Sensitive Ian, always worrying about what to do with Harry on holidays, didn't even mention him. "Maybe I could take off and ski one afternoon."

"I don't see why not," Alden said. "Celia, you'll have your getaway. Ian will get to ski. As long as we choose an inn that serves a traditional Thanksgiving dinner, everyone will be happy."

Ian slurped his coffee, grabbed another muffin, and stood. "I gotta go. Thanks for breakfast. I'll be home late." He kissed my cheek and made for the back door.

I spoke to no one in particular. "Yes, everyone will be happy."

FRIDAY, NOVEMBER 18   **5:30 P.M.**

I had trouble concentrating all day. In between clients, I jotted down things I'd need to remember: put timers on lights, turn down the heat, arrange for someone to plow the driveway in case it snows while we're gone. I noted things I'd need to pack: long underwear, boots, and extra gloves. This list didn't look anything like other family trip lists. The old lists were built around a boat.

I haven't been aboard her since that day. I don't go down to the harbor to see her. A visit there wouldn't bathe me in good memories as much as it would flood me with sad. I imagine she's still beautiful. Golden teak brightwork above, rich mahogany below. She turns heads in marinas everywhere, Harry would tell anyone willing to listen. Then, because he didn't want to embarrass me, he'd whisper, *just like you do, C.*

Parkas, scarves, thick socks, insulated ski pants.

Last night, I found myself putting in a ridiculous amount of time planning our trip. A few unexpected benefits of a vacation have arrived before we've even left.

Alden gave up reading his two hundred pages in favor of spending time with me looking over some brochures I'd found in an ancient folder marked FUTURE TRIPS. Ian showed me on his laptop how to search the Internet for inns. I couldn't believe we were all in the same room working on this.

First Ian, then Alden got tired of weighing the options and headed up to bed. I stayed up, mulling over the best place to unify my family. One family fell apart at the ocean; maybe I could put another together in the mountains.

I settled on a lovely bed-and-breakfast in Vermont, not three hours' drive from Wenonah Falls. The Heather Inn sits at the base of Killington Peak in the little town of Tama Ridge. I plan on telling Alden and Ian all the details tonight, unless Ian's going out, in which case I'll wait. I want to tell them both together.

This Thanksgiving perhaps I will truly have something to be grateful for.

MONDAY, NOVEMBER 21   **8:00 A.M.**

Last night, I finally shared the details of our weekend in Vermont with Alden and Ian. Alden's exaggerated happiness was a veiled attempt to cheer me after the tiff Ian and I had over his report card. After telling me he had no homework, he handed it to me. Leaving me to read it, he went into the dining room and sat down at the table like there was nothing to worry about, as if dinner had already been served.

"His grades might not be considered bad by other parents' standards, but they certainly don't reflect Ian's potential." I scanned it again and then handed it off to Alden. I regretted doing it the minute I saw disapproval grab hold of his lower lip. I was glad Ian wasn't there to see it.

"Bs and Cs are worrisome enough on a high school transcript, but it's the comments that have me upset," I said, putting out my hand to take it back.

I followed Ian into the dining room, leaving Alden alone in the kitchen.

" 'Distracted in class. Assignments missing. Inconsistent effort.' " I read from the ordinary piece of paper that held his lack of progress.

" 'Not working up to potential,' " Ian said. "I know. I read it. Relax, it's not that bad."

Alden walked in with a crock of soup. Ian used both hands to push off his seat; he walked to the opposite side of the first floor.

"Ian, don't walk away from me," I said.

He stopped and gestured for me to follow him into the living room. We sat down on the sofa facing each other.

"I don't want to talk about this in front of Professor Plum." Then he waited to see if his insult of Alden was effective enough to end the conversation about his grades.

"That was unnecessary and very unlike you."

He closed his eyes. "You showed it to him, didn't you?" He leaned back against the arm of the couch. He waited for my answer.

"I should've asked you first. I won't do it again." I put the report card on the end table behind me and reached to turn on the lamp. "You're such a smart boy. I hate to see you doing less than your best."

The light illuminated his face as he shared the reasons for his slip in performance. They were vague and immature for a boy as bright as he.

"Chemistry is impossible. My geometry teacher's boring and she grades really hard." He kicked off his shoes. About to curl his legs up under him, he caught my look and, instead, stretched his long legs out in front of him. Head down, he started picking at his fingernails.

"It's a good thing I won't be working anymore," he said. "Michael says fall cleanups are winding down. He won't need me again till things pick up in spring."

"When did you find that out?" I tapped his hands; he stopped fussing with his nails.

I didn't get an answer because Alden inadvertently did Ian a favor.

"Would you two like to join me?" He stroked his beard, as if he were the one who needed to make the decision.

On our way back to the dining room, Ian whispered, "Mom, this school thing isn't the end of the world. Trust me, I've got everything under control."

At least one of us felt that way.

When we sat back at our places, Ian kept scraping his spoon along the bottom of the bowl. With his head down and one elbow up on the table, he never took a bite.

"Celia, tell us what you've planned for our Thanksgiving trip." Alden handed me a plate of rolls. He took a perfect-size crescent and placed it on his bread plate.

I wasn't as excited as I had been. Ian's report card had dampened my mood. Nonetheless, our trip was in two days, and my hopes for the perfect holiday remained high. I shared the details of the Tama Ridge trip.

Alden stroked my hand. "We'll have a wonderful time."

Ian looked at Alden's hand on mine. He dropped the spoon with an intentional clang. "I think I'll go study." He moved his chair back, got up, and left. The only things reminding us he'd once been there were his place setting and his abandoned chair sitting lonely in the middle of the floor.

I thought he said he had no homework.

day 48 *without Abby*

It's a warm morning for November, still it's cool and quiet in the house. My kitchen has a week's worth of clutter on the counters. The dirty dishes in the sink aren't hopeful they'll get clean, since they're flanked by a single paper towel barely glued on the roll, and only a thin streak of dish detergent lines the bottom of the plastic bottle. The daily grind surrounds me as I move on to the family room, where two laundry baskets sit overflowing with clothes. Ethan's dry cleaning hangs from above the closet door. Newspapers dot the coffee table, they litter the rug.

Every mother, including me, has had the fantasy of being alone in her home with plenty of time to get these jobs done. She craves the solitude. Until she gets it.

I can't find the energy to clean. Mine is spent missing Ethan. I don't miss him as much as I miss Abby. This has everything to do with the fact that he's coming home. Eventually. I've kept myself busy the whole time he's been in New York, but it's been eight days, and I want him back.

On Friday, I got to Celia's early. She offered to start my session right then. Somebody else must've blown her off. Before she sat down, she tidied a stack of travel brochures on her desk.

"Thanksgiving." Her explanation came with a smile so quick I almost missed it.

I said nothing. The last thing I wanted to do was talk about Thanksgiving.

"I've missed Ethan a lot more than I thought I would. He's not coming home until Tuesday." I took my seat while I tried to take charge of the conversation.

"Maybe the business trip was good for the two of you. There's a reason for the expression 'absence makes the heart grow fonder.'" She smiled again, this time it lingered.

"Am I one of those women? The kind who only wants what she can't have?" I realized it wasn't true as soon as I said it. I waited to hear what Celia thought. It would be a good test to see how well she knew me.

"You'd know that better than I. But I'd guess it has more to do with it being safer to acknowledge powerful feelings from a distance." She put my file on her lap. She wasn't writing in it as much as she had in the beginning.

"Ethan and I have been talking more over the phone than we've talked in the last five weeks, face-to-face. Don't tell me we have a better shot at making it if he keeps traveling?"

"Well, that depends somewhat on you, Tessa. Do you plan to tell him how much you've missed him, when he comes home?"

I looked out her window. It was so convenient to go there when I didn't want to go where Celia was going. The park was teeming with people taking advantage of a late Indian summer. Runners and dog walkers didn't interest me. An old couple holding hands and a woman pushing a stroller competed for my attention.

"I know I should. I've been such a bitch to him lately."

Celia flinched when I said the word *bitch*. She hates it when I swear, which makes me want to do it even more. Sometimes I have the urge to hurt her. I don't know why, I do like her. She's nothing but good to me.

Maybe I'm not happy unless I'm pushing people. I push Celia. I'd like to shove Caulfield. The thing I really don't want to do is drive Ethan away from me. I can't seem to help myself.

Sick of analyzing my session with Celia, I crawled back into Abby's bed. I'm tired of looking at my messy house. Tired of this pain. Tired of my life. Just tired.

day 50 *without Abby*

Last night, I stretched out on my window seat, and waited. In a trance, I looked at the two maple trees diagonally across from each other on opposite sides of the street. One tree was bare, not one leaf on a single branch. The other tree held on to the few remaining leaves that clung to its sticklike branches. It was as if she was holding on tight, even though she knew she would lose them. She always loses them, but she keeps trying to fight it.

A mix of fear and gratitude hit me as his car sounds echoed around the curve of our street. When Ethan stepped out of the car, he saw me. He flashed a gorgeous smile and came in, leaving his bags in the car. I met him at the door, we hugged.

At first, we didn't say anything. We held each other, firm hands pressed against weary backs. He started stroking my hair, a gesture he knew simultaneously made me feel desirable and deeply cared for. I loved when he'd seduce me from the top down. We made love in the family room. I wondered if he registered this new freedom. It'd been so long since we'd been comfortable outside our locked bedroom. Always fearful we'd traumatize Abby if she woke to find us in the throes of passion. Last night there was no need for old lovemaking rituals.

There was an intensity to it, though not the ravaging, rip-your-clothes-off, hungry kind of sex. It was passion born of too much time gone by, so many words left unsaid between us, and our shared pain. It bonded us. I realized as we lay there in the warmth of each other's bodies, with the old chenille throw Ethan had grabbed from the back of the couch draped over us, that only he knew what it was really like. All these weeks, I'd felt like no one knew how I felt. I was a parent without a child. In that moment, I knew he loved her like I did. He was the only other person in the world who would look at her with a face that shouted, *She's so beautiful, I can't believe we made her.* Only he knows how deep her absence cuts my soul. Because of that, lying with him felt good. I let myself feel good. I decided to sink into it, knowing that in the morning when the reality of a new day without Abby would hit me, the feeling would be gone.

At first we were quiet. The usual silence that follows the pleasure. Then there was another kind of silence. It reminded me of the postsex silence characteristic of a one-night stand. The social awkwardness that comes when you share something so precious and deep with someone who doesn't even know your name. But this was Ethan. Our silence had more to do with where to begin again than with where to gracefully end something. As if each of us wanted to be the one to give the gift of starting over, we both talked at the same time. We laughed, and a sound long missing from this house cracked the ice between us.

He told me the trip was tiring and stressful, but the majority of the merger arrangement was worked out. Aside from some number crunching he could do from here, he was off until Monday.

I was elusive about what I'd done while he was gone. I didn't want to ruin the closeness that had taken nearly two months to recover. I thought, maybe I could tell him what I'd really been doing. Then decided not to take my chances.

As cramped and crowded as it was, we slept on the couch. On this night, even I couldn't face Abby's room on the way to find sleep. Funny, how we both sensed how fragile the renewed connection was between us. We sacrificed the comfort of our bed, as if holding on to each other through the night might help us carry this feeling safely into a new day.

day 52 *without Abby*

Thanksgiving was horrible. Too much food, too many meaningless conversations, not enough thanksgiving. It had been my turn to host it. Without ever discussing it, we ended up at Rosemary's. I did appreciate all she'd done to make it festive. I hadn't set out to ruin the day.

With Dad long gone missing, Mom and Abby dead, the families that should have been growing larger were growing smaller. Under the pretense of wanting a real New England Thanksgiving, Rosemary invited Kevin's brother's family out from Nevada. I knew she invited them because she couldn't stand a replay of last Thanksgiving, our first since Mom died. Poor Rosemary gets all the postdeath holidays.

She added people to the guest list in an attempt to change up the day a little. She cleared out her living room of its elegant couches and sleek chairs. A long table, with place settings for everyone, ran the length of the room. No kids table this year. She staged our seating with little cards tucked in front of our toile-patterned plates. New cobalt glassware zigzagged up and down the table. A long low arrangement of gourds, mums, and bittersweet added the perfect celebratory touch. She blended traditional recipes with new home accents. I noticed everything, except a place at the table for Abby.

Ethan pasted an idiotic smile on his face. It was his way of faking it for me and for Rosemary. I drank. The first glass of pinot grigio was crisp and cold. I let it linger on my tongue then slowly allowed it to trickle down the back of my throat. I lost count after the fourth, or was it the fifth, glass? Matthew wouldn't notice if his drunk Auntie took a little rest on the couch in the den. I didn't care what Kevin's family thought.

I don't remember eating much of anything, though I do remember how great everything smelled. Sage and cranberries, pumpkin pie.

I'm two for two on ruining Thanksgiving at Rosemary's. Last year for my loud argument with her over the sale of Mom's house. This year I didn't intentionally hurt her. I just couldn't handle Thanksgiving and socializing. Being a couple when we should've been a family.

The thought of calling Rosemary to apologize sickened me even more than the bile pooling at the back of my throat. But I did it. She's put up with a lot from me.

So I called. She cried. I cried. And so it's done. The first holiday fiasco is over. I can't wait for the first Christmas.

MONDAY, NOVEMBER 28   7:00 A.M.

I need to write it all down. I don't have anyone to talk to about the last few days. I don't know how it all went so terribly wrong.

My dream for a scenic New England road trip met reality less than an hour into the drive. The bumper-to-bumper traffic reminded me more of an evacuation due to bad weather than a Wednesday drive to a vacation destination.

Ian was comfortable enough in the back of Alden's Lexus, listening to music on that expensive contraption Harry gave him for the ride. Like Ian needs any more technology. Harry's always buying him things to make up for the things he can't give him. He wasn't even in the car and he had the power to steal from me the light conversation I'd been looking forward to.

Alden, aggravated by the stressful driving, spoke fewer than a handful of words until we got off the expressway. I wanted to say it was his own fault for making us squeeze that faculty reception in before we left. As we meandered through the leaf-covered back roads of Rutland County, our less than ideal beginning was followed by polite conversation. Nearing the inn, Alden and Ian started bringing my vision of the perfect holiday to life.

When we arrived at the B and B, I was thrilled with our rooms. Alden and I had a corner suite with a large high bed facing a picture window that captured a mountain view. There was a sitting area in front of a stone fireplace, where I could see us spending our evenings reading books or playing cards.

Ian's room was sunny and cozy. I thought he'd be hard-pressed to feel down in a place so intent on making its guest happy. Our innkeepers suggested we get comfortable in our rooms and then join them for a chat in their lovely parlor with its floor-to-ceiling walls of books and Americana artwork.

The inn was where familiar tension found us, and it began to creep in between us again. Alden, who almost immediately put back on his professorial voice, was willing to socialize with the innkeepers once he realized they were impressed with his research through the college. Even before I had my clothes out of my suitcase, Ian sought me out to complain.

"Please don't make me go back down there. I went to that stupid history thing and now we're supposed to be on vacation. It's hard enough to know what to say to Al." He threw his body across the length of my bed, and the down comforter sighed louder than he did. "I hate this."

"You know how important getting the department chair position is to Alden, we had no choice but to keep up appearances. He thanked you personally for going, didn't he?"

He rolled over, messing up my spread. I refolded my clothes and moved them to the top of the bureau.

"Let Al go bore them with all his stupid school stuff. You and I can go do something fun. I saw a bunch of art galleries on the ride in. Come on, please?"

In my effort to keep the peace, I came up with a compromise.

Alden and I would visit with the innkeepers for an hour while Ian scouted out the trails behind the inn. Then we'd all go in town together. It wouldn't be until after we fought during Thanksgiving dinner that I found out my choosing Alden over Ian had been the beginning of the end of my attempt to insert my family into the Norman Rockwell painting that hung in the parlor at the inn.

We got through Wednesday night with no more strain than is usual. By Thursday morning the tension started to rise. Ian arrived at the last minute for our buffet breakfast; he grabbed a plate and piled it high. I still don't know why Alden had to say anything.

"Ah, the emblematic adolescent dilemma, choosing between too much sleep and too much food. I see you've found a way to have both." Alden picked up his bone china cup. I almost expected his pinky to pop up.

Ian said nothing and ate nothing.

On our quiet drive to Killington Peak to collect information about skiing, I tried my best to lighten the mood. I talked a lot about nothing, trying to fill the silent gap, hoping I could bring them both back to me. For a brief period I succeeded.

When Ian and Alden met in the corridor of our inn, dressed handsomely for dinner, they shook hands, as if they hadn't seen each other the hour before. Off we went to the restaurant for what promised to be a meal of thanksgiving.

With warm popovers on our plates and drinks both alcoholic and non in our hands, I made what I thought was a simple toast.

"To our family," I cheered.

With glasses frozen midair, both Ian and Alden spoke.

Alden, with only his facial expression, questioned the phrase *our family.*

Ian spoke with words. "Let's toast something else. Dad's not here."

"I suppose I could be your dad for today," Alden said.

With that, the glasses came down.

"I've got the one I want. Being a dad isn't something you do for a day or a weekend." Ian pulled his roll to pieces.

Before I could stop him, Alden snapped, "Yes, I suppose with Harry for a father, no one knows that better than you do. I would think you'd be ready to trade up." He took a large swallow of his cabernet.

What had been a smoldering fire ignited. Ian stood up, and threw his napkin down on the table in my direction.

"See what I mean, he's not that nice. I can't believe you needed to be with a man so freaking bad you were willing to put up with this idiot." He backhanded Alden's water glass, spilling it everywhere.

Alden scrambled to wipe it up. My heart shattered at the same time the glass hit the floor.

Ian shouted at me from two tables away. "I choose Dad."

Other families watched our dysfunction like members of an audience watch actors in a play. Children stared, teenagers kept eating. Parents looked and then looked away. Whether they thought it was a comedy or a tragedy, it wasn't a Thursday afternoon matinee.

Curtain down. Thanksgiving was over.

day 55 *without Abby*

Ethan went back to work today. Aside from our terrible Thanksgiving, and my hangover on Friday, our weekend was okay. Saturday, we took a walk through the colorless harbor. Wrapped in winter, we bundled up in scarves and parkas. Ethan's gloved hand held mine. He didn't say anything about me wearing a pair of Abby's snowflake-covered mittens. The ocean was black and flat, no waves. Every once in a while we talked. Mostly we were lost in our own thoughts. Still it felt good to be together.

Sunday we read the *Globe*. Ethan made a full breakfast that left us satisfied until late afternoon. I scoured the paper.

I didn't tell him I was hunting, not reading. And I didn't bring up the investigation. He did.

"I only called Caulfield once last week," he said. "Partly because of the merger and Thanksgiving. Partly because I'm sick of hearing him say, *nothing new, kid.*"

Ethan mimicking Caulfield was the only funny thing about hearing there still wasn't any news.

"He told me you went there. Said you lost it."

I didn't offer to fill in the blanks. He didn't push me to.

"Caulfield said *Theresa should really get some help.* I told him the best help *Tessa* could get would be for him to get his act together and find out who did this."

Each on our own couch cushion, I met him in the middle for a kiss.

"It was nice of you to stick up for your crazy wife."

I don't know whether it was the fact that he stood up to Caulfield, or that we were talking about this, I decided to keep chipping away at the ice.

"I've been reading a lot about hit-and-runs."

He broke eye contact. When he spoke, his voice was unsteady. "Me, too. You know we're never going to know. If they don't know by now, they won't know. Ever." He used his fingers to rub under his eyes.

"I read that, too. I won't accept it." I sat up straighter.

"Maybe it's better not to know," he said. "Do you really think you could get through a trial? I don't know if I could. Have you read the laws for prosecuting this? Even if they find the guy and can prove it, eighteen months to five years doesn't cut it for me."

I tensed every muscle in my body to keep my anger on simmer, instead of allowing it to get to its usual roiling boil.

He left it there, either because he didn't want to wreck our reunion, or because secretly, he didn't mind if I got the answers for both of us.

I got up and went to make dinner. Toasted bagels with jam.

My eyes felt like they housed a pail of sand between them from a night that couldn't find sleep. And of all days, I had a full schedule, eight clients back to back with only ten minutes in between each one. I listened. I commiserated. They didn't know while I sat there pretending my focus was entirely on their predicaments, my son was becoming lost to me.

I expected the weekend to be uncomfortable after Ian's outburst on Thanksgiving. Silence blanketed the house like snow. Secretly I welcomed the break from refereeing. Ian has a right to his feelings; I only wish he'd chosen a more productive way to express them. I let Alden lose himself in the library, while Ian hid in his room. I started straightening up the studio, though with watercolor as my medium there's never been much of a mess. I boxed up half-used block pads and rinsed brushes stiff with neglect. I imagined our Monday work and school schedules would put everything between the three of us back on an even keel.

Nothing could have prepared me for Ian's decision. Yesterday

I arrived home at my usual time, expecting to open the door to wintry darkness. I turned up the heat and put some lights on. I didn't expect the letter. In the kitchen, he left me a piece of lined paper with fringed edges. Carefully folded in half, *Mom* stared at me from the middle of the table. Apparently when Ian said *I choose Dad* four days ago, he meant it literally.

Dear Mom,

I'm sorry I'm not telling you this in person. I can't take the chance you'll try to talk me out of it. I'm moving in with Dad, he said it was okay. I can't take living here with him.

You promised when he moved in everything would be different, we'd be a normal family. But kids don't feel left out in normal families. I can't stand his fancy food. I hate that every time I do something wrong he corrects me or gives me a look. And why does he always have to touch you when I'm around?

When Dad lived here I know things weren't easy, but at least Dad doesn't act like he's perfect. He doesn't walk around pouring tea, packing away our stuff, and pretending shit didn't happen.

I can't live here. It's too hard. I don't know how you stand it, but I don't have to. I know you aren't going to be happy I'm at Dad's, but I need a break. I know you hate any kind of fighting, and I really am sorry about Thanksgiving. I know you wanted the trip to, you know, bring us together and everything. Maybe it didn't look like it, but I tried. Not as much as I could've, but I did try. Anyway, things will be better this way. I'll call you tomorrow.

Love, Ian

He's been so quiet and withdrawn, always secluded in his room or spending time at Harry's. Without his letter, would I have even questioned his not being here?

I held it close to my chest and took the stairs to his room. There was hardly any difference between when he'd been here and now.

Dirty laundry clumps made circles on his striped rug, his bed perpetually unmade. His laptop gone. A conspicuous clear place outlined in dust, the only clue it once sat on his desk. Ian was at Harry's.

Ian's leaving storm had been squalling around me since the day I made Harry move out. It took less than two years for the final wind to blow.

I remember watching their good-bye from behind the French doors in the library. I didn't think they'd want me to be part of it.

"Please let me go with you," Ian said. He was holding a small box of Harry's things. Out of it poked a framed charcoal sketch, and the corner of a Little Mermaid photo album.

Harry tossed his single duffel bag down on the hardwood. He took the box from Ian, parking it next to the bag. Then he put both hands on Ian's shoulders.

"I'd give anything to take you with me. Hell, I wish I hadn't screwed us both out of me living here. But kid, I'm just beginning recovery. I can't promise I won't mess up."

"You said you'd never do it again. I believe you." Harry dropped his arms by his side. With his arms crossed, protecting his heart, Ian leaned back against the front door.

"Look, don't be mad at your mother. She's doing the best she can." Harry pulled Ian from the door to his chest. "When I get my act together, you can come visit me all you want." Harry's hug included two back claps.

"Where are you going?"

"I'm on the boat—until it gets colder. In the meantime, I'll be looking for a place to rent. I'm staying right here in Wenonah. Near you. And your mother."

Harry left, and Ian closed the door to me halfway that day. He shut it all the way yesterday. The day he chose to move in with Harry.

Ian may still be a believer in his father. When it comes to Harry Hayes, I remain agnostic.

day 57 *without Abby*

I wasn't sure Ethan knew what I meant when I'd said I wasn't done with it. He couldn't know I was becoming obsessed with finding the truth. Probably because I didn't tell him.

After he left for work, I brewed a fresh pot of coffee and laid out my stuff on the kitchen table. With my spiral-bound notebook and a chunk of Post-its, I got to it. I brainstormed two lists: one was what I'd done, the other what I needed to do to move my investigation forward. I'd already talked to Janie; she didn't see or hear anything. I'd visited Mrs. Dwyer, she wasn't any help either. I'd read about paint chip analysis, and people who leave the scene of a crime. The only ones solved after this much time were the ones where the guilty party came forward, or someone who knew something told. I knew what I had to do. I'd keep the story alive. I'd use my power to increase the sympathy, and in turn boost the chances of someone feeling guilty enough to step forward.

I drove into the *Globe.* I decided to ask the toughest softy ever to graduate Columbia School of Journalism if she would do a piece on hit-and-run crimes, and use my story to tell it. Melanie owed me big for helping her pass her undergraduate senior finals. It would be harder to refuse me in person.

It didn't matter that it was ten in the morning; the traffic was bumper to bumper at the Braintree split. I figured the cause could be anything from an accident to the sprinkles of rain that spotted my windshield. I willed it not to be an accident.

I drove around the parking lot three times. Fed up, I took my chances on an illegal spot near the building entrance, until a guard called me on it. Already worried Melanie would deny me the column inches, it didn't take much to tip me over. I'd made it through the traffic only to have the lack of parking and an apathetic security guard force me to lose it.

"Where do you expect me to park?" I asked. "I have an appointment with Melanie Reynolds and I can't be late." I gripped the wheel. The guard stood unfazed.

"I don't care where you park, so long as it's legal," she said.

I saw someone backing out of a space and wanted to rush over to nab it. I managed to get the space, even with the guard taking her sweet time to move out of my way.

When I entered the lobby, two more security guards moved only their eyes to take me in. Bored stood by the entrance like a cardboard cutout. Surly sat at the curved desk against the glossy faux marble wall, he spoke before I made it halfway there.

"Name." Surly didn't look up. He scanned the sheets of paper tucked under the metal clip of his board.

Melanie barreled through the double doors, which required the bored guard to move. "Tessa." She hugged me hard, then stepped back to look at me. Her movements were abrupt, everything about her quick. Even her smile ran down her face landing in a frown.

"How are you?" I was glad she didn't wait for my answer. I was tired of thinking up answers I could live with.

"Come on, let's go up to my office. There's so much I want to ask you."

She grabbed my hand, and before we had made it out of the lobby, Melanie had agreed to research the accident. We headed up two flights to her office. I gratefully accepted a swivel chair and a paper cup of water; my empty stomach was thankful I wouldn't be dumping any more coffee into it.

"I can't promise anything because it isn't my decision. I can definitely do the research and put a pitch together for my editor. The two of you have a lot in common. With solid information and tons of Starbucks, she's likely to say yes."

Her phone rang and she wrangled herself out of her Indian-style sitting position to lean in to see if the caller deserved to interrupt us. She dismissed it. I couldn't ignore the pace of the other reporters. Other phones rang and people talked loud. I wanted to blink and open to find I'd been deposited in the Wenonah Falls Police Station.

"I don't care how outrageous an angle you come up with, please get me a feature." The opening and closing of the door to the hall let intermittent blasts of cold air hit me. I pulled the belt of my coat tight, then sat on my hands to keep warm.

It was easier than I thought it would be, her agreeing to research the story. Sure I needed her and she owed me, but I didn't have to plead or beg. I was finding out who my real friends were.

"If you're okay with outrageous, you really should look into doing some TV. Get booked on CNN or Fox, and you're guaranteed to turn up the pressure on local law enforcement," she said.

"I'm not ready to go that route. Anyway, Ethan wouldn't want to," I said. "I'm going to place my hope in you."

day 59 *without Abby*

It was hard to go back to Celia's after taking last week off. She's like exercise; you don't want to go, even though you know you'll feel stronger afterward.

I let go of the handle to her waiting room door, convinced my time was better spent dropping in on Caulfield. Like magic, it opened. Celia was letting a teenage girl exit her office.

"Come right in, Tessa. I'm running a bit late today." Her desk had files in jumbled piles, not her usual neat stacks. In the two months I'd been coming here, Celia never ran late. I went to my corner, trying to think of something to talk about.

"How was your Thanksgiving," she asked.

"God, that was ages ago, wasn't it?" I hated it when she beat me to a topic. "Fine, I think. I don't remember much of it, thanks to Rosemary's good taste in wine."

Her body stiffened. She leaned in to me. "It's a dangerous game to play with alcohol when you're grieving. It may seem like an easy escape at first. It only brings pain to those around you and new problems to solve."

Celia went white, the muscles in her face tightened. I tried to lighten things up by tossing out my *poor Rosemary gets all the postdeath holidays* remark. She didn't find that the least bit funny.

"I remember you telling me that last Thanksgiving was challenging, too. It was shortly after your mother's death, is that right?" She opened my file to see if memory served. "It might be wise to take a deeper look at this, especially with Christmas looming."

Wow, when she put it that way, I couldn't wait to take a long look at how very good I am at ruining the holidays. Especially since it sounds like Celia thinks the likelihood I'll ruin Christmas is high.

Before I knew it, I was talking about Mom. One day, a trim, fit, sixty-year-old woman. The next day dead. She went for her regular walk that morning. Rosemary and I opted out, I can't remember why. I found her lying on the couch that afternoon. Sudden cardiac death, they said. No warning. No risk factors.

Broken hearts run in my family.

"Rosemary, Mom, and I did everything together. It felt more like we were sisters," I said. "Dad took off when Rosemary was four. I was two. I don't remember him. But I think about Mom every day."

Celia softened as much as Celia softens. Though to give her credit, I really do feel like she listens. I could've been her only client if she got paid per sad story.

"Mom was always honest about Dad when we asked. She'd say, *He couldn't handle family life, but I'll always love him for giving me my girls.*" I let my head fall against the back of my chair.

"Tell me more about the three of you," she said.

Either Celia was having trouble holding up her end of the conversation, or this was one of those times where a stream of consciousness was called for.

"My friends thought we were either crazy or lucky, all living in the same town. Still everyone envied the way we got along. Three women, no triangles, no one left out. There wasn't a single subject off limits. When Kevin and Ethan came along, it only made things better. She loved her sons-in-law, and they loved her. In fact, if I complained about something Ethan did, she'd usually take his side."

A glazed look fixed itself onto Celia's face.

"I know it sounds like we were the only functional family in America, but we were happy."

Celia stopped me from going further down memory lane. "I'm sure there was a wonderful bond between your mother, your sister, and you. Do you mind telling me why you and Rosemary argued last Thanksgiving?"

"Rosemary's idea was to be done with it. We'd lost our mother and she was ready to get rid of her house and her things, too. She said it was too painful to go there and see everything the way she'd left it."

"Ah, like Abby's room," Celia said.

"She was in charge of the estate. Without even asking me, she put the house on the market. She said she didn't think I'd object, but she knew exactly how I felt. You don't erase a life. You don't give things away, or sell sentimental things to strangers."

She winced, and I realized I was talking too loud. I lowered my voice for Celia.

"You immerse yourself in it," I said. "You bury your face in her clothes so you can hold on to her smell. You wait until you're ready. I don't know, maybe you're never ready. But you don't rush the good-bye. Rosemary did. And I let her know I was pissed. I did it last Thanksgiving."

Celia stared at me for a minute, she didn't say anything. She swallowed like you do when you have a sore throat.

"Tessa, I'm so sorry for your losses so close together. I know it's impossible to grieve the loss of your daughter without the support of the person you've come to lean on most."

For a second, it sounded like she was talking about herself. Since I wasn't able to pry, I let her pity me.

I wanted to be mad at Celia. Except today, she seemed kind of fragile. She looked tired. She wasn't wearing her pearls or her Mr. Rogers sweater, and she had a traveling run in her nylons, peeking out from under her hemline. This look would be par for the course for me, but it wasn't for Celia.

She'd put my lousy life into one sentence. She felt bad for me. I wanted to be mad at her, but couldn't be.

Maybe she is helping me, though I'm pretty sure not in the way she'd hoped.

MONDAY, DECEMBER 5   5:00 P.M.

    I got to the high school with time to spare, my usual punctual self. I canceled my last two sessions, disappointing one client, relieving the other. Parked across the street from the main entrance, I waited, missing the days when I could go in, sign him out, and see the children skip or run to meet their mothers. Ian had asked me not to come in to the school to dismiss him for his dentist appointment. He said he'd ask Harry for a note. Ten minutes became fifteen. I counted the minutes I had before I'd need to warn the receptionist we'd be late.

    A distant bell rang. Throngs of miniadults poured from the building. It was hard to notice faces amid the outrageous clothing. There were those in carelessly chosen combinations of torn jeans and dingy sweatshirts. It was the carefully planned bizarre looks of wide-leg pants big enough for three, black studded collars, and indecent skirts that achieved the goal of catching the eye.

    I needed to see Ian. Not only because we were running behind, but also because we hadn't seen each other since Thanksgiving weekend. Ian was one of the last to come out of the building. He walked beside a man with a military haircut, whose sleeves were rolled up enough to show off the traces of twin tattoos on his forearms. It's no wonder teenagers don't wear coats in winter when principals can't be bothered to set a good example. Principal Castigan held up the conversation, Ian's serious look said, *Are you done yet.* A look I was becoming well acquainted with.

Lacey stood off to one side of the steps, holding her guitar case. A boy, shorter by a few inches, leaned against her shoulder, deep into flirting. Her doelike eyes tried to catch Ian's attention. He nodded *hi.* Obviously disappointed, she offered a self-conscious wave and turned back to the boy.

I rolled down my window to signal Ian to come over, hoping I wouldn't embarrass him in front of his friends. His brows expressed surprise. I heard his principal call after him *see you tomorrow,* as if it were a challenge.

Dismissed by Mr. Castigan, Ian ran across the street and slid into the car.

"What are you doing here?"

"You've got a dentist appointment. Did you forget?"

"I called you this morning. I told Al to tell you it got canceled. There was a message on Dad's machine from last Friday."

He unhooked his backpack and tossed it on the floor of my car. Beautiful even with his hair uncombed, he had a faint shadow covering his chin and upper lip. Between the ketchup stain on his shirt and the jacket that couldn't be warm enough, it took everything in me not to play the mother. Someone wasn't playing father.

I skipped dealing with Alden's lapse in memory, or as I'm sure Ian saw it, his desire to be difficult. I shouldn't have worried he was angry because in his usual style, he settled me immediately with a kiss on the cheek.

"Mind driving me home? You can tell me how you are." He yanked the seat belt down and clipped it in one smooth motion.

I wanted to say, *I'm not well, Ian. I love you. I miss you. I don't want you to live apart from me. I would never choose Alden over you. I'll tell him to move out if you'll come home. Please, come home.* But I didn't.

Instead, I made a fool of myself. "I'm fine, how about you? You and Mr. Castigan seem tight. What were you chatting about?"

He looked out the window. "He told me to stop skipping school."

"You're skipping school? What is wrong with your father?" Leave it to Harry. I would never allow Ian to skip school when he lived with me.

"Nothing. I haven't been feeling good lately. Dad knows when I stay home. He just forgets to write me a note." Ian's hard stare told me to back off blaming Harry. "I get hot and sick to my stomach sometimes."

"Are you sick now?" I reached my hand over to feel his forehead. He shook my hand free.

"Mom, I'm fine. Can we go?" He looked across at Lacey. She had her back to us. As though connected to Ian's stare, she turned and started walking in our direction. "Drive. Please."

I started the car. "Next time you feel sick, please tell me and I'll take you to the doctor. You should know better. Your health isn't something to fool around with."

Lacey nodded as she walked past. "Are you and Lacey still—I haven't seen her around much lately?"

"I told you, she's not my girlfriend. She's busy with stuff, that's all."

He turned on the radio, I lowered it.

"How's work?" he asked.

"I'm busy, this is a tough time of year. A lot of my clients struggle with being sad, when everyone else is happy."

He hit the radio off switch. I hadn't been talking about our family, but the remark landed too close to home. I wondered who we would talk about first, Harry or Alden. Which of these two men pulling us away from each other should get our undivided attention?

I should've been the one to start, after all, I'm the adult. Ian, the prodigy peacemaker, went first.

"Mom, Dad's good. He's really stopped drinking this time. He's been to AA three times this week. I met his sponsor. The guy sails."

The hope in his voice hurt me.

"That's good." My hollow tone couldn't convince even me. "You know I could take you to an Alateen meeting? I think it would be good for you to talk about everything you've been through because of your father."

He closed his eyes for an instant. Even concentrating on the road, I could tell his light mood was a facade.

"This isn't just about Dad."

I should've known I'd have to be the one to bring up Alden. "Give it time. When you really get to know Alden, you'll see. He's a lovely man, smart, and centered. He's responsible and easy to be with."

"Easy to be with, are you kidding me? Look I don't want to talk about Al. I'm at Dad's now. I told you from the start I didn't like him. I still don't. It has nothing to do with some stupid kid thing about wanting your parents back together. You and Dad blew it a long time ago."

I couldn't come up with a single thing to say, Ian was telling the truth.

"You both could've tried a lot harder, you know," he said. "I heard all those arguments you guys had about going to counseling."

I pulled onto Harry's street. "Never mind, it's too late," he said. "You're married to weird Al. Nothing you can say will convince me to move back there."

"You have to give him a chance. Things could really be different with him." With everything Ian got off his chest, all I could talk about was a fantasy family with Alden.

"I'm not going to change my mind. I love *you*. I'll spend time with *you*."

It was getting harder to see the road through my tears. I willed myself not to cry. I wouldn't let him see me cry.

"How will we see each other? What about Christmas? Are you going to punish me because I wouldn't stand by and watch your father destroy himself?"

I pulled in front of the house, relieved I could stop steering the car. He lugged the backpack off the floor. "No, I'm not gonna punish you. You and I can do stuff. We can go out for a burger."

I must have made a face.

"Yes, Mom, a burger—with a large order of fries." His easy smile was back. "And Christmas, well, maybe we can figure that out another time, okay?"

"All right," I said. "Let's start with the burger and fries. Just you and me. When and where?"

If a burger was the way back to my son, I could eat it. I would do anything not to lose Ian too.

day 62 *without Abby*

The pillowy softness of our new feather bed made getting up this morning harder than usual. Every time I turn around, there's Ethan with some sort of present. Last week, a cobalt blue cable-knit sweater. Yesterday, a feather bed. Were these sweet attempts to blanket me in warmth to keep me from missing the cold reality of our first Christmas without her? Or was he bribing me to stay out of Abby's bed?

I hadn't been hungry for breakfast, though I managed to put on a good show making some for him.

Pushing a cup of weak coffee toward the center of the table, I started to flip the pages of a magazine. Ethan peppered his eggs. He brought up Christmas without ever saying the word.

"I was wondering what you'd think of a trip to California. We could visit my parents. Get some sun. I already told Chuck if we came, we'd stay in a hotel. We'd mostly be going there to get away from here."

I didn't say what I was thinking: *Are you kidding? There*

couldn't be anything worse than visiting your mother and father. Poor things don't remember who we are, and we'd have to navigate a nursing home full of sick abandoned old people to get to them. Then there's spending time with your brother's family. I've always loved Chuck, it's Cathy I can't stomach. I could already see her giving me that face. The one that said, poor, poor Tessa. Wow, Ethan, stay here or go there. Such crappy choices we have this year.

"That's an idea, I'll think about it." I nibbled a corner of my toast. Even that was hard to swallow. "What if something were to happen with the investigation while we were gone?"

Now he was the one who refused to say what he was thinking.

day 64 *without Abby*

My hand shook when I realized I had Melanie on the line. She'd only been researching the case for a week and she wanted to come see me. I braced myself for something. I hoped for anything.

"Don't get excited. I don't know anything about Abby's accident that you don't already know. I do think I have an angle for a piece that could get some pretty hefty attention. I want to run it by you."

She didn't mind coming down from Boston; we set the time at one.

When I answered the door I didn't know whether to laugh or cry. Melanie had the Charlie Browniest Christmas tree I'd ever seen, in her arms.

She held it out to me. Fragrant pine needles fell on the tops of my slippers and lodged in the feathery hair of her Clydesdale-like boots.

"It needs you," she said.

I hugged her around the tree. More needles fell. She dragged herself and the tree inside.

"It's the first week in December, you've got to get going on decorating. With such a cute house, you have no excuse not to decorate it. Oh, sorry, I *am* such an ass," she said.

I reminisced her foot out of her mouth. "Remember when you decorated our dorm room freshman year when I was in civ? You single-handedly started that whole light contest. I wonder if the kids in Greycliff still do it, or if they've adopted so many stupid rules it's sucked all the fun out of it. I'd ask you to decorate this place except I'd rather have you working on the piece."

I hung her down jacket on the coatrack, and we took chairs opposite each other in the family room. Melanie started building her case for an angle about drunk driving. She didn't tell me anything I didn't already know about the profile of people who leave the scene.

"I found the Web sites you told me about and I talked to a friend at BPD about hit-and-runs. He said the majority *are* drunks."

The phone rang and I ignored it. I only cared to hear what she had to say.

"Go ahead and get it."

I pulled my legs out from under me, went to the kitchen, and peeked at the caller ID.

"It's Ethan, I'll call him back. Did you talk to Caulfield yet?"

She shook her head while she picked at a thread poking out of her sweater; she stopped when it began to unravel. "It's impossible to get through to him, and he never returns calls. Don't worry, I'll get a statement. I do need to put some pressure on him. Every cop I mention the name to rolls his eyes."

She began to outline her idea for the piece. "I know you want this whole thing to be about Abby, but I had to sell the idea to my editor trying to help you the best way I can."

"You can do it any way you want. I trust you."

She reached over and rubbed my arm as a friend, but she kept talking like a reporter.

"I researched the arraignment logs. There's a huge increase in DUI arrests in the last two years in and around Wenonah Falls. I'd like to start the piece off talking about Abby's unsolved case, profiling people who hit and run. Since drunk drivers account for the majority of perps, I could end the article by putting a spotlight on the increase in arrests down here."

She put on her friend voice again. "Tessa, this is a long shot. You and I both know this may not be what happened. The best I can do is turn up the heat on Caulfield."

We didn't move or talk for what seemed like forever. It was more like a minute when I came to the conclusion: I don't have a lot of choices. If Caulfield comes out looking bad, then maybe someone else would take over.

"Do you have any names?" I asked. "Is anybody a repeater?"

"Yeah, there are quite a few repeat offenders."

She reached down into the leather bag at her feet and pulled out two sheets of paper stapled together. When she handed me the list, I knew this was the path we were taking. I didn't recognize any of the names. Then it hit me. This was no longer a strategy to shine a spotlight on this crime or Caulfield's inability to solve it. I could be looking at the name of the bastard who killed Abby. I made it to the bathroom in time to throw up.

FRIDAY, DECEMBER 9   5:00 P.M.

Last night Ian and I had dinner, if you can call it that. I met him at the tavern on Birch Street and ate a rubbery piece of meat and a handful of fries.

When I got to the restaurant, I took a booth near the open kitchen. It was too cold to sit near the door. Ian came in shortly after me, we hugged. He's always been such an affectionate child, even in public.

He grabbed a menu and opened it to the MAKE YOUR OWN BURGER page.

"You know, I would have been happy to pick you up."

He didn't look up. "I like to walk."

He kept scanning the page, though odds were he'd order the same thing he always did when burgers were on the menu. I didn't want to criticize Harry, I found myself doing it anyway.

"Your father didn't drive you here, did he? He's got to know he'd be in a lot of trouble if he drove without a license. Then since when did your father think the rules were meant for him?" Shaking my head, I ended with a pathetic laugh to cover over being so harsh. Ian and I knew there was nothing funny about the truth, or me criticizing his father. He sighed and I tried to start over.

"I'm sorry. Of course you'd tell me if he was driving." I paused to let him tell me. When he didn't, I moved on. "What do you think I should order?"

I didn't dare ask Ian if he was eating well or sleeping enough, since I'd already gotten off on the wrong foot. I hated seeing him so thin. I didn't like the dark circles under his eyes. I bet Harry wasn't paying one bit of attention to what he ate. Then Ian finished his own food and started picking at mine, so I let my concerns go.

Over the initial hump, I asked about his classes. He answered the same way he did when I picked him up at school. He offered vague answers about grades and assignments, and I realized I don't know if he's doing any better than last term.

Ian's been living with Harry for almost two weeks and there's little more than two weeks until Christmas, and I haven't talked to Harry. In this one conversation with Ian, I came up with a mental list of things he and I should discuss: Ian's sleeping, eating, and Christmas.

I couldn't imagine what we'd do about Christmas. I could deal with having Harry over for a meal. I could find a way to get through it. Alden wasn't likely to agree. As it was, he was put out that I had traded our Thursday night wine tasting for a burger with Ian.

Well that's inconvenient, he'd said, when I told him about my plans. My son had moved out, in part because of him, and he dared comment on the inconvenience of missing, of all things, a wine tasting. Alden wasn't acting as my ally, my port in the storm. He is another rogue wave.

Ian isn't likely to tell me if Harry's driving without a license. No, he wouldn't want to give me any reason to insist he come back home, or give me cause to cast aspersions on Harry. Something I do quite well without any help from anyone.

I'm outnumbered by men.

With Ian right in front of me, all I could think of were the people who weren't there. I stole a longer look at my son while he looked around the tavern and I wondered what it would be like to be sitting across from a teenage girl. A girl with light hair and expressive eyes like Tessa's.

Her face crowded my mind again. Like her animated persona, she insisted on flitting in and out without warning. Day and night. Whether I was at home or in the office.

Homework. Friends. Lacey. If I pooled the concerns I'd collected over dinner with Ian last night, with the ones Tessa raised in her session today, I had evidence of a tipping point. There was more than enough reason to meet with Harry. In fact, a conversation was long overdue.

Earlier today, Tessa went on about how a reporter friend of hers said the time of the accident makes no difference. Alcoholics don't just drink and drive at night. Something I know all too well.

I was glad Tessa was looking at the park when my heart rate quickened, sending blood throbbing up both sides of my neck. The streetlamps lining the perimeter of the park tripped on. I used the distraction as a chance to catch my breath. I willed myself to remove Harry's face from my mind. No matter how many early mornings I'd witnessed my drunken husband fall into our bed, it was ridiculous to think he had anything to do with Abby's death. The man I knew wouldn't last five minutes without telling someone about something so terrible. Besides, according to Ian, he'd been holding down his job at the Boatworks. Harry was reportedly in recovery. Again.

A sensible woman would pick up the phone and make the call to set up a meeting with him to put her mind at ease. A woman ruled by her heart would hesitate; she couldn't ask this vessel to hold any more than it was already trying to carry.

MONDAY, DECEMBER 12   **8:00 A.M.**

Yesterday, the snow fell heavily, as if challenging my resolve to go through with meeting Harry. We chose a restaurant. Neither his house nor mine would provide the neutral territory we'd need. I found myself waiting for the jingle bells that would announce Harry's arrival at Betty Ann's Café.

I dismissed the warm feeling I had when he walked in. He brushed the snow from his peacoat and shook the moisture from his sandy hair. It was cut the way I like it, not too short around his ears. He looked better than the last time I'd seen him, trimmer, healthy color spread across his cheeks. Ian could be telling the truth when he says Harry's stopped drinking. I caught him looking for me the way he had for so many years, as if he wanted to find me.

He slid into the booth, keeping his coat on. Harry wasn't friends with old man winter. Rubbing his hands together to warm them, he hunched his shoulders up and then leaned back against the seat.

"Bitter cold out there," he said.

I held my hands one over the other, flat on the table to keep them from trembling.

"Thanks for coming, Harry. I'm glad you agree we have a lot to talk about. Can we try to do it without arguing?"

"I never set out to argue with you, C. It's just so much fun, I find I can't resist." He leaned in and treated me to one of his marvelous smiles.

I shook my head and sighed.

He handed me a menu. "I'm kidding. I want to talk without fighting, too."

He teased like my funny old Harry, not the newer, harsher version of Harry. The waitress deposited a cup of coffee in front of him without asking if he was interested. Three plastic creamers and two sugars later, he stirred. I watched as he slurped his candy coffee.

"I know it's not good for me. You don't want to take away all my vices." He laughed. "Yeah, *you* probably do. This menu's impossible. Can I borrow your glasses?"

I pushed my glass case over to his side. "I didn't say a word."

"Those big browns of yours say it all, C. You're thinking I should just eat a piece of candy." He took another swig.

"So about Ian." I didn't like Harry talking about my eyes or knowing what I was thinking.

"I'll do anything for Ian," Harry said. "What's on your mind?"

"I think he's too thin. Are you cooking meals or buying take-out? What about school? He says he's been out a lot. Do you think he's falling behind on his studies?" I can't believe I launched right into it like that. Butterflies danced in my stomach. The café must have set the heat on high. I could barely concentrate, the place was so loud and busy.

"Celia, stop micromanaging him. He's fine. He eats and sleeps, for God's sake. He's in his room all night, what else could he be doing in there but homework?" He put my glasses in my case, closed it with a loud snap, and pushed them back over to my side.

"He could be getting caught up in that foolish MySpace business. I told him he couldn't have an account, then you said he could. We have to be together on these things." I dunked and re-dunked my tea bag. I needed something to do with my hands. Why couldn't I think of all the things I'd planned to say?

Harry got louder. "Look, I'm doing the best I can. I'm trying to keep the job and I'm back in the program. Jesus, he's fifteen. You want me to hold his goddamn hand?"

"Harry, please lower your voice. I'm not picking on you. I'm happy you're back in AA. But he does need some hand-holding. Maybe more than you can do right now. He should come back to me."

Never a good poker player, I showed my hand too early. The only thing that kept Harry from blowing was the arrival of the waitress. He relaxed his shoulders, and pulling his coat tighter, he ordered a breakfast loaded with enough cholesterol for both of us. I ordered something, too, overriding my original intention to drink and run. The waitress yelled our order to the cook back in the kitchen.

"Of course that's only one option. What do you think we should do?" I asked.

Harry was calm again. He placed his hand over mine, and the familiarity of it, rough from all the years he'd spent working on boats, was both painful and tender.

"I know what you want," he said. "But Ian wants to be with me right now. I'll give you an early Christmas present and leave out the part about why he feels that way. I can't lie, I love having him with me again. Stop worrying. Everything's going to be fine. Okay?"

I pulled my tingling hand free. Once again, I refused to let tears fall. The eggs came, and eating breakfast filled time. I knew we still had to talk about Christmas.

"Harry, would you like to come to my house—I mean the house—for Christmas breakfast? We seem to do okay with breakfast." I smiled. "Unless of course you have other plans."

"C, in our case I think four's a crowd. Don't you? I'm not sure Al and I are ready for a Christmas morning, especially in *our* house."

"No, Harry. Alden won't be there."

As soon as I said it, I wanted to kick myself. I was Ian, talking my way into staying out late or eating more junk. What was I thinking? I'd have to get rid of my new husband to make room for my ex-husband. Harry raised an eyebrow; the devil in him would sense the fun he could have at Alden's expense.

"Well, then, I'll come. With Ian. I won't stay long. You're not likely to be serving booze with brunch, are you?"

I drew a quick breath.

"I was kidding, C. Jesus, where's your sense of humor?"

"Harry, there isn't anything funny to me, about you and drinking." The vinyl squeaked as I scootched my way out of the booth. "See you Christmas morning at ten. I've got to go."

And for the second time in all our years together, I was the one to end it.

day 69 *without Abby*

I searched the Sunday *Globe* three times yesterday, even though Melanie told me her piece won't run until the eighteenth. I don't know why I have my hopes up. What good is one article going to do?

I've never been so bored. I could've read the sympathy cards that kept coming, but they just reminded me of what I should've been doing. This time last year, I wrote out our Christmas cards. I stuffed her picture, the one with her wearing the dark blue velvet dress and that silly little Santa hat, into envelope after envelope. No cards to go out this year. Funny, no Christmas cards coming in either. Oh, we got the occasional *Season's Greetings*. No *Merry Christmas*. No *Happy Holidays*. Certainly no pictures of little children in Santa hats.

I decided to decorate Melanie's tree. I went to the basement to get a few lights and some ornaments, and that's where Ethan found me hours later when he came home from work.

"Tessa, you scared me. There aren't any lights on and I called you. You didn't answer."

Then he saw me dripping with tears and snot, my hand frozen to the photo frame ornament she had made last year at Rosemary's.

"Come on, honey. Let's put that away."

"No," I said. "I want to put it on our tree. Help me, okay? Help me."

We took a single strand of colored lights, some star and bell-shaped ornaments, the picture of our daughter, and decorated our pathetic little tree. When we finished, we stood back to look at our weak attempt at Christmas.

"Well," Ethan said, "that fits how I feel."

More tears fell—his, not mine—and he started to move the tree. I thought he was going to bring it back to the basement.

"No, I want it. Leave it. When we take it down, it'll mean this one's over."

So he put the tangible reminder of our shitty little Christmas back on the table behind the sofa. I figured it was only thirteen days until we could do away with it.

day 71 *without Abby*

I've looked at the list a thousand times and have the twelve re-peaters names memorized. Lincoln Barnes. David Callahan. Neil Ford. Harry Hayes. Janet Howard. Paul Larkin. That's just the first half. Their names are indelibly written in my mind. I see the names while I sleep. When I woke up this morning, they scrolled one right after the other like a marquee in Times Square.

The names are stuck in my head. I can't tell Ethan or Rose-mary I have the list, they'd think I've lost my mind. I can think of only one way to get them out. I need to get the facts about these people down on paper. If I make them real, it might help. Help me hate them less. Or help me hate them more.

I've had the list for a week, but I haven't done anything with it because the odds these people are involved is absurd. Still I'm drawn to the list like Abby was to chocolate. I went back to the library, not to Wenonah Public but to Thomas Crane, in Quincy. I knew they'd have more newspapers archived. I was right. Between the library's collection and the Internet access to the Plymouth County arrest records, I would put a life to each name on my list.

Lincoln Barnes, twenty. Son of affluent real estate developer, Lincoln Sr. He was arrested for the third time in February. He blew a .15 after a bad accident. Fortunately, no one was injured or killed. As a third-time offender, he faced a mandatory minimum of six months in jail and an eight-year loss of his license. I could see him sitting at the defense table, all neat and clean in his navy jacket and khaki Dockers, playing his Yale card. Somehow his lawyer got his two priors thrown out. So what did he get? No jail time and eligibility for a work license in six months. He was back at Yale, probably celebrating by drinking out of a funnel.

David Callahan, eighty-two. I remembered David's story. Arrested across from the high school after he plowed through a crowd of people leaving a football game. He hit an entire family, sending all of them to the hospital with various injuries, none of them life-threatening. I'm sure their memories of a car coming out of nowhere, smashing into them, cracking bone, will hurt more in the long run than any broken leg or achy neck.

He was charged with driving under the influence of alcohol, driving to endanger, and causing serious bodily injury while driving recklessly. As I read further, rage percolated through me. Callahan was released on $1,000 bail. One thousand dollars for hitting a family. It took me forever to find out the status of his trial. Then I found it. Dear David had already stood before the ultimate judge. He died in August while awaiting trial.

Neil Ford, fifty-eight. Owner of Clean Closets, a dry-cleaning business in Corcoran Village. After two DUI arrests and two convictions, Ford agreed to enter a thirty-day inpatient treatment center. Following treatment, he bargained for six months house arrest, all to avoid jail time. His story was hard to find. His address wasn't.

Three down, nine to go. It took me all day to research these first three repeaters on my list. Only once during the day did I stop to ask myself why I was doing this. I have no idea if any one of these horrible people is *the* horrible person who did it. It makes me angrier to read their stories, as if I need any help with that. But I couldn't stop. I need to be doing something. Doing nothing isn't an option.

It was Celia who put a stop to me with a whisper. "Tessa, is that you?"

I should've known it was Celia. Only she would still whisper in a library.

"I didn't know you came here." I held her gaze as I closed my notebook. Like a teenager caught with porn, I covered some papers and shoved others into my messenger bag.

"I meet my husband here after work on Wednesdays. We like the Irish supper at Finnegan's across the street. What brings you here, are you working again?" she asked.

Her posture was perfect, and I hadn't realized how much taller she was than me. Then I remembered I mostly see her sitting down.

"No, sometimes I need to get out and I hate to run into people I know. Like to limit the pity parties." I glanced up at the clock hanging above the checkout desk.

"Well then, I didn't mean to disturb you. I'll be running along."

It was only when Celia turned to leave that we both saw a boy about six standing there, holding a stack of picture books. He screwed up his lips and blew, trying to get the hair out of his eyes. "Mrs. Reed, can you read these to me?" he asked.

Celia got down on his level, brushed the hair off his forehead, and helped him rearrange his books into a manageable load. I picked up the two books on dinosaurs he'd dropped and handed them to her.

"Hello, Bailey. I've already chosen the stories for today, but I think I can read one of yours at the end," Celia said. "Is that all right?"

His hair fell back down his forehead as he nodded. Puffing it out of his eyes again, he walked in the direction of the children's room.

Celia backed away from me, her eyes darting over what was left on the table. "I help out a little. I love—"

With all my papers safely covered or in my bag, I had relaxed my shoulders. I tensed them again, sensing the word *children* about to escape her lips.

"It's really time for me to go. I don't want to hit traffic on 3A. See you Friday."

I was glad Celia had interrupted me. If I hadn't left then, I wouldn't have made it home before Ethan. One lame explanation about what I was doing was all I could come up with in one day.

THURSDAY, DECEMBER 15   **8:00 A.M.**

I'd avoided the subject for as long as I could. With Ian coming to dinner tonight, last night was my last chance to tell Alden about Christmas. Ian loved the idea of Christmas breakfast with his parents. Unfortunately, I knew Alden wouldn't share his enthusiasm. Having already made a mess of things, I couldn't let Alden hear about our plans for Christmas from Ian. It needed to come from me.

I rehearsed in the kitchen what I'd say. I paced and whispered my words. It was no use. No matter how I said it, it came out sounding thoughtless and unkind. I walked into the library and took a seat opposite him on the ottoman.

"Alden, I've gotten myself into a bit of a jam. Ian would like to spend some time on Christmas with both his parents. And well, Harry isn't comfortable with us all spending time together." Alden glanced down at my wringing hands.

"I didn't think you'd much care for the idea either," I said.

"Could you do me the favor of disappearing for an hour or so on Christmas morning?"

Disappear. Did I actually ask my husband of less than six months to disappear on Christmas?

Alden placed his bookmark in the page before he looked me square in the eyes.

"Celia, where do you suggest I disappear to? Would the morning be sufficient, or is a longer leave of absence required?" He stroked his beard, running his fingers down his neck.

"That didn't come out right. I don't mean to sound callous. I found myself inviting them before I thought it through." I clasped my hands and squeezed.

For a man without children, his patronizing smile was well practiced.

"You're a grown woman, Celia. Don't you think you've acted rather juvenile? Say you've changed your mind. Certainly it will be awkward, but you can do it. Of course, only if you want to."

"I could, but I wouldn't want them to think you were responsible for the change in plans." I relaxed my hands by realigning the hem of my skirt. Deferring to his better judgment had been the better way to go.

He picked up his book, his signal the conversation was over.

"I can catch up on my proposal for the job, if you agree to owe me more than one faculty function. Does that work for you-and-yours?"

"I can do that," I said. When I was practicing in the kitchen, I'd planned to end the thing with a kiss reward. His bribing me made that unnecessary.

I'm walking a tightrope, with Alden on one side, and Harry and Ian on the other. I can see the easy way out is to let myself fall. The problem is that there isn't a safety net below.

FRIDAY, DECEMBER 16   3:00 P.M.

To his credit, Alden met Ian at the door. "I hope you're hungry, your mother made enough food to sink a ship," he said.

Ian acted as if he didn't see Alden's hand extended. "Yeah, I didn't have lunch. I can eat."

I'd hoped for apologies all around. Apparently too much time had gone by since Thanksgiving.

The meal was cordial. Alden ate. Ian ate. I picked. Back-and-forth conversation was next to nonexistent. It was boring for Ian, listening to Alden go on about his overachieving students and his run for department chair. I didn't want the whole evening to be dull, so when Alden reached for his book, I went to the hall closet to dig out the cribbage board.

When we were a family, we played all manner of card games. Fish. Whist. Hearts. On the boat, after an active day of swimming and sailing, we'd break into teams. Ian was always on mine. We'd sit around the galley table. I'd flip a coin to see who would decide what we'd play. The music of the night was laughter, high pitched and low. We'd laugh the most at Harry's dramatic antics when he'd lose. Only I knew he never ever tried to win.

I placed the board and cards down on the kitchen table. "Interested in a game?"

"Yeah, do you still have that raspberry cocoa with the marshmallows?" Ian opened the pack of cards and shuffled.

"I most certainly do. I keep it here for you."

It was easier to play with two than I thought it would be. Yet the light moment was brief, as light moments in my life so often are.

"Sometimes I wish everything could go back to the way it was," Ian said. "Everybody was really happy. You know, when she—"

The sound of the French doors leading to the library closed louder than was necessary.

"Well, I guess that's my cue that Al's had enough of me for one night. It's late. I gotta go."

"We can finish the game. We'll be a little quieter."

"Hey, when I lived here you always said *Go to bed, it's a school night.* It's no big deal. How about we go shopping tomorrow after school? You wouldn't mind helping me pick out something for Dad, would you?"

I jumped at the chance to see him two days in a row.

"No, I wouldn't mind at all. Your father's a bit tricky to shop for. Do you remember every year when I'd ask him what he wanted for Christmas? He'd always say socks and underwear."

"He still says it."

I whispered, as if Harry were the one in the other room, not Alden. "Maybe some year we should buy him the darn socks. How's three tomorrow at my office?"

He packed up the game; I gathered the mugs.

"I'll be there."

day 73 *without Abby*

Harry Hayes, fifty-four. Assistant manager, Sea Change Boat-works, right here in Wenonah Falls Harbor. His most recent arrest took place around the corner from Bright Futures; it was his second DUI. He pled no contest, got thirty days in jail, thirty days in treatment, lost his license for two years, with no eligibility for a hardship license because he lives within walking distance to his job. I got another address.

Between the time Ethan left for work and my appointment with Celia, I only had enough time to research one person on my list.

The list and those names have the power to pull me away from emptying the dishwasher, or draw me out of reading the mail. As much as I've started to try to do things, these faceless people keep calling me, as if they want to tell me their stories. Stories that suck me into a world where people care more for their gin than their jobs, and wives, and children.

This morning, I forced myself to stop. I dressed better than usual, since I was meeting Rosemary for lunch. I tucked the list into my bag. I don't leave home without it. If Ethan found it, he'd ask me questions I'm not prepared to answer. I wouldn't know where to begin, because I don't know what I'm doing with it, or why it has started to haunt me.

"Don't you look lovely today," Celia said.

Navy blue slacks and a crewneck hardly qualify as lovely. Then again, up until now, Celia must've thought all I owned were sweats. I parked my bag on the floor near my feet, and took my seat.

During my session, I waited for Celia to bring up seeing me at the library. Her discretion made me feel guiltier, even though I haven't done anything wrong. Yet.

I decided to test the waters. If I could tell her about the list, she might be able to loosen the grip it was starting to have on me.

"I called Caulfield twice this week. He hasn't called me back."

I hated having my feet on the floor. My tight pants prevented me from tucking them under me. I crossed and uncrossed my legs instead.

"In two months, Ethan and I have had four meetings and five phone calls with Caulfield, and all we know is that he has paint chip evidence from the scene. We don't know if that helps the investigation or if he has any suspects. He hasn't even told us the cause of her death. I can't believe we'll have to be the ones to ask for the autopsy results."

"This is really out of the scope of my practice, but have you thought about going to this detective's superior? This doesn't sound right." She had her arms crossed in front of her, too.

I felt myself relax as Celia stepped out of her scope of practice, whatever the hell that means. In that moment, I could see she genuinely cares for me, like she does little Bailey from the library. For a split second, I almost told her about the list, and what I was doing with it. When I blinked, her posture stiffened, and she'd put back on her shrink-wrapped face. It's as if her emotions have an on/off switch. I wonder if she's always been so good at flipping it.

"Ethan did go to the chief of police, a guy named O'Brien. He said the state police are involved now. Caulfield told me a month ago, they already were. I guess it's a special unit. It's called CARS. Collision, analysis, reconstruction, something. They use all the information they have from the scene to come up with what they think happened. I should call them myself. I've had it with Caulfield."

"Yes, perhaps you should. I think you have every right to be as involved as you need to be. You need answers," Celia said.

My bag tipped over, landing on my foot. The list was trying to get my attention.

day 75 *without Abby*

I can't stop reading it.

SAFE STREETS; A MATTER OF OPINION
STAFF WRITER MELANIE REYNOLDS

DECEMBER 18

WENONAH FALLS, MA—The annual list of the most dangerous states for pedestrians was released Wednesday by the advocacy group Safe Streets. While Massachusetts ranked twentieth, a number neither alarming nor comforting to local politicians, the mother of recently hit and killed four-year-old Abigail Anna Gray tells a different story.

Tessa Gray, a former freelance writer, says, "I don't care what the report says, my daughter wasn't safe on a neighborhood street in broad daylight. Local law enforcement has done very little to catch the person who hit and killed my child, in effect letting this person get away with murder."

National Highway Traffic Safety Administration (NHTSA) data indicate that 55 percent of pedestrians are killed on neighborhood streets and local roadways, making the places citizens believe to be the safest for walking, actually the most dangerous.

Detective Hollis Caulfield of the Wenonah Falls Police Department, who is heading up the investigation into Gray's death, says, "Wenonah has always been and will continue to be a very safe community. The tragic death of Abby Gray is still under investigation. Though our hearts go out to the Gray family, these kinds of accidents are difficult to solve, especially without eyewitnesses."

Little Abby Gray was killed the morning of October 5 on Beach Rose Lane, the same street as the Bright Futures Preschool she attended. After Abby failed to come in from recess, Abby's teacher Janie Beck found her unconscious by the side of the road. Doctors declared her dead on arrival at South Shore Hospital. Investigators under the direction of Detective Caulfield say that skid marks found at the scene indicate speed was a factor. The detective refused to elaborate on further evidence recovered at the scene.

The Wenonah Falls Police Department hasn't just been plagued with coming up empty on finding the person who fled the scene of the Gray accident. Police logs and arraignment records reveal an alarming increase in arrests related to alcohol and driving, particularly in Wenonah Falls. Officer

Caulfield admits to significant alcohol-related issues in Wenonah but claims, "The problems we have in town related to drinking and driving and any connection to the Gray case are unsubstantiated. After all, the incident occurred at ten in the morning."

Nearly one quarter of all hit-and-run accidents involving alcohol do occur during the day. According to NHTSA more than seventeen thousand people in the U.S. were killed in crashes involving alcohol—an average of about one every half hour, with significant numbers of accidents occurring during daytime hours. With the number climbing each year, the NHTSA reports that motor vehicle crashes involving alcohol remain the leading cause of death among children ages two to fourteen years old.

Leading experts from the advocacy group Safe Streets say, "The investigations into hit-and-run crimes regardless of the profile of the driver are a race against time. The longer it takes police to find persons responsible, the more difficult it is to obtain proper evidence to get a conviction."

When asked if the police have any suspects, Detective Caulfield said, "I'm in no hurry to point a finger at anyone. We're going to take our time putting the evidence together. Sometimes you have to accept that you may never know what happened."

Gray said in response to the detective's position, "I won't accept not knowing what happened. The people of Wenonah should be outraged that a coward hit a child and left her dead at the side of the road. And even more outraged that police aren't confident they can solve this crime. Whether the driver was drinking or not, someone killed a child and didn't stop. Who knows what else this person is capable of doing?"

To that end, Gray has a message for the mystery motorist whose actions have forever changed her life: "You hit a person, my beautiful daughter. Your conscience must be killing you. Please come forward. Someone please come forward."

If you have any information about this case call Wenonah Police at 781-555-6629 or Melanie Reynolds at 617-555-9987.

day 76 *without Abby*

The shrill noise woke me, and I froze. I'm conditioned to think tragedy. I was glad Ethan was still in bed. He took the call. It didn't take long for me to realize it was Chief O'Brien.

"Set up a meeting? Sure," Ethan said. "Thursday works. No, I don't have to check with her. We'll both be there."

As he placed the phone back in the base, his eyes locked with mine, his expression a cross between hope and fear.

"It was the chief," he said. "We've got a meeting." He got back into bed but kept staring straight ahead. "Tessa, I think we need a lawyer."

A shiver ran through me. I twisted my body in bed so I could get a better look at him.

"Honey, this thing is a mess. I think Caulfield is as bad as we thought and O'Brien's going to start backpedaling now. Melanie went pretty easy on Caulfield in that article, but she raised enough red flags. We've got O'Brien's ear now. I want someone to represent our interests."

I got out of bed and moved to the chair by the window. I wanted to look at Ethan without screwing up my neck. I must've moved too quickly because I felt dizzy once I landed in the chair. A lawyer.

Like the flash of an old-fashioned camera, all I could see were orchestrated press conferences, our faces—her face on the local news—again. It sickened me. I knew then that this would get a lot worse before it got better. If it ever got better.

"Why do you think he called so early?" I asked.

"I think if someone challenges him or Caulfield today about what Melanie wrote, he can tell the press he meets with us routinely. *Our next scheduled meeting is Thursday to discuss the ongoing investigation.* He's trying to cover his ass. Tessa, are you okay? You don't look so good."

"As good as it gets. It's a lot to absorb this early in the morning." Part of me wanted to crawl back in bed. The other part—the journalist in me—couldn't wait to write down our questions for O'Brien. Something was finally happening.

"Go ahead, get the lawyer."

MONDAY, DECEMBER 19   **6:00 P.M.**

The light snow and white lights outline the evergreens in Verity Park the way a child would paint winter trees. It's one of the prettiest sights of the season, and a carbon copy of it sits on a piece of paper in the bottom drawer of my desk. I only dare look at it occasionally. Today I had the strength.

I visualized it before I pulled it from the artist's portfolio I keep it in. The watercolor strokes are etched in my mind, as well as on the paper.

Looking at it, I can't believe it's almost Christmas. Another Christmas future. Time and the heaviness of longing force me from my Christmases past. I can remember exactly where she was when she painted these trees, decorated with crimson and copper-colored ornaments, a gold star perched on what she called its tippity-top. Sitting on side-by-side stools in my studio, I taught her how to use a rigger brush, the perfect tool for making branches with striations that look like rope. When she finished, she made it a gift to me. It's a treasure to me now.

The riches of my weekend came in the form of my shopping trip with Ian. The mall was overcrowded, though that didn't matter to me; we were together. He got such a kick out of me buying Harry the socks and underwear.

I had to pay for more than Harry's gift.

Once again Alden was annoyed I went out. He'd tried to surprise me with tickets he'd bought to see a French film at the theater in Corcoran Village. He gave me the cold shoulder on Saturday morning, eating his breakfast behind *The New York Times*. I didn't care and I didn't confront him. I let him slight me until he'd felt I'd had enough.

Later, over dinner, he was harsh. "Remember, I don't care much for Christmas. Never have, really. Don't expect false sentiments and lavish gifts. It isn't my style."

I couldn't tell if that's how he really felt about Christmas, or if he was still mad at me for choosing to go out with Ian.

"I've always loved it," I said, choosing not to make eye contact. There wasn't much conversation after that. He made it clear, the week wasn't likely to be holly jolly.

I've lightened my client load for the next few days. I'll take Thursday off to get ready. I'll keep my Friday schedule as is, since some of the clients I worry about most have Friday appointments. Tessa for one.

I knew she'd want to talk about the article in the *Globe* yesterday. Even I found it hard to read and then not talk about it with someone, one of the most difficult parts of my job. I tried to use Alden once as a sounding board about a tough client. He dismissed me.

"Celia, I don't believe I'm comfortable with your breach of confidentiality. Don't you have a colleague you can discuss these things with?"

Knowing I'd get a similar response, I read the article and kept it to myself. I wondered if it could really help her. Maybe someone who knew something would come forward. Sometimes people don't because they think someone else already has.

I thought back to our conversation last Friday. She was uncomfortable with me. More distant, less eye contact. She kept playing with a wisp of her hair, looking out the window as she spoke.

I hadn't thought she'd be the kind of client who'd be unnerved by seeing me outside the office. Not Tessa, so in touch with her feelings, direct and passionate. It had to be something else. As she fidgeted, I remembered the way she'd shuffled her papers in the library. She shoved them into her bag without a care, acting as if she had something to hide. I didn't bring up seeing her there. I didn't want to push her away from me. She needs me, and I need to help her.

Tessa talked about the investigation. She holds on to it like a rope dangling from a cliff. I've held that rope before. She doesn't realize nothing can stop you from falling, because you can't hold on forever.

Holding on to a painting doesn't help much either.

day 78 *without Abby*

I wrote out the questions. Ethan found the lawyer. He called me this morning and said our first appointment with Pat Benedict was this afternoon. It wasn't until we were standing in the art deco office that I realized Pat was a woman.

Even behind her enormous desk I could tell she was all legs. Taller than Ethan and certainly me, she reached across the desk, stretching out one long arm to shake my hand and with the other she covered it.

"Mrs. Gray, pleasure to meet you. I'm so sorry for your loss. Let's see if together we can get you some answers. Please sit down."

"Call me Tessa." I sat down in a kohl leather chair, it swallowed me up. I was a little kid sitting in the grown-up's chair.

"I spoke to your husband at length this morning. He and I are definitely on the same page about how to proceed. I'd like to hear more from you. What are you hoping I can do for you?" Elbows on her desk, she laced her long fingers together and rested her chin on top.

I didn't mind her confidence. I didn't mind her professionalism. I wasn't sure I liked her being on the same page with Ethan.

"I'll pay anyone, even you, to find out who killed my daughter. I want to look into the eyes of that person and I want to know why."

"Sorry, Pat. Tessa's been through a lot. She and Abby were inseparable." Ethan took my hand.

Pat rounded her shoulders, she softened her tone. "I take no offense. I don't blame you for being skeptical about what I can do to help. I do want the same thing you do."

I knew I shouldn't be taking my frustration out on this pretty stranger. It was typical of me to start off not liking her and wait to see if she had the power to win me over.

"I haven't had a chance to catch Tessa up on everything we talked about," Ethan said. "Do you mind telling her about Hugh?"

"I never mind talking about Hugh, but this meeting isn't about me. It's about the two of you and Abby."

Ethan nodded, encouraging Pat to go ahead.

"It might help you to know, I understand firsthand what you're going through. My brother and I were in a car accident when I was nineteen. Hugh was twelve. A drunk driver broadsided my parents' car while I was driving. Hugh was killed instantly. The driver of the other car got out without a scratch. He got seven years and is out of jail as we speak."

In an instant, I was on the same page with her and Ethan. A page no one would be on if they had the choice. "Is that why you want our case?"

"I'll work hard to find out what happened to Abby," she said. "I won't lie. You might not like the answers I get, or feel any satisfaction once you have them. I understand why you need them."

The more she talked about our upcoming meeting with O'Brien, the more I liked her. We were connected through Abby and Hugh. I couldn't keep my eyes off the picture on the bookshelf behind her onyx-colored head. Staring out at me was Pat. She looked exactly the same, only fifteen years younger. She had her arm slung around the skinny shoulders of a boy with Down syndrome; Wenonah beach framed the shot.

After a confident Pat declared us ready for our meeting, we shook hands and left.

"She's a pistol, huh?" Ethan said.

"You couldn't have found an old fart lawyer who smoked cigars? Do people take someone that pretty seriously?" There was his irresistible smile. "She's really smart," I said. "I think I could trust her. She's in."

He placed his lips on my cheek and whispered. "She's not as pretty as you. And I did ask around, she makes things happen."

I felt stupid for needing reassurance. I linked my arm in his and we walked to the elevators. We had a lawyer.

day 79 *without Abby*

Caulfield didn't show. Ethan and I walked in, and there was O'Brien. A secretary was setting up to take notes, a defensive move, I thought at the time. There was a detective with one of those spiky *GQ* haircuts and two days' growth of beard; he looked almost excited to be there. Then I remembered he was the one who'd picked up my bag the day I blew up at Caulfield.

"Hello Mr. and Mrs. Gray. I'm Jack North, the detective taking over the investigation."

I let slip a gasp. He *was* young, cutting right to the chase without all the usual Wenonah Falls Police formality we'd come to know and hate.

O'Brien jumped in, trying to do damage control. "With Detective Caulfield's retirement weeks away and the investigation still open we thought it best to get Jack on board in a more direct way."

"I don't mean to be rude," I said. "Or maybe I do—but Jack

here doesn't seem old enough to tie his shoes, never mind lead an investigation."

Pat marched in, her good old take-charge self. She said each name as she shook hands. Then she plopped down in the folding chair right next to me, her briefcase making a racket when it came in contact with the table. Sitting next to me was strategic. There was tall Pat, little Tessa, then Ethan. We looked more powerful on our side of the table. All they had was dull O'Brien and the kid detective.

"Tessa, Detective North looks young, but off the record"—Pat sent an intimidating look over to the secretary—"we'll take North over Caulfield. Let's get to it, shall we?"

It was clear Pat Benedict was in charge and that these men already knew her. North nodded his head, pleased Pat had tossed him a bone.

O'Brien stuttered. "Well then. I imagine you would like to know the status of the investigation?"

Bolstered by Pat's compliment, Jack started. "We're working very closely with CARS—Collision Analysis—"

Pat interrupted. "The Grays are well aware of the role CARS plays."

"Yes, well," he continued. "They've analyzed the skid mark and the small glass sample found at the scene. The skid mark was short and inconclusive for tire make. The glass was of a fairly common type. They generated a list of possible vehicle matches. Unfortunately, it's long."

As he hesitated, Pat jumped in. "Is that it for forensics from the scene?"

O'Brien was best at playing defense. "There was a small paint sample." He paused, then almost whispered. "We've temporarily misplaced it."

"I'm sorry," Pat said. "How do you temporarily misplace evidence in a vehicular homicide?"

"This is a complete sideshow," I said. I wanted to put my hands around yet another police officer's neck.

"I'm confident Jack will be able to put his hands on it once he has a chance to get things organized," O'Brien said. He sat up straighter, trying to switch to offense. "He's going to sit down with our contact at CARS tomorrow to see if there's anything else he can look into."

"This is bad for you, Chief. Very bad," Pat said. "Is this Caulfield's doing?" Her voice was louder now, and a tiny drop of spit escaped from her mouth and flew across the table. Ethan and I were speechless.

"I'm sorry Mr. and Mrs. Gray," O'Brien said. "You have my complete assurance that I will look into this misconduct further. I'm being honest when I tell you I don't believe the paint transfer is the solution to this case. Detectives who've seen it tell me it's very small. At any rate, are you comfortable letting Detective North get hold of things to see where we are and what else we can do?"

What else could we say? Caulfield was out. Pat and Jack were in. As we nodded, I could feel the heat in the room rising. These days the source of the initial flame usually came from me, but this time it was coming right off Ethan's steel blue suit.

His lips were pursed, his knuckles white from gripping the conference room table. I'd never seen him like this. I was strangely calm. I'd already known the investigation was irreparably damaged.

O'Brien continued. "I hate to follow difficult news with more difficult news. We have the autopsy results. If you like, we could discuss the report at another time."

"The Grays are prepared to hear the findings. Unless they've changed their minds since we discussed it yesterday?" She dropped her right hand under the table, found mine, and squeezed it. She looked at me, then Ethan. We both gave her the go-ahead.

Jack took over for O'Brien. His voice sounded more like a doctor giving bad news than a cop.

"Your daughter—Abby—died of a head injury. Apparently when her head hit the ground. She had some superficial injuries from the actual car hitting her, but that wasn't what caused her death. I'm very sorry."

I don't know what he or anyone else said after that. All I could hear was Abby's head hitting the pavement.

The house looks beautiful. I draped as many strands of lights as I could find around banisters, doorways, and along the mantel. The lights cast shadows in so many directions, the library reminds me of a church. I tossed evergreen and winterberry branches on tables and bookshelves. I haven't decorated like this since before Harry and I separated. Ian would notice. It looked like Christmas, our old Christmas.

I've already been grocery shopping. All I have left to do is wrap my gifts. It felt strange buying a gift for Harry. I certainly couldn't have him over for Christmas and not give the poor man a gift. I'll keep it out of sight until then, no need to further upset Alden.

I've been trying extra hard to be kind to Alden, and he's returning the favor. Maybe we just had a rocky moment. It certainly is a bit wicked of me, getting all excited about breakfast with Ian and Harry on the first Christmas with my new husband.

I gave Alden an early present last night: a fine-looking brief-case, the one I saw him admiring a few weeks ago in a catalog. We had dinner in front of the fire. I served his favorite pasta dish and opened a fruity merlot.

"Very thoughtful, Celia. You seem to have a great deal of holiday spirit. And energy I might add." He made a sweeping gesture with his hand around the room.

He liked my artistry, though I doubted he'd come around on the plans for Christmas morning.

"It does look nice, doesn't it? I'm trying to find a way to make both you and Ian happy this Christmas. Thank you again for Christmas morning. I really do appreciate it."

He changed the subject, either because he was still hurt I'd invited Harry over or because he was uncomfortable talking about my feelings. I went with the topic of his gift, since that's where he seemed more at ease.

"I'm glad you like your present, I really wanted our first Christmas to be memorable."

"The case is perfect in every way. And if I get the job, the university's new department chair will have an accomplished wife on one arm and a smart case on the other," he said.

"Perhaps I could use your other case," I said. "I rather like the old one."

4:00 P.M.

Tessa brought so much pain into the office today, there was barely enough room for the two of us. She started the session by refusing to sit down. She stood, looking out the window.

"I need a minute. I'm too angry to sit. Ethan and I met with Chief O'Brien yesterday. What an ass."

Though I despise her swearing, I tried to calm her by lowering my voice. "Start wherever you like," I said.

"Caulfield lost evidence. He actually lost the paint sample, which could be the only thing they have to narrow down the car that hit Abby. O'Brien kicked him off the case, which is fine, but he replaced him with a detective who doesn't even shave yet. This case looks more like a circus act than a police investigation."

I gestured for her to sit and she did, tucking her feet under like she does every week. "You told me you and Ethan hired a lawyer. Is he going to be able to help you?"

"She, our lawyer's a she. Pat Benedict," Tessa said. "Do you know her?"

I told her I didn't know this Pat. I asked her to tell me about the rest of the meeting. She looked out the window again. Though her face was turned from mine, I saw her anger dissolve into tears. She let them run, making no attempt to catch them.

At first I was comfortable with the silence, the distance of our chairs and our bodies. How many times have I done this before? Then I disregarded what professional ethics dictate and I went to her. I wrapped her in my arms, letting her sob like a little girl.

I let her decide when she was done, handing her the box of tissues. Then I moved back to my proper place.

She took a few minutes to gather her thoughts and breath. I didn't rush her.

"Celia, I'm really sorry I messed up your sweater." Then she looked right at me. "I'm not crying because they screwed up the investigation. I'm a mess, because they told us how she died."

I'm not sure who was more surprised, Tessa or me, because when she finished telling me, I reached for a tissue from the box.

day 82 *without Abby*

Ethan and I spent Christmas with Abby.

It was ten o'clock when Ethan begged me to get up to open my present.

"Come on, Tessa, I can't wait another minute. You're either going to love it or hate it. I can't stand the suspense."

I propped myself up in bed, pulled the covers up under my armpits, and accepted the pretty package he handed me. It was clear it was a DVD, no disguising it. When I opened it, my favorite photo of Abby graced the cover. I looked up at him; his eyes were crinkled, his mouth slightly open. He waited, trying to read my reaction.

My voice shook when I asked, "What is it?"

"I took all of our movies and had them edited onto one. You know, with music and everything. Are you mad? Do you think you can watch it with me?" he asked. "I waited for you."

I didn't mean to pause. I didn't mean to let him think for one single second that this wasn't the most bittersweet present I'd ever received. It took me a minute to breathe.

"I love it. It's going to kill me to watch it. But I love it and I want to watch right now."

He hugged me so tight it almost hurt. When he let go, I kissed him. Deeply. Lovingly.

We ran downstairs like Abby did last Christmas, so eager to see what Santa had left her. He'd set the family room coffee table with holly place mats and napkins. In the center of the table was a bowl of fresh fruit, cinnamon coffee cake, and a small quiche cut into wedges. Two new candy cane–patterned mugs sat at each of our places. He put the DVD into the player. We waited.

And there she was.

Twirling in the backyard, her curly blonde hair flying. Her little dress looked like an upside-down tulip. She was laughing, showing off for the camera. She was alive.

After that sweet beginning, set to the song "Castle on a Cloud," the movie really started, right from the beginning of our life with Abby. I was standing sideways by our car, looking huge and awkward, pregnant. So proud to display my big fat belly, I stuck it out even farther. I mouthed the words *in labor*. Ethan said from behind the camera, *We're off to the hospital.*

The whole movie was about three hours long, and we watched it three times. The first time, we cried the entire time, gripping each other's hands. By the third time, we laughed through our tears. It was so good to be with her.

It was the first Christmas we didn't go to church. Or visit with family. Or eat a big dinner. Or open lots of presents. It was our first Christmas without Abby. It was better than I'd ever thought it could be. Ethan risked our relationship with his gift, and I loved him for it.

Christmas was wonderful. It was stressful at first, trying to get Alden on his way without pushing him out. I didn't want Alden and Harry to come face-to-face. I knew it would ruin the day. For Ian's sake, I wanted Christmas to be everything Thanksgiving wasn't. I delivered.

Alden packed his new briefcase and left around nine-thirty. His gentle kiss on the lips told me he'd forgiven me for asking him to disappear. He left as if it were any other workday.

With one arm and one leg inside his Lexus, he called back, *Merry Christmas.* After telling me to enjoy my breakfast, he told me to save some room for dinner. He'd be back just at noon.

Knowing Ian and Harry are always late, I had time to get out my gifts and light a fire. At ten minutes past ten, I looked out the window and saw them trudging up the street through the snow that had fallen overnight. Ian was carrying a Macy's shopping bag. Harry had both hands buried deep in the pockets of his peacoat.

The two of them were deep in conversation, oblivious to me watching from the picture window.

In they came, bringing the cold with them. I'd already made a pot of hot chocolate. Ian's swimming with mini-marshmallows, Harry's topped off with a peak of homemade whipped cream.

"Do you want to sit by the fire to warm up or are you both hungry enough to eat?" I asked.

Harry glanced over at Ian. Ian looked to me. I took charge. I didn't want any awkwardness to color our morning.

"I say let's eat a little, open our gifts, and then eat some more," I said. "How's that?"

Harry finally spoke. "Fine with me. C, did you happen to make my old favorite, that sour cream coffee cake with the cinnamon crumb topping? I think I smell it."

I tried to temper the smile I knew was creeping up my face. "Yes, I did. Ian likes it a lot, too."

Funny how a silly little coffee cake can bring a family together. I was surprised at how easy it was to talk to Harry with Ian there. We talked about insignificant things like food and snow. Our conversation was light, and light was nice.

Though the words we exchanged were superficial, the gifts we exchanged were not. I let Ian give Harry the socks and underwear. When we bought them, it seemed like a funny present, but in the giving it became strangely intimate. Harry's mouth turned up in a semismile as he glanced at me and thanked Ian.

"Finally, I got what I've always wanted. Speaking of things you've always wanted, here C. This one's for you."

He handed me a slender jewelry box, clearly wrapped by him.

"Harry, you didn't have to get me a gift. It's gift enough that the three of us are celebrating Christmas and we're all getting along so nicely."

"Go on, open it. Don't make a federal case over a little present."

Classic Harry, getting all tough to protect having his feelings exposed. I said *thank you* as I opened the tape-covered package.

I couldn't believe he'd done it. There lying inside a cherry red velvet jewelry box were two birthstone wheels, one ruby, one emerald. They hung from a gold box chain. The mother's necklace I'd always wanted but could never bring myself to buy.

Even I realized my mouth had dropped open. Ian knew the significance of my gift, knowing his birthstone was emerald and hers ruby. He didn't say anything but jumped up to help me clasp the chain around my neck.

I choked out the words, "I love it. Harry, I absolutely love it. Thank you." I placed my hand over my gift, holding it to my chest.

"Well, I knew you wouldn't get it for yourself. You know me, always a day late and a buck short. Glad you like it. Now what about Ian? Have you got something for the kid?"

Though I had several gifts for Ian, the timing couldn't have been better for my gift to Harry and Ian. I practically skipped over to the tree and picked up two identical presents. I handed each a shirt box.

"Open these together, they're the same thing. I hope you like them."

Harry and Ian locked eyes for a second and then like two little boys in a race, they tore open their presents. It was Harry's turn to be surprised.

Harry unfolded his maroon sailing jacket, stood up to try it on, and ran his hand over the black stitching *Crew of Summer.* Ian did the same.

Five years after Harry wooed me aboard *As You Like It,* our growing family required a bigger boat. The newer version was longer and brighter—Harry's dream boat—and he knew his way around it like he'd owned it all his life. We both loved it. Still, seeing the new owners of *As You Like It*—the boat we'd had our first date on—sail out of sight was like closing a photo album full of memories.

"Harry, the last time I saw you speechless, you were saying good-bye to a boat." I rubbed the arm of his new jacket. As if I'd touched a hot stove, I drew back my hand.

"Wow, C. I love it," he murmured into his chest, still looking down at the writing. "I only wish there were two more."

His comment hadn't meant to sting. He missed us being a family, and for a moment so did I.

Ian looked from Harry to me to see if all this loose emotion would unmoor another holiday.

I got the morning back to a safe place with food. "Well, the gifts this year were a hit. Let's see if I was able to do the same with breakfast. Ian, take off your jacket. You don't want to get bacon grease on it before you've had a chance to wear it on the boat."

The rest of the morning flew by. Like an old Cinderella, I suddenly realized the time was near twelve. Alden, precise being his middle name, would be home any minute. As much as I hated to end our family Christmas, I knew I needed to respect Alden's sacrifice and not rub his nose in my happy family, one that at the moment didn't seem to include him.

I starting picking up discarded boxes and bows, giving not-so-subtle cues to Ian and Harry it was time to leave. Ian crumpled wrapping paper while Harry loaded the dishwasher. I couldn't remember the last time he'd done that. Each moved quickly, not bothered by my nudging. They left the way they came, walking through the snow, talking. I watched them, wishing they could have stayed all day.

When Alden returned, I was still beaming over how the morning had gone. I let him think it was because he was home.

"Celia, you may very well change my skepticism over this commercial holiday of yours. Your elation is rather contagious. Now let's get cooking, shall we?"

He handed me a bottle of Bordeaux like it was a bouquet of flowers. I opened it, poured us both a glass, and hid my disinterest in food behind sips. Though the thought of eating again made me seasick, eating more than I wanted was a price I'd gladly pay for juggling the desires of both of my families.

winter of

PART TWO

the heart

day 89

New Year. Same old life. Ethan and I always go to Rosemary and
Kevin's for New Year's Eve. This year was different. I hated every
minute of it. Stupid people screaming in Times Square blasted
from out of the new plasma screen TV set up in the den. Perched
on kitchen stools, Rosemary and I watched Kevin and Ethan chop
and sauté. Their process time-consuming and inefficient. The
smell of garlic lodged in my nose for hours before we finally ate
real food. It was so late I was nauseated by the time I picked up
my fork. It took so much energy to socialize, you would've thought
there were more than the four of us celebrating. I should've tried
harder to get out of it, but Rosemary made me feel guilty.

"Tessa, you can't break with tradition. We can't start off the
New Year without you and Ethan. I'll be able to put Matthew to
bed early and we can have a nice dinner just the four of us, no
kids."

"But you had Thanksgiving. Aren't you sick of hosting?"

"We could go out to dinner if you want. It's just that it's always so loud and expensive. And with all the crazies on the road, I'd be a wreck wondering if we'd get home in one piece."

She didn't mean to reopen the wound. Her simple expression meant nothing to her while those same words cut me. Sometimes after they've been spoken, they beg to be taken back, the person instantly realizes the thoughtless turn of phrase. That was in the beginning. Now, I'm the only one who feels the twist of the blade.

"Why don't we bag the whole thing? You and Kevin can have a nice romantic dinner, and I can go to bed. I hate watching a bunch of drunks stare at a stupid disco ball dropping down a metal pole."

"You'll disappoint the guys. You know how much they love making Chinese food."

What I didn't tell her was how I dreaded the thought of ushering in a New Year. What I wanted more than anything was to have stopped time right before I sent Abby to preschool on October 5. I didn't want to raise my glass to what would be my first full year as a mother without a child.

day 92

I was starting to get pissed I hadn't heard anything, when Pat called. She had grand plans for bringing the case back into the media spotlight. She'd organized a press conference at noon the next day, the three-month anniversary of Abby's death.

"I know it will be a painful day, but you said it yourself, we have to go after the public's sympathy," she said. "We need media attention. It could help us get people to give up any information they have, and we need to keep the pressure on the police. No one is more aware of this than you are; we've lost precious time here."

"I don't think I can talk."

"You won't have to," she softened. "I'll talk. Jack will talk. O'Brien's going to run the thing."

"Can you come over here to get some pictures of Abby? I'd like them to use new pictures of her. You know, for the news."

day 93

I fainted. North had just finished telling the press the little bit of evidence they had and how the public could help us. I went down. When I came to, a sea of faces blocked my view, making it hard for me to remember where I was. Though it took me a minute to find Ethan, his face a mix of love and concern, the speculation was impossible to miss.

Reporters buzzed.

"The stress must be getting to her."

"Do you think that's the first time she heard they don't have much evidence?"

"She didn't eat this morning, she's fine." Pat's commanding voice rose above the rest. "Get out of our way."

I never felt my feet touch the floor as Ethan and Pat carried me to the nearest conference room. Apparently the press conference was over. With a cold cloth on my forehead and a glass of water in my trembling hand, I beat Pat to it.

"Well, that went well. Don't you think?" I asked.

"As long as you're okay, Tessa, I couldn't be happier," she said. "This press conference will lead the local news, it could even make the nationals."

I was glad she, Ethan, and I were the only people in the room, because anyone else would've found her coldhearted. But I get Pat. I wonder if she's gotten into as much trouble as I have over the years for seeing it and not being able to control the impulse to call it.

Ethan took the rest of the day off. On the ride home we were quiet; I replayed the day in my head. I forgot he was there until he spoke. "Are you up for the cemetery?"

I almost laughed at how ridiculous it sounded, but I didn't want to hurt him. A few months ago he would've asked if I was up for a drink. Now his idea of a pit stop on the ride home was a trip to our daughter's grave site.

"No, but you should go if it helps you. Drop me off at Morgan's Pharmacy, I need some things. I can walk home. I could use the fresh air."

"No, Tessa. I'm not letting you walk home after you fainted. You're not up to it. Either you're getting sick or the stress is getting to you."

He should've known better than to order me around.

"Ethan, don't tell me what to do. You do what you need to do and I'll do what I need to do. Drop me off. On your way home pick up some takeout. We'll watch the news together when you get back."

I got what I needed at Morgan's. When I fainted I knew the aisle I'd have to visit. It surprised me that Ethan hadn't remembered the last time I'd done it.

Once again he came home to find me frozen to an inanimate object. Last time it was Abby's photo ornament. This time, I was sitting on the couch, watching Abby on the news, watching myself fall to the ground during the press conference. All while I was holding the stick that had turned blue, minutes before he walked through the family room door.

Tessa's pregnant.

When she told me, my hand flew to my necklace. In the two weeks since Harry gave it to me, I've come to see it as my personal amulet. The men in my life have been peaceful since its arrival. If only a necklace could protect Tessa from the heaviness that comes with being a wife and mother, I would give her mine.

"Ethan and I tried for two goddamned years to get pregnant and now it happens? This isn't ironic, it's cruel."

It was another session where she paced and I sat on the edge of my seat. This time I didn't bother to encourage her to sit down. I focused on trying to think of what to say.

"You certainly have a lot to sort through," I said. "I'm here to help."

"Ethan sobbed when he figured it out. I was sitting there with the pee-covered stick in my hand and he started bawling. He's ecstatic and I can't even be happy."

"Give it time," I said. "There are so many emotions for you to understand. Of course it's overwhelming. You'll adjust to the idea. Have you told anyone other than Ethan?"

"No. I'm afraid to. People will think I'm a horrible person. I would if I were them. You don't replace your child with another child. Oh God."

Her little body made a loud wheeze as she dropped into the upholstered chair. She hugged her knees to her chest. Her yet-to-be-largess still allowed for it.

"Perhaps you should take your time sharing your news."

"Why? In case I lose this child, too? That's great advice, Celia, a real vote of confidence."

"I meant give yourself time to deal with your feelings. You don't owe anyone an explanation. You and Ethan want this child and what's most important is for the two of you to figure this out, together."

She dropped her head on her knees.

"You do want this child, don't you?"

She raised her head and locked her eyes on to mine. "I don't know, Celia. I don't know if I do."

I knew I wanted Ian from the minute I realized I was pregnant. Though two under two wasn't my preference, it only meant our family was complete sooner than I had planned. It helped knowing Harry would be over the moon.

Without fanfare, I told him one night after dinner. As was our routine, I cleared the table and he loaded the dishwasher. Ordinary circumstances sprinkled with extraordinary news.

"We'll need to clean out that mess of a room upstairs. There's plenty of time, though I would like to do it before I get so big I can't get out of my own way. Let's paint the walls anything but pink, I have a feeling it's a boy."

Without warning, he grabbed me and dipped me, like we were dancing. He hollered so loud, I worried he'd wake her. Secretly, I wouldn't have minded. It would have been nice to wrap her up in our joy.

Tessa wouldn't have a sweet memory of sharing her news with her husband. Her second child announcement was tainted. As she spoke—while I listened—I heard her story echo my own, though it rang in a slightly different key. Firstborn daughters lost. A future that held the promise of a second child. The question wasn't whether or not this child would change her, it was whether or not one child could be enough.

day 95

Ethan's driving me crazy. He cleaned out the cupboards of coffee and diet soda, all I could find this morning was that crappy herbal tea. I went to get a breakfast plate and he practically did the fifty-yard dash to save me from reaching up to pull one down. I know he's trying to take care of me, but I had to set him straight.

"Look, Ethan, I know you're excited about the baby. I know you're trying to be sweet and helpful. But you need to knock it off or I'll tell you who the real father is."

He looked the way a puppy does after its owner swats its nose. I can be such a bitch.

"I'm kidding. You have to leave me alone, though. We went through this when I was pregnant with Abby. It drove me crazy then, and I have a sneaking suspicion this time you'll be a lot worse."

"I can't help it. It's a miracle. I never thought I would ever feel happy again." He hugged me for the millionth time as he put his hand on my flat stomach.

I'm feeling a lot of things, happy isn't one of them. Sure, he can jump to happy. I'm the one who's queasy in the morning, pissy during the day, and exhausted at night. We don't even know this baby.

I can't believe he's moving on. He can be so simple sometimes. Lose Abby, be depressed. Tessa's pregnant, be happy. I don't want to move on. It'll be as if Abby never existed. This baby will never know his sister.

I want a boy. If I have a boy it won't be like I'm replacing her. Blue instead of pink. Little jeans instead of little dresses. Trucks instead of dolls. It would be different, and different might be okay. I don't know if I can love this baby the way I loved Abby.

Yesterday, Celia promised me I can.

"When you hold your second child in your arms, you feel a love you didn't know you were capable of," she said.

She kept putting her hand to her throat, touching a necklace, not her pearls. Then she tucked it inside her sweater.

"Each child becomes yours the minute those tiny fingers curl around yours." Her eyes got shiny. "Tessa, you'll love your baby. You'll open your heart again."

I go back and forth between hoping she's right and fearing she is.

MONDAY, JANUARY 9   **8:00 A.M.**

I'm a bit queasy this morning. I'm so susceptible to the power of suggestion. Ian was sick all weekend. Harry called me to cancel our Saturday plans.

"He tossed his cookies late last night into this morning. He's been okay since. Just really tired, not wanting to eat. Won't be going out to eat with you today, that's for sure."

"I thought you said he was better. Do you think it's the bug? Or did he go out with friends last night?"

"There you go again, assuming someone tied one on. I wish to hell he would get out of here once in a while. All the kid does is spend time online."

"See, I told you he shouldn't get caught up in those sites. They're addictive, and you have no idea who he's talking to."

"And you say I can't let things go? Look, maybe he'll feel better tomorrow. I'll have him call you."

After Ian still didn't feel up to going out yesterday, I went over to see if there was anything I could do.

Harry was working in his office off the den, which made it easier for me to take charge. The Sunday paper was strewn all over the living room. A plate with toast crumbs and a glass of fizz-less ginger ale sat on the coffee table.

Ian's room looked like it had been throwing up clothes for much more than a weekend. I shooed him out to the couch and began to put his room back in order. Clothes, dirty and clean, seemed to live on surfaces rather than in drawers. The room had such a boys' locker room odor to it, January or no January, I opened the windows to air the place out.

When fresh sheets were on the bed, the room vacuumed and dusted, and all traces of clothes sorted dirty and clean, I found his journal. I didn't know he kept one. I touched its faux leather cover, knowing his hands touched it when the deepest of thoughts were on his mind. Thoughts I wanted to know, but dared not know.

If I ventured inside, I could find out whether or not Harry was drinking. Did Ian still talk to Lacey? Was he getting pulled into the vortex of the Internet, or was it as harmless as Harry seemed to think? I wondered if Ian wrote about how much he despised Alden. Or me.

It would be so easy. One page I told myself. I could read just one page. Without looking inside, I cracked the journal enough to run my hand over the first page. It fell to the floor in swirling motion. I recognized it immediately. Harry had been responsible for choosing her memorial card. I don't know why I assumed he would pick something religious. A dove soaring toward heaven. Saint Thérèse, the Little Flower, patron saint of children. But no. Harry chose a red sun setting over a calm seascape. He said she would have picked it. I hated his choice but couldn't argue. He was right. It was exactly what she would have chosen.

The pounding of my heart startled me. I picked up the card and placed it back inside Ian's journal. I closed it. I'd always been afraid someone might read mine. I wasn't going to jeopardize my closeness with Ian. He'd given me no reason to invade his privacy. I didn't need to confirm any suspicions or know more about his life than he was willing to share with me. I slipped the journal back into his underwear drawer and looked toward the door, afraid Harry or Ian would catch me.

With a clean room and a cleaner conscience, I checked on Ian to see if there was anything else I could do.

"Would you like some chicken soup? I brought all the ingredients to make homemade."

"I'm not hungry, Mom. You can leave the stuff and go. I'm fine. I just want to go back to bed."

"Maybe I should call the doctor. Can I help you back to bed? Then I'll make the soup. You and your father can have it for dinner. Would you like to change into some clean pajamas?"

Irritated but not irate, he begged me to stop. "I'm not four, okay? Leave me alone."

As I reached over to brush the hair off his forehead, I offered an explanation that seemed only to make matters worse. "I didn't mean to hover. It's hard not to want to take care of my baby."

I must have moved from mothering to smothering because he blew.

"Cut it out. I'm not your baby. Why don't you go and take care of that overgrown baby you have at home?" Ian's tone was enough to draw Harry from the office.

"Hey pal, knock it off. Sick or no sick, you don't talk to your mother that way. Ian, back to bed. C, you can head out now, Ian will call you when he gets up." He raised his voice as Ian brushed by both of us, "To apologize."

I left Harry's with my tail between my legs. Later that night when Alden and I were reading, Ian followed his father's orders.

"Hi, Mom. Sorry about before," he said. "I wasn't feeling good. I couldn't take all the babying. We okay?"

"Of course. I only wanted to make you feel better. I don't get to mother you anymore. Perhaps I got a little carried away. I hope you're not angry I cleaned your room."

"No, I'm not mad. I'm sorry you had to see the mess I've made. You didn't have to clean my drawers." He hesitated in a way that told me we were talking about the journal.

"Just so you know I did put some things away, but I left what was there untouched. I won't go in your drawers again. I respect your privacy too much."

"I'm sorry I was mean. You were only trying to help."

"Sometimes when a boy is fifteen, his mother should wait until she's asked."

TUESDAY, JANUARY 10   8:00 A.M.

It's hard to believe I've known Alden only a year. We surprised more than a few of our family and friends when we married within six months of our first meeting. Easy trips to museums led to exotic dinners. He introduced me to Malaysian and Creole cooking. He treated me to repertory theater and evenings at the symphony. When he proposed after an experimental version of *Candide,* I didn't think twice about accepting. His desire to please me told me all I needed to know. The next step seemed logical. Our being together made sense. We'd be each other's companion; I thought he could be Ian's rock.

It had been a few months since Alden had planned an out-of-the-ordinary evening. I hadn't expected much of a celebration of the anniversary of our first date. He surprised me when he picked me up after work last night.

I opened the door to a waiting room I thought would be empty, and there he sat. In his pinstripe suit, he held a bouquet of blush-colored roses. Reminiscent of our first date, he stood and handed them to me, only this time they came with a kiss.

"I originally thought we'd have dinner at Pierre's, but I then realized something more memorable was in order," he said.

From his pocket he produced two opera tickets. He displayed them in a fan so I could read them, Mozart's *The Marriage of Figaro.*

"For tonight? This is so sweet."

"Are you up to it? You won't mind staying out late on a work night?"

"Of course I don't mind. I can't think of a better way to celebrate."

As the muscles in his face slackened, his posture took on a less formal stance. I realized then, he'd been nervous. He'd spent time planning to surprise me, and he'd worried I might not like his spontaneity. I kissed him again, even though I know he hates public displays. It was my waiting room and we were alone, after all. Alden kissed me back, deeply, right in front of the picture window that looks out on Verity Park.

day 99

Over one hundred calls have come through the Wenonah Falls tip line since the press conference last Thursday. Pat called to warn me. The story is officially back in the spotlight.

"I wanted you to know, when you turn on the TV or pick up the paper, you're likely to see something about Abby," she said. "With all these tips coming in, some local media have assigned reporters to stay tuned to what's going on."

"That's good, right? More media, more tips. How many of the leads are credible?"

"Most of them are bogus. North and another detective are going through them now to see which ones could be legit." She paused. "Tessa, I know he looks young, but he's in his thirties and he's good. This is his chance to stand out, so he's going to work hard for you, for himself."

She seemed to know a lot about Jack North. I wanted to know more about the tips.

"Are you going to tell me what the callers said? I mean, we're paying you to get us what we need here." I tossed out my first test question.

"Most of them involve any kind of car you can name. Some callers name specific people. When you dig around, you find out that the person pointing to someone else has an ax to grind. You know, rough divorce, disgruntled employee, one kid trying to get another kid in trouble. The detectives know how to filter the clots from the cream. They're looking for themes."

"Look, Pat. I get you. I know you already know what the themes are. You and *Jack* seem pretty tight. Even if you don't have an inside track on the tips, you're clever enough to get the information another way." I wasn't going to let one more person play around with me. "So, are you going to tell me, or do I have to go badger North myself?"

"You do get me." Her laugh was airy. Then she spoke straight.

"There's nothing between the detective and me. That doesn't mean I don't know how to get what I need. You're going to need to trust me. When I can tell you what I know, I will. If I don't tell you something, there's a reason. I'm not going to baby you, I bet you hate that. You've got to promise me you won't interfere with the investigation. Agreed?"

I found a way to keep her talking, but I didn't agree. I wouldn't make that promise to anyone.

day 100

One hundred days. I've spent one hundred days without Abby. The weather is mocking me, its vivid sunshine and high temperature for January. It should be dark and cold like me. I spent the morning touching her things. I took out her Barbies to see what she'd left them wearing. Her favorite—the one she named Trixie—was dressed like the vixen she sounds like, in revealing evening wear. With the gown askew, her plastic breasts poked out, reminding me why I'd objected to Abby having these stupid dolls in the first place.

Girl-deprived Rosemary used to say, "I insist, Tessa. Every girl Abby's age has these sexist playthings. Deal with it. Don't start worrying about an eating disorder for God's sake. We'll agonize over that when she's thirteen."

She'll never be thirteen. She's four. She's been four for one hundred days. She'll be four for the rest of my life.

MONDAY, JANUARY 16 **8:00 A.M.**

Things were going so well. Harry and I could talk without fighting. Ian and Alden hadn't fought since Thanksgiving. I'd found a way to douse the flames that so often ignite between these men I love. Then Harry met Alden. This time was worse than all the other times before, combined.

Since Harry still can't drive and the weather had turned cold again, I thought dropping off a few groceries would strengthen the olive branch between us.

"Alden, do you mind staying in the car while I drop off these bags?" I asked. "It will only take a minute. Then we're off to St. James's and out to breakfast." My mood was light. I hadn't anticipated any objections.

"Celia, since you've already bought the provisions, I'll permit it. Please, I ask you, don't make a habit of this. He's a grown man. He should feel the consequences of his actions. If he finds it a trial to get groceries in January, it seems a proper penalty to me. Especially after all he put you through."

In retrospect, I should have guessed Alden wouldn't appreciate my gesture, but surprisingly Harry didn't either.

"C, what brings you by? I thought we agreed you'd call whenever you wanted to see Ian. The place's a mess." He kept his voice low and the door only partially open. He didn't invite me in.

"I brought you a few things." I lifted up both plastic bags as evidence. "I know it's hard for you to shop in this weather. I thought if Ian would like to go to Mass and breakfast, he could join us."

"I can get my own damn groceries. Jesus, I know the kid's thin, but I manage to put food on the table. As far as church goes, good luck. He's not up yet."

My motives were good. Two out of three people found them offensive. Church was the place I brought my unintentional wrongdoing, praying this was simply a small detour on the road to peace in my so-called family. It wasn't. Apparently we will be taking the long way around.

Alden and I went to Betty Ann's for breakfast after Mass. With our order of omelets and corn bread placed, the familiar bells rang. I looked up to see Harry and Ian walk in. Harry looked around the café, trying to spy an empty table. At once, four awkward glances darted from the door to our booth and back again.

"There's plenty of room at our table. Please join us," I said.

Alden looked at me like I'd lost my mind. Ian's my son. I wasn't going to eat in the same restaurant and not sit with my child because two grown men couldn't find a way to be civil.

He quickly found the social etiquette he's good at using in public. Standing up, he reached his hand out to Harry. Harry nodded his head, ignoring his hand. He slid in next to me. Alden sat back down. Ian shot a harsh look at Harry as he took the outermost edge of the booth on Alden's side. I knew immediately I'd made a huge mistake.

I directed my attention to Ian. "How about a nice hearty breakfast?"

Alden's cheery mood was put on. I wondered if he thought he could fake closeness with Ian to impress Harry. "He loves a good breakfast. What'll it be, son?"

I tried to sail over his remark. "There's our waitress, want a stack of strawberry pancakes?"

"No, thanks. I'm not hungry. Dad dragged me here, said we didn't have any food in the house."

Alden spoke to Ian, but looked at Harry. "That's funny. Didn't your father tell you that my wife brought groceries over this morning before Mass?"

"You didn't tell me Mom came over." I hated seeing that look come across Ian's face, disappointment merged with sullen.

"Look, kid, you were sleeping. I didn't have the chance." Harry raised his voice, casting a warning glare at Alden. "I didn't feel like getting out the damn skillet. Is that a crime?"

Alden shot back, "No, that's not illegal. I just don't think *I'd* add lying to my list of things I role-model to my son."

Harry, Ian, and I stopped breathing. Harry took his time standing up. He grasped Ian's upper arm, making it clear there'd be no pancake order. He looked like he was doing everything in his power to restrain his body. He didn't restrain his voice.

"Look, you don't have a son. You do have a wife who, in case you forgot, used to be mine. I sure as hell haven't always done the right thing. But don't sit there all high and mighty, when you didn't waste any time taking her away from us. Ian, we're out of here."

The waitress, who looked like she'd seen this scene before, came and deposited our eggs on the table with a slam so loud we didn't hear the door do the same. "Is there anything else you need?"

What a silly question. There was so much more I needed. But she was talking about food.

day 106

I've always loved Dr. Hilliard. His grandfatherly look makes me trust he's got all the experience he needs. Even though I have to put my feet in that ridiculous man-made contraption, he has the ability to make me feel like I'm anywhere but where I am, upside down and exposed. I like that he examines me with his practiced hands but does the doctor talk in his office down the hall. When I have my pants back on.

"Thanks for the flowers and the note you sent. It meant a lot," I said. "I admit I didn't read it at first. I wasn't up to reading cards until recently."

"I meant it when I said I feel very sad any time a child I've delivered dies. These children feel like mine in some small way." He glanced over at a bank of photos.

All you had to do was look at his striped walls papered with pictures of children and you'd believe him. His children. His children's children. Patients' children.

"Does that make you more happy than sad to be delivering another baby of mine?"

"Every life is precious. Abby's life was cherished, and this child's life will be, too. Bringing a child into this world is never an easy task. That means you, Miss Tessa, have a lot of work to do."

"I'm overwhelmed, all right."

"I'll be honest with you. I'm concerned about the effect your mood will have on this baby. There are stronger and stronger links being made every day between the mind-body connection of a mother and her developing child. I'm not telling you not to be depressed, since that's impossible. But I do want you to stay on top of things," he said.

"I won't take antidepressants. I took them for the first month only because Rosemary fed them to me. I didn't have the energy to fight her. But I have been seeing a therapist once a week."

"Are the sessions helpful?" he asked.

"I hate to admit it, but yes. The therapist's wound a little tight, but she cares about me, and she's helping me talk about things I can't seem to with anyone else."

"Excellent, good therapists are hard to find."

"Like good doctors?"

He broke into a smile revealing his perfect teeth. The warmth I felt coming from this kind man, his genuine concern for me, made me wish for a minute he were my father, not my gynecologist.

"Tessa, do you have any questions for me before you head out to schedule your next visit?"

"I do, but I don't want you to think I have a problem. I mean, it only happened once, and I don't even know if I was pregnant yet."

"Go ahead, you can't imagine the confessions that take place in this office."

"I got drunk on Thanksgiving. Could one big binge have harmed my baby?"

He flipped open a date book and used his long index finger to count. "I would say you can leave that worry right here in this office. While there's no safe amount of alcohol to consume during pregnancy, what's done is done. Given your estimated due date, your baby was likely only a few days', perhaps a week's, gestation. Our biggest concern about alcohol comes a bit later, when brain development is in full swing. The most important thing is that you're not drinking now. I don't recommend any drinking at all during pregnancy. Knowing you, Tessa, I'm certain you'll do what's right for your baby."

I left Dr. Hilliard's office with my next appointment scheduled in February, a due date in summer, and confidence he would get me safely from one date to the next.

day 109

Ethan called my name so loudly, I startled awake. I'd fallen asleep in Abby's rocking chair. I rotated my neck to work out the crick. I must have been out for a while.

Knowing he wouldn't come to me, I made for the stairs. He stood at the second-floor landing. His jaw was clenched, and he was waving a piece of paper.

"What the hell is this?"

My mind raced, trying to conjure up where I'd left the list and my notebook. I could've sworn I tucked everything back in my messenger bag and left it in my study.

"Tessa, why do you always have to do everything by yourself?"

"I can explain." I stalled, not having a single idea how to justify what I was doing with the list and my investigation.

"When were you planning on telling me?"

"I was—"

"I would've loved to have gone with you," he said. "This is my baby, too."

The last thing he said faded into the herringbone wallpaper as he took the stairs down to the family room. I followed. He dropped down on the couch at the same time he tossed my prenatal instruction sheet down on the coffee table.

I curled my body into the window seat, glad I hadn't said anything about the list. He still didn't need to know.

"You didn't miss anything. It was a routine doctor's visit. There will be plenty more for you to come to."

"That's not the point. You could have said, *Hey, Ethan, I'm going to the doctor today.* It wouldn't have been that hard."

His look was all little boy, as if I hadn't picked him for a game during gym. He put his hand on his forehead and closed his eyes. He was working hard not to be mad at me. Ethan couldn't live with himself if he yelled at me pregnant. He's not very good at yelling at me not-pregnant either.

"I didn't mean to leave you out," I said. "I need time to warm up to doing this again, that's all."

"What about what I want? Do you ever worry about that?" He got off the couch and left me without saying another word.

I hate when he drops things so easily.

MONDAY, JANUARY 23   4:00 P.M.

I collected my messages in my usual automatic way, pen in one hand, message pad in the other. I started paying attention when I heard Harry's unmistakable tone fill my office.

"It's me. Call me after work. I've got something to tell you."

He sounded flat. He always did hate to apologize. I was so eager to call him back I almost skipped listening to the rest of the messages. When the fourth message was from the high school, I realized Harry hadn't called to mend fences.

The secretary from Wenonah High was calling to see if either Harry or I could call to set up some time to meet with the principal. All she said was that he needed to talk to us about Ian.

I paused the machine to call Harry.

"Sea Change Boatworks. This is Harry Hayes. What can I do you for?"

"I got your message, and the one from school about Ian."

"I told you to call me after work." His tone was gruff, the way it is when he talks from work and customers are staring him down to get off the line. "Lewis isn't here, and it's busy."

"For goodness sake, it's January. How busy can it be?"

"I already called them back. I set something up for two tomorrow."

"In the middle of a workday? You couldn't have pushed for something more convenient? Did they say what this is about?"

"Look, you don't have to come. It's probably something about him not working up to potential. I can handle it." He said something I couldn't hear. Then I realized he wasn't talking to me.

"Of course I'm coming," I said. "You could've been more thoughtful about the time, that's all. I'll have to reschedule clients, and at this late hour—well, it's going to be difficult."

"I get it, I get it. Come if you want, don't if you can't. Call me later. I'm trying to close up, and I still have customers."

Click. Dial tone.

I hate being shut off like a light. I had more to say and I wasn't about to wait to hear more from Harry. I wouldn't be blindsided by Principal Castigan either.

After five rings, Ian answered in that voice that pretends not to be sleepy.

"Ian, it's mother. Were you napping?" I hadn't meant to make it sound like an accusation. "It's five o'clock."

"I guess I fell asleep studying. Mr. Gordon should bottle this chemistry. It'd make a great sleeping pill."

"School called your father and me. Do you know of any reason why Principal Castigan would want to meet with us tomorrow?"

Had we been on cell phones, I'd have thought the call was lost. "Ian? Are you there?"

"Yeah, I'm here. He's pissed I've been out a lot. He keeps saying I could be doing better. I'd like to see him take chemistry with Mr. Gordon."

"Why wouldn't we be meeting with the guidance counselor

or your teachers, if it's about grades? A meeting with the principal implies something more serious, am I right?"

"I don't know. I wish everyone would leave me alone. School.
Dad. I can't take it if you start on me, too."

"We all want to help you."

"Everybody yelling at me isn't going to help me get my act together. The new term starts in a week. Tell everyone to back off.
I'll try harder."

"No one is yelling at you. We're only concerned because colleges take a hard look at every single year. There isn't a great deal
of room for error."

"College." His voice was low, discouraged. "Look, you probably
want me to get back to the books. I'll call you later."

Click. Dial tone.

Once again, I had more to say without the opportunity to say it.

WEDNESDAY, JANUARY 25   8:00 A.M.

Never in my life have I sat in a principal's office because I'd
done something wrong. Sitting there yesterday, I had the distinct
impression Harry and I were about to be taken to task for bad parenting. Something, I'm afraid, that can't be solved with a detention.

Books, papers, and manila folders managed to fill the office
despite its bigger than expected size.

Mr. Castigan was dressed more like a principal than the last
time I saw him. I wondered if we warranted his covering the tattoos
and wearing a tie, or if I'd seen him on an off day a few weeks back.

"Mr. and Mrs. Hayes."

"She's Reed, I'm Hayes," Harry said.

"Forgive me, Mrs. Reed." He didn't get up. He didn't shake our
hands. I don't think he cared what our respective names were.

"At any rate, we called you here today to share our concerns
about Ian." He gestured to Ian's guidance counselor, Miss Lapin,

who sat in the corner. I secretly wished Principal Castigan would turn her chair around, then she'd be the one in trouble.

"As you know, Ian is a very bright young man with enormous potential to do well. Lately, he's been having a difficult time getting *to* school and getting *into* school. Is there something going on we should know about? Anything you want to share?"

I clutched my purse close to my body. I didn't have any light to shed on it, so why I spoke is a mystery. "We realize Ian's grades were less than his best earlier in the school year, but we've been right on top of things this term. Haven't we, Harry?"

Harry's eyes told me to hush. He sat in his chair reserved for bad parents, and scratched the back of his head. I wasn't the only one who was puzzled. Principal Castigan gave us a look that shouted, *not another set of ignorant parents.*

"That's even more disturbing, since right now he's getting Ds in everything except English. He skips class even when he is here, which lately, isn't very often. He's been absent twelve days so far this term."

I was about to ask if he'd been absent again lately, when Harry jumped in. "He's had a tough winter, that's all. Colds, the flu, you understand. That can really put you behind the eight ball, even if you are working hard."

I know Harry Hayes and he was making excuses for Ian. I decided to forfeit the appearance of unity, knowing full well it would upset him.

"Mr. Castigan, Ian's home situation has changed. He went to live with his father at the beginning of last term. Not to disparage Harry, but I'd like to know more about your concerns so I can help him. Even if it is at a distance."

"Gee, C. Thanks for throwing me under the bus."

"What do his teachers say about his schoolwork?" I asked.

Surely Principal Castigan had mediated parents at odds before, because without getting out of his seat, he stood right up to Harry's indifference. "According to his teachers, he isn't the same outgoing kid he was last year. I'm going to cut to the chase. We think Ian's depressed. We think his poor attendance and failing grades are symptoms of a bigger problem. We'd like to recommend he see a psychiatrist, and perhaps it's time for a trial of medication." Miss Lapin nodded to everything the principal said.

A psychiatrist. Medication. These strangers—educators, not doctors—were telling me my son was depressed. They weren't qualified to make that determination. He'd been through a lot. The stress was getting to him. He wasn't depressed.

Harry came out from under the bus. "Wait a minute. The kid's fine. Christ, his mother's an expert at depressed. She's a therapist, don't you think she'd know if he was? Look, thanks for the information, we've got this under control."

He got up, so I got up. Even little Miss Lapin stood. Harry marched out of the office and I followed. All I could hear ringing in my ears, besides the click-clack of my heels on the floor of the corridor, was the word *depressed*. School election posters papered the hall walls. Lacey was running for school council rep. A boy named Marshall Kirby for class president. Offices Ian was apparently too despondent to campaign for.

I looked over at Harry, his eyes focused on the exit door. I tried to keep in step with him. His feverish pace told me he was boiling. Had I been asked to cast a ballot as to who Harry was angry with, it wouldn't have been the principal, though he had interfered in Harry's parenting. It wouldn't have been Ian; I've never seen Harry incensed with Ian. I'd have to vote for myself.

day 113

We knew they were coming. I paced the kitchen floor while Ethan ran around cleaning. You would've thought we were expecting real estate agents instead of our lawyer and the police detective. Pat, North, Ethan, and I sat around the empty kitchen table like we were in a restaurant waiting to be served. I hadn't bothered to offer drinks. They said they had information. Oddly enough I was excited. Would I stay excited if North had made an arrest? Their good posture and tilted heads told me they thought the news was good. When I heard it, I thought, not good enough.

"We've identified two persons of interest." North raised two fingers.

Pat took out her notes. "One man is a two-time DUI offender, just out of rehab. The tip came from his ex," she said.

Like a game of tennis, North took his next swing. "The problem is after questioning him, I can't rule him in or out. We have forensics going over his vehicle. Then we'll know more."

"What's his name?" Ethan asked my question. I listened to the kitchen clock tick.

"Neil Ford. He lives in Wenonah Falls."

I knew this name. His was on the list of repeaters Melanie gave me. He owned Clean Closets in Corcoran Village. I said nothing about Neil Ford, or my list. It was safely tucked away in my lingerie drawer. Like an addict, I knew exactly how long it had been since I'd touched it. Three days.

"Who's the other person?" I asked.

"A kid. Twenty-year-old, named Nicco Julian. He's got a pretty long rap sheet, all misdemeanors." North spoke from memory. "His boss said he came in late to work on the fifth. Julian was shaky, had a gash over his eye and a dent in his car. He claims he was in a minor fender bender. We've got forensics on his vehicle, too."

"How long before you know more?" Ethan likes timelines. "Now what?"

"If you're a religious man, I'd pray for patience and some luck. We need forensics to prove without a shadow of a doubt it was one of these cars. Since no one can put either of them at the scene, a car with DNA and some additional circumstantial evidence that points to one of these men is what we'll need to arrest someone."

"So now we wait," Pat said.

Like that wasn't what we were already doing.

day 115

My body is changing. If I conceived this baby the night Ethan and I made love for the first time after losing Abby, I'm nine weeks. I like thinking it was that night. That's the closest I've felt to Ethan since we entered this nightmare.

My breasts look their best when I'm pregnant, partly because they're nonexistent when I'm not. My stomach is already slightly rounded. It reminds me of a batch of dough. With Abby, I didn't show for so long I had trouble believing I was expecting; only the nausea was there to remind me. Celia told me when she found out she was pregnant with her son, she landed in maternity clothes by eight weeks. She was easy in the way she offered tidbits of her pregnancy story with me. I've lost some weight over the last three months, so it'll take me a while to need them.

I can't wear the ones I've coveted for nearly five years. The periwinkle capris with the white flowers, the turquoise mesh skirt slung low on my belly, the jeans that are more comfortable than any of my regular jeans. No, I won't be able to wear my Abby maternity clothes. I saved them for nothing.

I've been less dizzy this last week. I get up more slowly now, letting my blood pressure catch up with my movement, and I'm eating better. I make it a point to let Ethan see me taking care of myself. The more I eat and make it look like I'm taking walks, the more he leaves me alone. I'm not where he is—excited and ready to be a family again. I don't begrudge him. It's all he's ever wanted. I never thought a man could want and need to be a father as much as a woman needs to be a mother.

I remember the day after I told him I was pregnant with Abby, he came home bearing gifts. I heard him pull into the driveway and I met him at the back door, thinking I could bribe him into taking me out to dinner.

"Close your eyes for a minute," he said.

When he told me to open them, he'd dropped his briefcase at his feet and his hands were behind his back.

"Pick a hand."

"What are you doing?" I smiled and shook my head, knowing he was about to do something adorable.

"Oh, here. You have to open both of them anyway." An embarrassed look flashed over his face.

He produced two gifts. One wrapped in rainbows, one in blue tissue. I sat on the bench near the door; he squeezed in beside me.

I opened the lightest one first. Out of the box tumbled a cocoa-colored stuffed bunny. I hugged it and then Ethan.

"Isn't it soft? There aren't any buttons or anything for her to hurt herself on. And I knew you'd love the color. It reminds me of a Tootsie Roll," he said.

"Tootsie Rabbit," I said. "That's what we'll call him. What's in the other box? Don't tell me you bought a baseball glove."

He handed me the box wrapped in blue. I lifted the lid, and inside was a small wooden boat.

"It's beautiful." I rested my head on his shoulder as I ran my hand along the length of it. "But what if we have a boy who wants the bunny or a girl who wants the boat?"

He knew I was teasing. He was an expert at ignoring my sarcasm. "He or she can have them both. Or we could have more babies." He caressed my stomach and kissed my neck.

Today, after seeing Celia, I decided this time I'd be the gift giver. Actually, it was Celia who gave me my idea. She said Ethan and I didn't need to be in the same place about this baby. She used words like *journey* and *parents-to-be*. I was walking out the door and she placed her hand on my shoulder.

She said, "Especially after a loss, you should take your time getting to the place where you're ready to be a mother again, and you can allow Ethan his own way. You're a bright woman, Tessa. I know you'll find a way to let him channel his enthusiasm without, as you like to say, *pissing you off*."

When Celia said *pissing you off,* I almost laughed out loud. I stifled it because I didn't want to embarrass her. The way she spit it out looked like Abby the first time she tried broccoli. It was really kind of sweet how she tried to connect with me using words I like to use to get my point across. Sharp, biting words. Her advice was good advice.

I stopped at Papier's Stationers on the way home. I'd kept a baby book for Abby. This baby deserved a book, too. Only I couldn't be the one to keep it. I'd let Ethan record this baby's journey. It was the first thing I bought for my second child, and I handed it off to Ethan. You would've thought I handed him a real live baby.

He held the book out to take in the cover, its stars and moons dancing top to bottom. "You want me to do it?" he asked. "Are you sure, I mean I'd love to, but are you sure?"

I didn't tease him. I didn't make light of my gesture. "I think it would be better for you to do it."

He opened the book to the front section. "See how it starts with reflections," I said. "You fill in how you feel, knowing the baby's coming. I think you'll say lots of sweet things. Every baby deserves to be wanted."

He closed the book and placed it on the counter. He didn't want his tears to stain the page. Maybe it isn't so easy for him to start over.

I looked over my shoulder as I unlocked the office. Dropping my things on my desk, I bumped the candy dish I keep for clients. Mints skittered all over, making me even more ill at ease. It's unnerving to be here alone on a Saturday. No other professionals in the building, no clients in the waiting room. I've left my door open so I won't feel like I'm in a box. My expansive view won't be enough to settle me. Today I could use the boat.

I came here to call Alden, to tell him I've got to catch up on my paperwork. The truth is I can't talk to him about what just happened at Harry's. Not yet. I need time to collect my thoughts before going home.

I'm not sure we did the right thing, blindsiding Ian the way we did. Imagine waking up to your parents reading you the riot act?

I got to Harry's at eleven. As we expected, Ian was still in bed. "Okay, pal. Time to get up. Your mom and I need to talk to you."

His beautiful face emerged from under his down comforter, going from sleepy to surprised when he saw both of us standing there. He popped up, pulling the covers with him. He looked at Harry, but spoke to me. "What's the matter?"

"Please get dressed and meet us in the kitchen," I said. "We need to talk."

"Just let me just hit the bathroom." Again, he looked to Harry. I left, Harry lingered. The unmistakable sound of Harry whispering traveled down the hallway. I couldn't make out what he said.

We sat around the kitchen table. Ian took forever to spread cream cheese on one of the bagels I'd brought. Harry hid his face behind his coffee mug. Of course the next move would be mine.

"Ian, as you know, your father and I met with Principal Castigan and Miss Lapin."

"They said it's time for me to get my shit together, right?"

"I'd prefer you didn't swear. We've got some difficult things to discuss, and I'd like to do it respectfully."

"Sorry," he muttered with a mouthful of bagel.

"Going into the meeting, I was afraid they were going to tell us you're not working up to your potential. It seems they read it as something far more serious." I clasped my hands together. "They think you're depressed."

He swallowed what was in his mouth and threw the bagel half, cream side down, on his plate. "Depressed?" He said the word louder than was necessary. "Look, just because I don't sing and dance my way to class doesn't mean I'm depressed. I'd like to see another kid with my life act all happy."

"What's wrong with your life, exactly?" I asked. Harry was strangely quiet, but the fierce look that flew from his face to Ian's carried a warning.

Ian got up to leave. "Ask Dad. I'm sure he could tell you a ton about what's wrong around here."

"Get back here, kid. Your mother and I aren't done." Harry pushed Ian's chair out, making it clear he needed to sit back down. His tone was uncharacteristically controlled. "We get it, we screwed you up. Okay? We know we're crappy parents. If you don't want to be treated like you're depressed, you're going to need to do things our way. Get back to class. Stop wasting time online. Get the hell out of bed. If you can pull it together, we'll back off on what the school wants us to do."

Ian's eyes became a river, the buildup of tears spilling over the bridge of his nose. "What do they want?"

I softened my voice and placed one hand over his. "They want you to see a psychiatrist and maybe start medication."

There was a moment of silence. "Maybe I should." He lowered his head, and two perfectly round drops landed on the table.

"Jesus, kid, snap out of it. Straighten up at school. Like I told you, we don't need anyone interfering in our business making things more complicated than they need to be. Not everyone needs a shrink or pills to feel better."

The last remark was a dart to my heart, his malice aimed directly at me.

It was as if Harry shook Ian out of his self-pity. He sat up straighter. "You're right, I'm good. Everything will be fine."

"Wait a minute, you two. We can't pretend everything is all right. Ian, are you still angry with me for asking your father to move out? You can tell me."

"Let's not go over that again," Harry said. "He's fine. He had a tough fall after you and Al got married. Then moving in here. He'll buckle down, he'll get through it. Time heals everything, right, C? He's a sensitive kid who's been through a load of crap." Harry turned to Ian. "I'm sorry, kid. You don't know how sorry I am."

With that, it was his crappy mother's turn to fight the tears.

MONDAY, JANUARY 30   9:00 A.M.

The weekend went from bad to worse. I left the office late Saturday afternoon and found Alden waiting for me in the kitchen, his back glued to the ladder-back chair at the head of the table. Not one muscle in his face moved.

"Celia, did you intentionally keep me waiting, or were you thoughtless? You know how important dinner with the dean and his wife is to me."

"I lost track of time. After I left the office, I couldn't find my cell phone. It'll only take me a few minutes to get ready." I put my purse on the counter, closed my eyes briefly, and turned back to face him. "Or would you prefer we drive separately? I could meet you there."

Dislodging himself from the chair, he rose, smoothing out the creases that had formed on the inseam of his pants. "I know what I want. What about you, Celia? Would going separately suit you? Or for the sake of appearances should we go together?"

I let his inference go unchallenged. I couldn't bear another curt discussion in which I wasn't just a crappy mother but a crappy wife, too. "I know we both want to ride together, so if you can manage a bit more patience, I'll be right back."

I didn't wait for his answer. I walked, without urgency, up the stairs and down the hall toward my room. I stopped when I got to the two doors opposite each other. If I opened his door I'd be hit with what's left of Ian's life here. If I opened hers, I'd be faced with the life I erased. I touched my fingertips to my lips and placed a kiss first on his door and then on hers. I couldn't bring myself to open either.

Once in my room, I took no extra time deciding what to wear. I didn't need to make an impression on the Rutherfords. At faculty events, the dean gave me little of his attention, and his wife made it clear she didn't care for me. I chose my wine-colored dress, the one that never needs ironing. I took the necklace Harry gave me out of my jewelry box; as if it were liquid I poured it around my neck. I ran a comb through my hair and applied a touch of lipstick. I took the stairs back down. Alden stood in the foyer, his coat and mine draped over one arm. Without speaking, he handed me my purse, and we were off.

On the ride to the restaurant and throughout dinner, Alden measured the words he gave me as if they needed to be rationed. Enough to leave Wes and Fran Rutherford with the impression we were a happy pair, enough for me to know we weren't. On the ride home, the car was filled with words unspoken. It wasn't until we pulled into the driveway that Alden chose a few careful ones to say out loud.

"I don't recall ever seeing that necklace. Where did you get it?" He wanted to hear me say it; I knew he knew the answer.

I placed my hand over it to give me the courage to have this conversation. His gaze was set on the two precious gemstones. He couldn't possibly know their true value. "This was my Christmas gift from Harry."

During dinner with the Rutherfords', Alden had placed me on a conversation diet. After I told him about the necklace, he decided it was time for a fast.

day 120

I sat on the window seat, mesmerized by the raindrops collecting in the puddles along my street. I'd spent the last two mornings reading cards and letters. It took me two months to register that there were postal bins of sympathy collecting in my study. It took me three months to want to read them; four to be able to.

Like any good writer, I couldn't resist separating the bad writing from the good. The floor beside me was littered with adverbs and run-on sentences. I made an exception when it came to reading the bad writing of a friend. At times, I imagined using the letters as research for a book or an article on grief. Reading like a writer, it was easy to break them into categories. Category one: Letters that reminded me people were insensitive or unacquainted with real loss. These letters were filled with such trite phrases, I almost wanted to write back to clue these people in to never again write: *In time this won't hurt as much as it does now. Time heals everything.* Or, *you'll have another child and then life will be worth living again.*

Even before, I couldn't have written that, reread it, and still put it in the envelope to bring it to the post office. At no time did they stop to think about whether or not these sentiments would sound thoughtless to the woman who will live the rest of her life missing her daughter? There won't ever be a day when she won't wonder who took a car and crashed it into her life.

Category two: Letters that remind me people are beautiful, kind, and good. I took comfort in knowing there are people out there who know what it means to lose the child of your heart. There were strangers who took the time to write to me, to steady me. They knew the words I needed to hear, because they'd lost Teddy to cancer or Liza to SIDS. These letters made me feel something I could never tell anyone—except maybe Teddy's mother or Liza's dad.

Today I spent my day submerged in pain, and it felt good.

day 121

Ethan kissed me awake and asked if I felt up to a walk before he left for work. He was partially dressed, fighting to get a sweatshirt over his head. I pulled the comforter up and made a face.

"Too early."

"Promise you'll get out later? It's going to get colder later this week, and then you won't want to." He pulled the drapes closed, giving me permission to stay in bed.

"Speaking of going out, I thought I might go see North," I said. The room was dimmer and he was tying his shoes, making it hard to read his expression.

"It's been over a week since he told us about those two men."

I could see Neil Ford's name on my list. I'd read it dozens of times, sitting on the end of this very bed. I'd scanned it for Nicco Julian's name, too; his wasn't on it.

"I can't figure out whether they measure time differently than we do, or if they're intentionally closing us out."

After Ethan tied his second lace, he chimed in. "What about Caulfield? Are they really looking into the mess he made, or do they hope we won't push it?"

I sat up. I couldn't go back to sleep now. Ethan stared at what I was wearing. He didn't have to say it; my ratty T-shirt screamed, *Tessa, you've let yourself go.*

"I don't think I'll call ahead. I'd rather see North's reaction to me just showing up. I don't care if Pat's aggravated." I could've gone and done it, but I didn't want Ethan mad at me again. For once I told him what I was going to do before I did it.

"Do you want me to go with you?" he asked. "I could skip the walk and go in late, if you want me to."

"To tell you the truth, I'd rather go alone. You know, slip in, get the feel for what's going on down there. If we both go, it kind of makes it a bigger deal. If that's okay."

I got up and pulled a fresh shirt out of my lingerie chest. Like a quick change artist, I took off one tee and put on the other. He'd been walking toward me when I had the first one off. My turning-him-off skills were faster than his turning-me-on ones. I ducked behind him and threw my embarrassment in the hamper.

"Thanks for telling me you're going. You want to call me later to tell me how it goes?" He put his arms out for a platonic hug. I was willing to give him that much.

At least I did one thing right. I told him. And I still got my way.

When I got to the Wenonah Falls Police Station, the female officer in the cage let me right into the detectives' open area of random desks and cluttered tables. I guess you get special privileges when you're the mother of the dead girl. I made it halfway across the room when I noticed, through the glass, two officers cleaning out Caulfield's office, neither one of them Caulfield. When a light hand landed on my shoulder, I jumped and turned to face Jack North.

"Hey, Mrs. Gray. I didn't mean to startle you. I thought you heard me. Do you want to step in here to talk?" He pointed over his shoulder to the conference room.

North wore a navy blazer, his ID badge hung from his neck. I walked with him to the room, looking back in the direction of Caulfield's office.

"I'm glad you dropped in, it keeps us on our toes," he said. He sounded older each time I spoke to him.

"What's with the officers cleaning out Caulfield's office? I thought he wasn't retiring until the end of April. And why isn't he doing it?"

We were still standing inside the door. The room was dim, one lone lightbulb carried the burden. "He may not be retiring. He's officially under investigation." North gestured to the table and pulled out a chair for me.

"I'm not telling you anything Chief O'Brien wouldn't tell you. He's taking the misplaced paint sample and a few other things pretty seriously."

He gave it to me straight. His was the first honest face I'd seen in this shady place. A face that made me hesitate to hurl my hatred for Caulfield at him.

"Why do I always have to find things out because I push you people? Is this a real investigation into Caulfield or lip service?" I tossed my bag across the table, it slid farther than I intended.

North reached to stop the bag before it went the distance. He didn't try to calm me.

"It's real, Mrs. Gray. Internal Affairs is in on it. It might be a while before we know more." Then he stood still, not the least bit uncomfortable with me and my fury. "You're absolutely right. Someone—I should have come to tell you."

He knew more, and I knew I could get him to tell me. His lack of experience and good nature were no match for me.

"Detective, you're going to get me some coffee. Real strong coffee. Then we'll go over the details you do have. I deserve details."

He was easy. He went straight for the door.

"When you get back, you'll call me Tessa and my daughter, Abby. She's not just a victim of an unsolved crime." I sat down. "She was my little girl."

The coffee must have been sitting on the burner since Tuesday. I sipped the sludge while North told me what Caulfield had done to screw up the investigation. After the paint sample went missing on Caulfield's watch, North reinterviewed the first responders and the officers who took the initial crime scene evidence. He'd been able to confirm that several autopsy photos were missing, and so was the transcript of the interview with the old woman, Mrs. Dwyer. I wasn't sure he was supposed to tell me all he did. I had no intention of stopping him.

"You have every right to be furious. Mrs. Gray—Tessa—I want you to know if Detective Caulfield's actions are criminal, he'll be dealt with. O'Brien's very respectable."

"Furious doesn't begin to describe it, detective. How the hell am I supposed to trust you now?"

"All I can say is that I'm not going to rest until I find out what happened. I want to know what happened almost as much as you do."

"Don't even think about comparing your need to know to mine." I closed my eyes. I couldn't look at his fresh face and happy hair for one more second. When I opened them he was still looking at me, no fear of eye contact.

"I want to believe you when you say you'll find out who did it. Tell me it's not too late?"

"It isn't. I've got a lot more I can do. We're waiting on the forensics on those two vehicles. I've got officers keeping their eyes on the two suspects, informally of course. I'll find the paint sample and those autopsy photos. Good Catholic boy that I am, I've put a call into my old friend Saint Anthony." North smiled. "I will personally conduct a new interview with Mrs. Dwyer. Even though she's getting on in years, she might remember something new that didn't seem significant at the time." He pulled his enthusiasm down a notch. "I'm not giving up, and neither should you."

"I won't until you tell me to." I attempted a smile. "Okay, I probably wouldn't give up even if you *did* tell me to." My tone turned serious. "I really need to know what happened to her."

"I know. So do I." We both stood up at the same time, only the table had us on different sides. "Tessa, I hope you won't think I'm prying. When's your baby due?"

He took me aback with his confidence that I was expecting. "August." I placed my hand over my stomach. "What made you so certain I was pregnant?"

"Good Catholic boy who's got a sister with six kids. She holds her hand over her stomach, too. I first noticed it when I startled you in the squad room. It's an instinct I guess, protecting your child when you're frightened," he said. "Your baby is lucky to have you for a mother."

I muttered thanks and left the station. There was nothing left to say. I got all the way to the lobby before the tears hit my sweater.

day 122

What if. The weatherman keeps saying, what if all this rain were snow? It's a ridiculous question really, because it isn't snow, it's rain. What if it rained on October 5 and they all stayed in for recess?

Celia told me we ask *what if* questions to help understand where we are. Like a reference point on a map, we have to wrap our minds around where we are, so we can start accepting where we're going.

"What if North *can* solve this?" I asked Celia. "I mean, what if he makes an arrest?" It took us less and less time each week to get into our places. "I want him to, but I don't know if I'm strong enough to go through a trial or more media coverage."

The light came out from behind Celia's eyes. "Tessa, I don't think I've ever met anyone stronger than you. Your determination is a powerful tool, enviable really. You're using it right now to prepare yourself for what you may need to face."

I was curled up in my client chair, comfortable this week in my favorite sweatpants and zip-up hoody. Celia looked pretty comfortable, too. She'd abandoned her therapy dress code and was actually wearing pants. She looked tired, though. I couldn't help wondering, what if she got sick of hearing me whine?

"I'm feeling more confident with North on the case. He's young, but he has drive. I don't think he wants to solve this for the credit he'd get, or his reputation. I think he wants to solve it for me and Abby."

I'd never told her about the list, so there was no point in telling her it was safely tucked away in my lingerie drawer in the hopes that North could solve this the old-fashioned way.

"He said he'd do whatever it takes. I hope it's not too late."

"This is good news. I've not heard you express confidence up until now. What's the detective working on?"

"He's got two suspects. These days they call them persons of interest."

"Men, women?" She uncrossed her legs and leaned forward.

"I'm not supposed to get into it. North asked me not to talk about the details with anyone. Except Ethan. I don't know if it's because I could ruin the investigation, or because he had second thoughts about how much he told me."

"You can share the details here. Our conversations have been and always will be confidential." Like a shopper drawn to tabloids, Celia wanted to know more.

"It's not that I don't trust you, I just don't need to get into all the details. It's funny, I've only met North a few times, but I'm starting to trust his way of doing things."

Celia leaned back in her chair and pursed her lips. "Know I'm here when and if you're ready to share."

"I do have one question. What if North catches the bastard, how will I feel then?"

Maybe I should drive in to Boston and take in a couple of galleries on Newbury Street, on my own. I'm in no rush to go home. Alden's curt and careful words have me on edge when I'm there. He makes me wish I could have my house back—and Ian right along with it.

"Pass the cream. We need shampoo." Alden speaks only to convey essentials.

He knew he was entering a tight spot when he agreed to marry me. Ian made no secret of his lack of feeling for him. Right up until he moved in, Alden assured me that with patience and kindness on his part, Ian would come around. I thought his careful nature and measured practicality would steady our home. Instead his lack of connection to Ian only brings more tension. If I brought it up in conversation, I'm afraid I'd yell, *If you really love me, you'll help me try to keep my son close. Conflict or no conflict, make a move to invite him over or at least encourage me to see him by myself.*

I suppose if I called him now and invited him to join me for a carefree night in town, he'd take me up on it. But would we talk like partners in a real marriage, or would we be two separate people standing side by side, looking at someone else's ability to capture feelings in oil?

What would I tell one of my clients to do, if she described a marriage like mine to me? Would I advise with my mind? *No marriage is ever perfect. It isn't wise to make rash decisions. You should consider couples counseling.* Or speak from my heart. *You seem to be the common denominator in your marriage failures. Maybe this is the best you can do.*

Because then there's Harry. He's short on words in person and on the phone. I called last night to see how Ian's getting on with the new tutor. I tried to make small talk, even asking about the Boatworks, but I got no response. I worked hard at making casual conversation, Harry didn't bother to try. At least when he handed me off to Ian he was considerate enough to cover the phone before he yelled, *Ian, it's your mother.*

Then there's Ian. He gave me cursory details about this boy named Robert that Harry hired to help him study. According to Ian he's *geeky,* but he'll do. Ian doesn't hide the fact that he's resigned himself to having a tutor. I tried to act upbeat, complimenting his efforts thus far, and I offered him a well-deserved break.

"I'd love to spend some time with you this weekend. We could head to Boston, there's a new exhibit at the Institute of Contemporary Art. Then we could browse around Boylston Street. What do you say?"

"I can't. I spaced out last term, so I've gotta go back a ways to understand the stuff we're doing now."

"It'll just be the two of us. Come on, we both need to do something fun."

"Fine. I'll ask Dad and call you back. Can I go now?"

When the call ended, loneliness was my only companion.

Alden's detached. He's angry about the necklace and anything associated with my family. Harry's disconnected. He made it clear at breakfast, he's jealous of Alden. Harry's complexity isn't new to me; my connection to him is as intricate as the knots he ties on the boat. The surprise is Ian's distance.

Even after I made Harry move out, he forgave me. He has every right to blame me. A child should expect his mother to make everything perfect, build a secure family life for him, not one so fractured. His mother shouldn't let anything bad happen.

Ian has moved away from me and he's moving away further still. My son, sensitive and split. School life. Two homes. Father, mother, stepfather. Time with Harry or time with me. I'm having a hard enough time trying to put the pieces of my own life together. Some puzzle pieces are nowhere to be found, while others simply don't fit.

Life should be easier, his and mine. If everyone stopped being so selfish, everything would be fine. How can I be the mother Ian needs if all my energy is being sucked out of me by two men unable to see the priority is Ian?

I'm done spending my precious energy tiptoeing around Alden's feelings. And Harry's moods. I've handled outburst after angry outburst. I've been brushed off and dismissed for the last time. They either get in the game to help Ian or get out of the way so I can.

MONDAY, FEBRUARY 6   **8:00 A.M.**

I won't back down. I can't concede. I've made up my mind to put this family back together. Even mismatched plates set a beautiful table. I'm going to speak up and speak out. I decided to start with the man closest to me, in proximity that is.

I found Alden grading papers at the writing desk that found a temporary home in the alcove off the library. Cleaning out my studio has proven harder than I expected. I had to interrupt him; it was time to call a truce and talk about what was going on between us.

"I won't pretend there's nothing wrong," I said. "I take full responsibility if I've hurt your feelings in any way. We've got to clear the air."

"I don't know what you're carrying on about, Celia. I've been a bit quiet lately, that's all. I'm fine."

"Please, don't make this more difficult than it needs to be. I know you were hurt by my accepting the necklace from Harry. In fact, I know you're bothered by the very existence of Harry. He's Ian's father and we all need to figure out a way to coexist in peace. For everyone's sake, most importantly Ian's."

He puffed out a false laugh, pushing his glasses on top of his head. "You don't think I'm bothered by a silly piece of cheap jewelry, do you? I'm not a sentimental fool like—"

"Alden, stop. This is exactly what I'm talking about. I won't tolerate you, Harry, or Ian casting anyone in this family as villain. This is our family, however imperfect."

He tipped his head and caught his glasses before they fell off.

"Yes, *your family*," I said. "If you're going to stay in it, you'll need to find a way to put Ian first. That includes finding a way to be civil to Harry." I realized my arms crossed tightly across my body conveyed anger and inflexibility, so I let them drop by my sides.

I've seen Alden choose to be quiet before. I've never seen him speechless. He put the cap back on his red pen and carefully pushed back his chair, adjusting his posture before he stood. Shoulders back, breath controlled. If I'd had to guess his next moves they would've been: coat, keys, door. Instead he walked over to me, lifted one of my hands, and kissed it.

"Where would you like me to start?"

4:00 P.M.

I finished hearing seven clients tell me their incomparable stories. Now I can continue with mine. Alden and I kept talking. We didn't untangle all the threads of hurt tied together during our short lives as a couple. I neither reacted, nor wavered in my need for him to know, Ian comes first. Second to no one, not even me. Alden said he would try harder.

The next member of the family to be brought on board this peace train was Ian. I would save Harry for last.

After leaving Alden a hearty chicken plate to eat when he got home from his faculty reception, one I successfully opted out of, I picked Ian up at Harry's to head out for a bite to eat.

Still early, it was quiet for a Saturday night at the Birch Street Tavern. Ian hugged the corner of his booth, his sweatshirt sleeves pulled down, making it look like his hands had been amputated. The hood covered his beautiful, too long hair.

"I'm famished, how about you? Are you feeling okay?" Once again, my mothering made him cringe.

"Can we talk about the energy crisis or your clients? I'm getting so sick of everyone always asking me whether I'm sick, tired, or hungry. I say *I'm fine* so many times a day, I could die."

"Well then. I'll try not to annoy you with any more questions about health or school. I do have something else I'd like to talk about."

"What? You look all serious." He sat up straighter in his seat. "Is it bad? Did you and Dad have another fight?"

"I'd like to order first and then I'd be happy to tell you what's on my mind."

Waiting to order, he rolled and rerolled his napkin, then he tore his straw wrapper into tiny pieces.

Orders placed, I was about to speak. Ian beat me to it. "So, what's the matter?"

"My goodness, I've certainly got your attention." I put my napkin in my lap.

"Last time you had something to talk to me about, I was *depressed*," he said.

That wasn't the last time I'd spoken to him. I didn't correct him, since he had a right to his feelings, his irritation with me justified.

"I haven't spoken to your father yet, but I certainly plan on it. I wanted to talk with you first."

"God, Mom. Just tell me what I've done."

"I'd like to set up some ground rules for the four of us. I know you don't care for Alden, but we're a family now, and we need to start behaving like one."

He let his breath escape. "Is that all? Look, I'm not having this conversation. I told you he's your problem. I don't have to deal with him if I don't want to."

"Yes, Ian, you do. I know this isn't easy for you. It isn't easy for me, either. Alden's my husband, and you and your father are going to have to start acting respectfully toward both of us."

"I'm not trying to be mean to you. I don't like the guy."

"All these acrid remarks flying back and forth between you, Alden, and your father. Don't you think it hurts me? Every time we're together I get a sick feeling in my stomach, afraid one of you will start something."

"I'm not trying to hurt you, Mom. Dealing with Al is more than I can handle. I have to keep Dad going to meetings. I've got school on my back. There's too much to figure out."

"You don't have to make sure your father goes to meetings. He's a grown man. And you've got the tutor. You can talk to me, Ian. Let me help you." My tone was pleading.

His head was down. I couldn't see his beautiful eyes under that silly hood. I knew they were filling with tears. I handed him my napkin, neither one of us comfortable with crying in public.

As Ian composed himself, I thought I saw Alden walk by the restaurant window. We were so far from the front, I had to be mistaken. I looked at my watch, reassuring myself that he had to be at least one merlot into the reception.

The clanging plates hid the sound of Ian blowing his nose. He made a quick swipe of his eyes. "I'm good. Dad's good. I'm gonna focus on school and I'll try to be nicer to Al. I guess if you've talked to him maybe he'll stop correcting me all the time. I'll try harder."

"Great. Next I plan on talking to your father. He plays a big role in all this, too." I waited a second. "Ian, I want you to see someone."

The food arrived and the waitress moved on to a new party. The tavern had grown busy and the noise level had risen.

"You've said it yourself. You've got a lot going on. Sometimes a professional person—someone outside the family—is better able to help you make sense of all these powerful feelings, these grown-up issues."

He dropped his head again, I didn't hear him. I want to believe he said yes.

On to Harry.

day 126

Rosemary's suspicious look includes a one-eyebrow raise with a one-sided lip lift. She gave it to me when we went to lunch. She ordered a sauvignon blanc. I ordered a grapefruit and soda with a twist of lime.

"No pinot?" She teased. "You're either hungover or pregnant. Which is it?"

"Geez, Rosemary. You can't even wait for my formal announcement."

"Shit, Tessa. Don't you play with me. Are you?"

"Do you mind not telling everyone in Vincini's? I'd like to keep it quiet, okay?"

So much for discreet. Rosemary barreled out of her chair and hugged me so hard she nearly knocked my pregnant self off my seat and onto the floor. I'd had the sense people watched me as I walked in. After Rosemary's public display, it was obvious people were staring.

"When did you find out? Does Ethan know? Oh my God, a baby."

"Promise you won't be mad. I've had so much to figure out, I definitely didn't do things the way I would have if this had happened before."

"Why would I be mad? What did you do that's so terrible?" She took a gulp of her wine. Poor thing, she never knows what I'll do next.

"Nothing really. I've known for a while. So has Ethan. I didn't tell you before now because I didn't even know how I felt about it. I hate to say it, I wasn't even happy when I found out. It's like God is playing with me or something. This was the only thing I wanted five months ago and now—"

"We'll help you figure it out." Her skinny arm reached across the table and took my hand. "Ethan and me. You'll be a wonderful mother to this baby, just like you were to Abby." She held on, squeezing hard.

"Thanks for not being hurt I didn't tell you sooner. All I can say is thank God I've got more time because I don't know how I'm going to do this. One minute I'm consumed with missing Abby and focused on the investigation, and the next minute I'm buying those god-awful prenatal vitamins and underwear two sizes up." I snapped my waistband under my shirt.

"Don't take offense, but I've got a million questions to ask about the baby. How far along are you?"

"Eleven weeks tomorrow. Don't worry about offending me, with everything I've been through, I'm building up a really tough shell."

Her smile dampened. She was sad I'd waited so many weeks to tell her, though she would never say so. After I told her what little I could about the baby, a child no bigger than my fist, I filled her in on my meeting with North.

Lunch with Rosemary was like always. We gossiped, we cried,

we even laughed. No matter how much we squabble at times, she's my sister and I love her. I wish my baby hadn't already lost his sister.

day 128

It's been a week filled with days out. Today I met with Pat. She'd called to say she needed to catch up with me, this time she wanted to meet in person. I met her at her office, right near the courthouse. The lobby was crawling with good-looking professional types; upscale lawyers' office meets plastic surgeons to the stars.

There was no chance I could mistake her waiting room for Celia's. Fresh flowers tumbled out of enormous urns, contemporary furniture killed my back. I didn't wait more than five minutes, when Pat came out to get me herself. As I stood up, her eyes dropped for a split second to my stomach.

"So when did North tell you," I said.

Pat cocked her head and fixed a curious look on her face.

"Yes, I'm pregnant," I said, putting one hand over my newly rounded stomach.

"Tessa, you should've been a detective. Come, let's talk in my office."

She didn't go behind her desk; I sat in the same chair as the last time, and she sat where Ethan had.

"How'd you know I knew?" she asked.

"Come on, Pat. People glance at a woman's stomach only if they think she's pregnant or getting fat."

"That obvious, huh? I hope you're not upset he told me. I think he thought I already knew. How are you feeling?"

She crossed her perfect legs. Her short skirt and I would never have gotten along. She controlled it with style.

"Better. I'm less queasy this week and I'm not as tired as I was."

"I'm glad you're feeling well. I guess I meant, are you okay with it. You know, are you happy?"

"I'm working on it." I took off my jacket and laid it over my lap. "Once the baby starts moving, it'll get harder to stay detached. Nature's way, you know?"

"I've heard that from my friends."

"Any babies in your future, Pat?" I stopped myself. "You don't have to answer that. Lately, I'm not filtering a damn thing. I've always hated it when people would ask me when I'd have another."

"I don't mind your being direct. That's what I like about you. Sure, I'd love a baby. I have to find a donor first."

"A donor? Are you thinking of—"

She smiled and cut me off. "No, Tessa, a husband. I'm blunt like you, remember?"

"North's kinda cute," I said.

"You said it yourself, he looks seventeen. I have two rules for dating." Pat tapped two fingers into her hand. "I won't date anyone who looks younger than me and never someone thinner."

We both laughed. Given why we know each other, I never expected to laugh with Pat Benedict.

Her receptionist knocked lightly on the open office door. Handing Pat what looked like a phone message, she apologized for interrupting. When she left, we got back to the real reason we talk.

"I wanted to meet face-to-face instead of our usual phone update because I wanted to see if you were okay. And I'm afraid I have something I wanted you to hear from me, in person."

"Can't be that bad, right? What could be worse than what's happened already?" My words sailed over my nervous laugh.

"It looks like Caulfield's in trouble. I know Jack told you he's under investigation for mishandling Abby's case."

"Yeah, I found that out no thanks to you or him. If I hadn't gone down to the police station this might be the first I'd have heard of it." I dropped my coat on the floor; I didn't bother to pick it up.

"I'm sorry about that. You're right, there's no excuse for my call coming in after you'd already gone there." She reached down for my coat, stood, and hung it on a coatrack by the open door. She closed us in her office, which signaled to me this was about to get worse.

"Look, let's not get all junior high. Tell me what's going on." I gripped the arms of the chair, now that I didn't have my coat to cling to.

"At first, people guessed he botched things because he'd mentally checked out of the job. Eyes on retirement, you know? Something came out today. The word is that when they dug around a little, they learned he'd accepted a bribe. Apparently, he looked the other way when an old sailing buddy was stopped for driving under the influence. Caulfield drove the guy home and let him off without charges. I have a feeling he won't be seeing any gold watch." She was back beside me, arranging her skirt and her legs.

More than anything, I wanted to be gripping Caulfield's throat instead of my chair. I had a strong urge to run, but my body had forgotten how to move.

"That son of a bitch. I knew the minute I met him, there was something rotten about him. Ethan begged me to give him a chance. I should've trusted my gut and demanded somebody else. I told myself it was the retirement thing, too. Oh God, what if he's hiding something about Abby's case?"

Pat reached over to put her hand on my arm. I swatted at her like she was a bug.

"Don't touch me." My voice was too loud for her space.

"I know it's upsetting to hear about Caulfield, but we don't know if there's anything bigger or if this is an isolated incident. We'll have to see what else the investigation turns up."

"You don't really think Caulfield made just one mistake, do you? Once you look under the rock, you're going to find a snake. Tell me the truth. How bad is this?"

"I don't know. Most cops and lawyers see him as lazy. Every once in a while there's been a rumor about things like this, but nothing anyone can prove."

"Oh great, now the focus will be on everything he's ever done wrong. No one will be focused on Abby. Damn him."

"This isn't all bad. Caulfield was off the case already anyway." She dared to reach out to me again. This time I let her hand rest on mine. "O'Brien's focused on Caulfield. North's still focused one hundred percent on your case. He's committed to finding out what happened."

I heard phones ringing outside her door. Someone's justice was still being served.

"What's North doing about Abby? Can he fix things or is it too late?"

"I know you've waited a long time and it's not over, yet. There isn't a lot of evidence, that's true. At some point, I think you'll know. I wouldn't blame you for getting angry with me for talking feelings instead of facts. But I trust him. You'll know."

She glanced at her watch and apologized for needing to get going. She had to be at the courthouse for a hearing by one.

In less than an hour, I went from almost happy pregnant woman to a baby myself.

"I know you think it's irreparable," she said. "I don't think it is. Jack's not done with this. Not by a long shot."

She said, Jack, not North. Maybe she really does know.

Harry's hardly ever easy. Last night was no exception. I stopped over after work, mostly to meet the new tutor, though I had every intention of taking Harry aside and asking him to join Alden, Ian, and me in our peace agreement.

"Hi, C, come on in." Harry gave me a peck on the cheek. A gesture so automatic, it seemed he only realized he shouldn't have done it, midkiss. That greeting was past history, a story that brought back old feelings. He headed toward the kitchen, leaving me and my rosy cheeks in the hallway.

I could see Robert was as Ian had described him, a little geeky. His black-rimmed glasses looked like protective science goggles and were pushed too high up the bridge of his nose. His books and notebooks were angled in a schematic pattern on the table. I wondered if he'd have a panic attack if my spontaneous son decided to rearrange them.

"Hello, Robert. I'm Ian's mother. I hope you know how much we all appreciate you helping Ian with his schoolwork."

Robert stood, and with his arms and legs akimbo, he hit the table and winced. He hesitated, grappling with whether or not to extend his hand. "Oh, I help a lot of students who aren't doing well in school. Nice to meet you, Mrs. Hayes."

"Reed," Ian, Harry, and I said in unison. Harry's voice trailed him as he left the kitchen.

With one word, we outed the divorce and my remarriage. "It's Mrs. Reed," I said.

"Oh, sorry." The smart boy stuttered.

Ian, the expert at sidestepping the broken branches of his family tree, recovered. "No big deal, let's get back to it, okay? I'm getting a little fried and I need to eat."

"Yes, please continue," I said. I hadn't meant to interrupt. I left the kitchen, peeked into the living room, and was relieved when Harry wasn't there. We'd have more privacy if we talked in his study.

"Harry, do you have a minute?" I stood on the threshold. He was concentrating on a mound of papers. "I've got some things I need to talk to you about."

He swiveled his desk chair and leaned forward. "What's up? Come on in, and take a load off. You don't have to stand."

When we were married and he was organizing paperwork for the sale of a catamaran or a yacht, he'd never drop what he was doing to listen to what I had to say. I liked this recent turn of events, the one where the men in my life wanted to hear what was on my mind. I'd spent my life listening, now it was my turn to talk.

I took a seat on the rose-and-cream-plaid sofa, the one we bought for our first apartment. Tattered for sure, it still looked perfect next to Harry's big oak desk.

Harry watched me run my hand over the sofa's arm. "I should probably get it covered," he said. "Still, I love the old girl, as is."

"Some things are meant to carry their wear and tear." I was back in our tiny apartment building looking up at Harry from under one end of the sofa, while he held on to the other and tried to climb the stairs. We struggled for what seemed like an hour to get that sofa up to our studio. We rested it every few stairs to steady our breath and our grip. Once it crested the apartment's landing, we fell onto it, laughing. Things weren't always so tense between us.

Here it sat worse for wear, like the two people who had owned it. I forced my eyes from the sofa, and they landed on the wall. I'm surprised it wasn't the first thing I noticed when I stepped into that room. The familiar watercolor, with its giant swells and storm clouds, was framed and centered above Harry's desk.

"I never get tired of looking at it," he said.

As if a wave from the painting took hold of me, the strength of its undertow tried to drag me down. "Why that one? It's so— angry." I locked eyes with Harry, exaggerating the intimacy of the moment. All I was trying to do was stop looking at it.

"You really let yourself go. It's better than any of that photo-realism stuff you used to show me in those books of yours. To me, this is your best piece."

I tried to pull Harry back to the office in his rented ranch. All I could remember was the day I painted that boatless ocean. What I couldn't remember was what I'd come to talk to Harry about. "I want to thank you for helping Ian find the tutor. Is it working out, do you think?"

"Hell if I know. Ian says he's only helped with homework so far. First test is next week, I think. Could you follow up on the test bit? You know it's not really my thing."

"I appreciate you asking me. You make sure the tutor keeps coming, and I'll follow up on the results. This is great, we're working together."

"You always were easy to please." He ran his hands through his hair, leaning back so far in the desk chair, I thought he'd topple over.

When he righted himself, I launched into the real reason I was sitting in Harry's office, surrounded by our things. "I wonder if you'd be willing to do something else for me."

"Shoot. I'm in a good mood. The kid's doing better, don't you think?"

"Ian does seem better. I think there's even more we can do. You might not find this as easy." I don't know whether I was speaking too softly, or if I'd really gotten his attention. He leaned forward again, his elbows digging into his knees.

His eyebrows came together. "What's the matter now?"

He looked like Ian did in the tavern the other night, curious but wary. Do I really speak up for what I want so infrequently that the men in my life are taken off guard?

I straightened up and tried on an air of confidence; I didn't want to sound demanding. Harry doesn't like being told what to do. His response to my next suggestion could go in countless directions.

"I'd like Ian to see a counselor."

He glanced up at the painting, lost at sea. I waited, still.

"You said yourself, he's doing better. Why not let's see how he is, in say, a month? Let him concentrate on school."

"I could consider that, if you'll agree to something else. I'd like all of us—you and Ian and Alden and me—to work harder at how we talk to each other. Ian needs us to stop all the arguing."

"Wow, that'll be tough. Between you and me, that Alden is one tightly wrapped son of a—"

"Harry, this is exactly what I'm talking about. You can't talk that way about him to me. He's my husband." I didn't say it to hurt him. I was stating a fact. He pulled his head back, as if I'd slapped him.

"I don't want you talking this way in front of Ian," I said. "I wouldn't be the least bit surprised if your dislike of Alden is what's colored Ian's opinion of him."

"Oh, please. Ian's capable of forming his own opinion. You ever think maybe the guy's an ass and you can't see it?"

I stood up to leave. "I am not having this conversation with you."

Harry stood, too. "Of course you're not. You'll run from this conversation like you ran away from the boat. And me. Going gets tough, Celia gets going."

"If you need to get things off your chest, go to counseling." As soon as the word slipped out of my mouth, I longed to take it back. This argument was a broken record from our marriage collection.

I heard throat clearing over our raised voices. Harry and I turned at the same time to see Ian's fed-up face and Robert's ill-at-ease one, standing side by side in the hallway.

WEDNESDAY, FEBRUARY 15   8:00 A.M.

Last night, the sweet woodsy smell of wine and mushrooms met Alden at the door. My veal marsala was my Valentine's Day gift to him along with flutes of sparkling zinfandel and chocolate-covered strawberries.

"Celia, how did you find the time to make something so special? I thought you had clients today."

"I finished early enough to stop at Harvest Market and get the meal started. I can make it from memory. It's one of my signature dishes. Haven't I made it for you?"

I was glad he changed the subject as soon as I realized the last time I made it, I hadn't even met him yet.

"How long will it be before we sit down? I have a little something I need to tend to."

"Twenty minutes and I'll be ready to serve. Meet me in the library when you're finished. I've set the table in front of the fire. We can have a drink first."

"I'll be there in ten minutes."

Both our food and conversation were rich. Alden consumed every last drop of sauce, using his baguette as a sponge. For all the attention he paid to eating, it was a wonder he could talk as much as he did. If he had a dial for vocal speed, I would have guessed it got stuck on high.

While I cleared the table and went to get the strawberries, Alden threw another log on the fire. When I returned, the reason for his nervous chatter was perched on the table in front of my dessert plate.

"I thought we agreed no gifts. You said this holiday was commercialism at its worst."

"Perhaps I've been struck by the arrow of a certain winged boy. It's true I've always thought it silly to express sentiments on a contrived day. Until I loved you."

I could no longer see him clearly through the film of tears. I reached for his hand across the table, he reached for the gift. His smile grew as he pushed it toward me. "Open it, please."

Given its shape, I knew at once it was jewelry. When I removed the scarlet ribbon and gently lifted the cover, the arrow in my own heart dislodged, leaving me disenchanted. Inside the box, lying on a bed of cherry velvet, was an ornate diamond necklace. My dazed expression didn't betray my feelings right away.

"It's a remarkable piece, isn't it? Can I help you put it on?"

"Remarkable, yes. It's actually quite, ah, extravagant. It must have cost you a fortune." I couldn't stop staring at the sea of diamonds encrusted in a pendent arranged like a heart. The piece was closer to the size of a magnifying glass than a coin.

"It was worth every penny to see your expression. I certainly surprised you." He clapped his hands.

"Yes, I am surprised. It's so—" I hesitated, praying the words would come. "Wow. Where in the world will I wear something—so lavish?"

"You don't like it," he said. His smile slid down his face.

"I do, it's lovely. I don't mean to seem ungrateful, I wonder if I can carry off such a dazzling piece of jewelry. I don't know if it suits me. I don't think my lifestyle agrees with it, do you? Simple jewelry is more my style. Like a single strand of pearls or—" I didn't say Harry's necklace, but Alden was smart enough to fill in the blank.

Alden closed his eyes, and then he saved the evening like the gentleman he is. "I see what you mean, Celia. Perhaps you'll accept the gesture of extravagance as an expression of the depth of my feelings for you, while you exchange the necklace for something a bit more everyday."

"I will. Please know I think both the gesture and the necklace are stunning."

As we ate our strawberries, the only sound in the room was the crackling of the fire. Without intending to, I'd found the dial to slow his speech. I just hadn't meant to shut him off.

day 134

Ethan and I agreed, no gifts, just a nice meal and time to talk. I called Rosemary for her beef stew recipe. I figured I could handle throwing a bunch of ingredients into a pot, not much I could screw up there.

"Why don't you come over here for dinner? I have plenty of food," she said.

"No, thanks. Ethan and I had another big fight about Abby's room. He's as stubborn as I am. God forbid he admits it. My peace offering is an edible valentine. It's easy, right? You know I'm no Julia."

"It's so easy you should let me make it for you. You could nap while I throw it together." Rosemary was getting really good at coming up with excuses for coming over here to check on me.

"Cut it out. I can make a stew. Why are you treating me like I'm five?" I could tell there was something else going on.

"I'm only trying to help. Ethan said you're a little stressed with everything."

"Jesus, Rosemary, are you two talking behind my back again?" I could feel my blood pressure rising. "What did he say?"

"Ethan and Kevin went out for a beer after work on Friday. Kevin asked him how you're doing, that's it. God, relax." Her pause on the other end told me she was choosing her words more thoughtfully. "I know things have been really hard for you lately. This whole thing is unbelievable. But I love you both. I worry about you both. Ethan's like a brother to me, and he's having a really hard time. All of this is happening to him, too."

It was a good thing that's all the sisterly advice she dared to get away with.

"Come on, go get a piece of paper and a pencil and I'll give you the recipe. I'll hang on. Or do you want me to e-mail it to you?"

I'd lost interest in the stew. "Rosemary, is he okay? You don't think I'm going to lose him, do you?"

"Tessa, you couldn't lose him if you tried. He's true blue. All you have to do is play nice, okay?"

Nice isn't as easy a game to play as it once was.

It took me four outfits to find the one that didn't make me look like a sausage. I've got to break down and go buy some maternity clothes. I set the dining room table, not both ends, but the two seats facing out the picture window, and I lit two pillar candles. When he came home, I met him at the door with a kiss and a beer.

"You look pretty. What smells so sweet, is it you?" He kissed me on the neck like he was going to take a bite out of me.

"I made us dinner, including German chocolate cake for dessert." I stuck my stomach out in an exaggerated gesture. "I figured if I'm going to get fat, I might as well enjoy the ride."

"I got you something. I know I wasn't supposed to, but I couldn't help it."

He moved into the kitchen. He put his briefcase on the counter while I stirred the stew. He restuck the bow that had fallen off the flat box and handed it to me. Rosemary was right, Ethan's one of a kind.

Inside the box was a double picture frame with writing on the bottom, OUR BABIES. Tucked into the left side was my favorite baby picture of Abby. She's sleeping with her tiny index finger slipped between her bow lips. The other side was empty except for a blue Post-it note Ethan had written on and stuck to the glass: ABBY'S SISTER OR BROTHER—PHOTO COMING SOON.

I wrapped my arms around him and he whispered in my ear, "We'll never forget her. She'll always be part of our family."

day 135

The looks on their faces were as varied as the sizes of their stomachs. There was joy, fear, apathy. I wondered what my face revealed about how I felt about my baby.

Ethan came with me to my twelve-week checkup. His face said, *overjoyed*. There were two other men in the waiting room. The older man skimmed magazines, his three-hundred-dollar briefcase parked at his feet. The creases in his pants were so sharp they could injure a passerby. I couldn't care less about this salesman, who was probably there to convince Dr. Hilliard to recommend his revolutionary hemorrhoid cream.

It was the pimply, scared-looking teenager, a soon-to-be dad I'd guessed, who captured my attention. Was he drawn to his girlfriend because she was beautiful or easy? Did they love each other or were they sitting there because their hormones got the best of them eight weeks ago?

I was making up his story in my mind when the nurse called Ethan and me in. Ethan jumped up like a jack-in-the-box. His eagerness to be part of this was already bugging me. I'd invited him in a weak moment, right after he gave me the picture frame. I figured if I took him to this visit, maybe I could get to the next few alone.

"Have a seat on the table, Mrs. Gray. Do you need a hand?"

I shook my head after I was already up there.

"I see you've already had your weight and blood pressure taken. Did you leave me a urine sample?"

I nodded.

"Great. You don't need to do anything now except wait for the doctor. He's right on schedule. He'll be in here in a sec," the nurse said.

I can't imagine being enthusiastic about pee, but I smiled, and she left.

"Why don't you have to get changed?" Ethan asked. "I forget what happens at this visit." Ethan was in the mood to talk, I wanted to get this over with.

"He's only going to examine my belly and talk to us. The big thing is you might be able to hear the heartbeat."

Before Ethan could say anything, Dr. Hilliard filled the doorway, stretching his long arm out to Ethan as he entered the exam room.

"Ethan, so good to see you again. Please accept my condolences. How are you holding up?" Dr. Hilliard had a wonderful way of making you feel like you are the only family he ever took care of.

"A little better now that we're having another child. Don't get me wrong, I miss Abby every minute of every day, but I still want us to be a family." Ethan squeezed my hand and I squeezed it back. I didn't do it to share in his delight. I did it because I wanted to hurt him. He winced as Dr. Hilliard made his way over to me.

"Well, then let's see how your baby is doing. Tessa, any complaints?" Dr. Hilliard asked.

I made a lame attempt to add lightness to the moment. "About the pregnancy or Ethan?"

"Let's start with the pregnancy." Dr. Hilliard smiled.

"I'm fine. I kind of popped in the last two weeks." I stroked my stomach. "Do I seem a little big for twelve weeks?"

"You look a little big, but you're thin and this is your second pregnancy. It's not unusual to experience things a bit earlier than you did with your previous pregnancy. After I examine you, I'll have a better idea."

He held my shoulders as I laid back on the table, the crinkly paper protesting. In a deft manner, he lifted my shirt and massaged the rounded mound of me. Ethan circled the exam table to get a better look at what Dr. Hilliard was doing. I put my hand on his in an effort to apologize for being such a brat. I didn't need to wreck this for him, even if I'd rather be anywhere else.

The gel was warm and the heartbeat loud. There was no doubt I was carrying life. Ethan cried. Then I cried. I'm pretty sure for different reasons.

After the gel was wiped off and the rhythm of the room was restored to quiet, Ethan blindsided me with the real reason he'd wanted to come.

"Dr. Hilliard, I'm worried about Tessa's ability to bond with this baby. She misses Abby so much she still sleeps in her bed sometimes. She's under a lot of stress."

I pulled my shirt down over my protruding stomach and gripped the sides of the table, getting ready to launch myself. I was not going to sit there while two men discussed whether or not I could bond with a baby. The reason I constantly felt like shit was because I'd been a little too good at bonding with a baby. Ethan kept looking in Dr. Hilliard's direction; he didn't dare make eye contact with me.

"Tessa, please wait," Dr. Hilliard said. "Though I have every confidence you'll accept this pregnancy as time goes on, Ethan has a valid concern. I'd like to do an ultrasound. It will help me confirm your due date, better assess the size of your uterus, and I believe having a picture of your child will help."

I stayed seated on the exam table and covered my stomach with one hand. "Are you concerned about how big I am?"

He put one of his strong hands over one of my small ones. "Only slightly. I think a baseline ultrasound, in your case, is a good idea. I want to take every precaution I can to ensure that five to six months from now you're holding a healthy baby."

"What are some of the reasons for Tessa being bigger than she should be?" Ethan's voice cracked.

Dr. Hilliard held my hand more firmly. "There are a number of likely pregnancy complications, none of which I suspect. The most common reason for bigger than expected size of your uterus is multiple fetuses."

I wrenched my hand free. "Multiples? You've got to be freaking kidding me."

"Tessa—" Ethan reprimanded me then turned his attention back to Dr. Hilliard. "I apologize for her. See I told you. She's having a really hard time with this whole thing."

"No need to apologize, Ethan. Tessa, your response is very common. If I had to wager a guess, I'd say you're carrying one child. To allay your anxiety, I'll get you on the schedule for tomorrow or the next day. Will that help?" He looked at me with eyes that could melt an iceberg.

I said, "Fine."

Ethan said, "Great."

Dr. Hilliard said, "Anything else, then?"

I wanted to ask, what else could there be but more than one baby? I shook my head instead.

day 136

She took the black-and-white image from my hand and a smile crept over her face. Celia's pretty when she smiles, she just doesn't do it very often. After all, what is there to smile about when you have me for a client?

"Some mothers feel reassured to find out they're carrying one child," Celia said. "Some feel a little bit sad. I wonder how you're feeling about your news."

"Are you kidding? I can barely imagine having one baby, never mind twins. I'm relieved."

Dr. Hilliard was kind enough to call ahead and ask the radiologist to come in and tell us right then whether or not I was carrying one big baby or twins. Dr. Beryl slipped into the darkened room while the technician slid her wand across the width of me. I prayed she'd perform magic and tell me there was only one child. Better yet, that I was just getting fat from not exercising and eating too much cake. The radiologist told Ethan and me that there was only one baby. This time I was the first to cry.

"The radiologist said I was a little big for twelve weeks, but she had no concerns. Everything is as it should be." I didn't tell Celia my guess was that no one told Dr. Beryl the rest of my story.

I went on to tell Celia my other news. "She asked us if we wanted to know the sex."

Celia leaned forward, and for a minute she looked like any other mother. She wanted to know so she could start imaging the real person hidden inside me. "And did you?"

"Typical of us lately, Ethan wanted to know and I didn't. Dr. Beryl said she could tell him separately, or we could think about it and if we decided we wanted to know, we could call her anytime."

"What did you and Ethan decide?"

"I'm so sick of everything being so complicated so I said, *Go ahead and tell us.* She told us—it's a girl. I'm having a girl." I reached for the box of tissues.

I cried because I'm having a baby. I cried because I'm having a girl. I cried because I wanted to spin the clock back and have this baby be Abby.

FRIDAY, FEBRUARY 17   **4:00 P.M.**

I'd finished my session with Tessa, she was my last client of
the day. I didn't rush to file my client folders or empty the waste
can of a day's worth of tears. Instead I looked out my window
and watched her walk at a snail's pace to her minivan parked between my building and the entrance to Verity Park.

Before she reached her van, she veered from it and took a seat
on the bench inside the park gate. I didn't think she should be sitting outside; it was too cold, and it was getting dark. I shouldn't
have watched her wrestle with her thoughts. I was only to witness the struggle when I'd been invited to do so.

It wasn't long before she resigned herself to leave. I couldn't
tear myself from watching. When she turned, heading away from
the building, she looked up at my window. We exchanged a
glance. Hers said she couldn't shake her sadness. I hoped mine
said, *take care.* She wiped her eyes and nose, the cold outside and
the pain inside making them run.

The ring of my phone pulled me from the window. Once I retrieved it, I looked back to see Tessa, but she was gone.

Ian's strong deep voice betrayed his childlike request. "Mom, I was wondering if I could take you to the movies tomorrow, for your birthday. You could drive and I could pay. Unless you're already doing something."

"There's nothing I'd rather do on my birthday than spend the day with you. What time should I come by? Fivish, six?"

"I thought we could go in the afternoon, in town, if that's okay."

Of course he'd want to go during the day, out of Wenonah Falls. A teenage boy going out with his mother on a Saturday night would pay for more than a movie ticket; he'd pay heavily in school on Monday morning.

I couldn't think of a better way to spend my fiftieth birthday. I wondered if Alden could be persuaded to see this from my vantage point, this being his first challenge in peacekeeping.

MONDAY, FEBRUARY 20 **8:00 A.M.**

On my birthday, there were more than a few surprises. Ian's plan was to spring for a movie at our favorite theater in Boston. When I picked him up at Harry's, I received the first of my birthday gifts.

"Happy Birthday, C. Come in for a minute. This I have to see." Harry stood back to let me in. It was hard to get past his huge grin.

I stepped into his entranceway and saw Ian walking backward toward me, his hooded sweatshirt covering his head. He turned and with a flourish removed the hood to reveal his new haircut. Short all around, parted on the right, the wavy blond curls usually on his forehead were smaller and swept to one side.

"Happy birthday." He was even more handsome because of the glow coming off of his face. "Like it?"

"Wow kid, I hope you know CPR. I think she's having a heart attack."

I tried not to go overboard with compliments, but he looked marvelous. "You didn't do this just for me. You like it, too, right?" With my hands on his shoulders I turned him around so I could see the whole of it.

With his presentation over, Ian went right back to business. "Yeah, it's cool. Literally. Dad, have you seen my Red Sox cap?"

Struck by his new look, I stepped out the front door and headed to the car. Ian leaned in to Harry and said something. The only word I could make out was *don't*.

After a French film that I loved and he slept through, Ian's next gift was that we would stop by the house and pick up Alden. He told me he'd already called him and we'd go out to dinner together. He smiled when he said, *on Al*.

The plan proved to be a ruse. When I walked through the door of my home, I was met by what at first I thought was a mirage. Alden and Harry were standing next to each other with big grins on their faces. Both were holding soda. Alden's was in cut glass, Harry's in a can.

The "happy birthday" I heard was in unison. I took notice of three separate terms of endearment—Celia, Mom, and C.

Alden sautéed fresh tilapia, made a field green salad, and homemade mashed sweet potatoes. There was no doubt in my mind Harry set the dining room table. Hanging from the chandelier was a cluster of black and white balloons. The table was set with black paper napkins topped with forks placed on the right instead of to the left of our plates. No matter how many times I'd corrected Harry on table setting, he still hadn't committed this etiquette to memory. What had once annoyed me was now rather charming. Though I'm certain it gave Alden more fuel to torch Harry's character, he gave no indication it bothered him. A gift, in and of itself.

"Don't get the idea that I picked black to razz you about your age. I thought you'd like the decorations to match our dining room." Harry winked so only I could see.

"This is so touching. I can't believe you're all doing this for me. Ian, was this your idea?"

"No, it was Dad's. Al and I—we agreed it was a good idea."

"Luckily Al offered to have it here and cook. Do you remember the time I forgot the rolls in the oven and we ended up calling the fire department?"

Harry put his soda down on the counter so he could use his hands to talk. Even Alden laughed as Harry told one kitchen disaster story after another. This line of conversation got us all the way to dinner.

"Harry, Ian, can I pour you a celebratory glass of wine? I've opened a lovely sauvignon blanc," Alden said.

Ian looked at me. "Dad and I don't drink." His voice was sharp, his words hard. Harry's mood remained light.

"Thanks Al, but I've been sober since November tenth. Even C's special day isn't reason enough for me to go back to drinking the juice. There's that little thing called a DUI." Harry put his arm around Ian's shoulder. "And I've got my boy to take care of."

"Well we've all driven a bit under the influence when perhaps we shouldn't have. Unfortunately, you were unlucky and got caught. I wasn't aware you considered yourself an alcoholic. Do you attend meetings?" Alden made no eye contact with anyone as he slipped a piece of fish into his mouth.

Alden was well aware of the type of trouble Harry had with alcohol. Everyone at the table knew it, too. It had been too good to be true. Here it was, the fuse that would end my party with fireworks.

"How about that movie, Mom? Best French film I've seen in a long time," Ian said. "You would've loved it, Al, it was kind of a mystery slash love story, right, Mom?" Alden had tried to toss a grenade on our dinner party. Ian was committed to the cease-fire.

While Ian and Harry found creative ways to rearrange the fish and field greens on their plates to make it look like they were eating, I forced myself to eat Alden's cuisine, though I was full of anxiety. I hoped Alden wouldn't be offended that they didn't care for his meal. I prayed we could keep the conversation away from any other land mines.

"Never could get into those foreign films," Harry said. "Presents, now those I've always been able to get into. C, let's get you opening some gifts. You go sit in the library. Ian and Al and I will get this table cleared. We'll meet you in there."

The three men stood; I hesitated. I tried to think of something I could do to stay near, in case a referee was required. I wasn't eager to leave the three of them alone, but I'd already seen the cake in the kitchen and knew Harry would stick with his ritual of cake with presents.

I took my time getting to the library and sat in the middle of the couch, knowing it would force everyone else to sit safe distances from one another. Fifty birthday candles illuminated the path from the kitchen to the library. They sang a pitchy version of "Happy Birthday" on their way toward me. Ian carried my favorite cake; Harry and Alden trailed behind. The evening was moving to its natural close and I was hopeful again we could make it through in one piece.

"It's your favorite, Black Forest. Dad and I got it at McGrath's." Ian stuck it out in front of me. I feared he'd drop it before it made its way safely to the coffee table.

"I haven't had something from McGrath's Bakery in years. Alden, have a nice big piece, you'll love it," I said.

"Thank you, I'll pass. I'm still full from dinner. Perhaps, I'll have a piece later—with you." Alden emphasized the words and spit them out in Harry's direction.

Harry reached for the first piece. "I'll take Al's piece. I'm never too full for chocolate and cherries."

I half expected Alden to say Harry couldn't have cake, because he hadn't eaten his dinner, but he handed me a gift instead. It was Ian's.

I turned my attention to Ian. "You didn't have to get me a gift. The movie and your haircut were more than enough. Alden, don't you love Ian's new look?"

Alden glanced at his watch instead of Ian's hair. "Yes, he looks rather respectable now. Shorter hair is more appropriate at your age. Have you thought about colleges at all? What about my university? I could take you on a tour."

I hoped Alden didn't see Ian roll his eyes. "I haven't thought much about college. I'm only a sophomore, it seems like a long way off."

Ian's gift was a champagne-colored cashmere cardigan with tiny pearl buttons. Just the right size, I wondered if Harry had helped him pick it out, and who paid.

"I know you keep a sweater down at work, so I thought you might like a new one," Ian said.

"It's perfect, Ian. I love it." I rubbed the soft fuzz against my cheek.

"Here, open mine," Harry said. "Sorry for the crappy wrap job. You know me and presentation."

I took Harry's recognizable gift, a book wrapped in tissue paper. It took me a minute to realize I held a limited edition copy of *The Count of Monte Cristo*. When I lifted my eyes from the book to Harry, his face was lit up like the candles on my cake.

"How do you like that addition to your collection, C?" Harry easily matched Ian's earlier gift-giving enthusiasm for the haircut.

"It's remarkable. Where in the world did you find it?" I caressed the cover of this book I've always treasured.

"Remember that book dealer we met when we took the boat down to Newport? God, that had to be twelve-plus years ago. I've never been able to get that store out of my mind. So I called the guy to see what he had. I couldn't believe it. You love this book, and I thought that's it. That's C's birthday present."

"Did Summer and I go on that trip?" Ian asked.

I gripped the hard cover of my book.

"You did," I said.

"Who's Summer?" Alden asked. His eyes were glued to the last gift on the coffee table.

Without warning, I heard air gust, luminous zigzags bolted back and forth between Harry and Ian. Everything compressed violently until my head felt like it would burst. She'd entered the room in the form of a pop-up thunderstorm.

I managed to thank Harry. The words I spoke were faint. I couldn't stop flipping the pages of my copy of *Cristo.* Alden, so intent on trying to slip his gift between his body and the sofa, missed the entrance of our uninvited party guest.

I sat still in my place, unsure of what Harry would do next. He could've chosen center stage, using theatrics to revel in my dishonesty, not in the least beneath him. Instead Harry kept the focus on gift-giving. Ian didn't move or say anything.

"What do you have there, Al?" Harry asked. "You didn't show us up now did you?" Harry leaned across me to egg Alden into giving me his gift.

"Celia can open it later. It's getting late, and there's still some cleaning up to do." As Alden tried to tuck his gift farther away from Harry, he dropped it on the floor.

Harry tried to snatch it up. "No, Al. She'd like to open it now."

As Alden grabbed for it, the box opened, and a gift card to the local mall slipped out onto the floor.

Ian picked it up and handed it to me. "Whoa, have a little cash."

I plowed forward, since I had no right to reprimand these boys behaving badly. "Why, Alden, how generous of you. I've been meaning to shop for some new work clothes, thank you."

"I thought a gift card practical, given your birthday falls so close to Christmas and Valentine's Day. This way you can choose whatever you like and it's certain to be your style." I couldn't tell if his snippy explanation was because he was still hurt over the diamond necklace, or because Harry had embarrassed him.

I didn't have a chance to smooth things out before Harry took advantage of his position of power.

"Al, you've got the presentation thing down. Your meal looked like a piece of artwork from the gallery on Surfside Street. You've got the French film thing going on. But one husband to another, presents aren't supposed to be practical. They're supposed to be fun, exciting. You know, extravagant."

Alden's face reddened, and I felt its heat on my cheek. "Since your marriage is over, and ours is still going strong, I don't believe I'm in need of any tips from you. And by the way, my name is Alden. If you'll excuse me, I'll clean up while you say your good-byes."

Under his breath, Harry delivered the final jab. "Not as strong as you think, pal."

With that, my party was over.

spring

PART THREE

rain

148

When my last pair of pants had my waistline screaming for a nightgown, I knew it was time to buy maternity clothes. While the clothes had gotten trendier, the stupid store names hadn't. I drove to the mall and found a store called Bun in the Oven or something equally ridiculous tucked in between a lingerie store and a baby boutique. I'd already collected a handful of comfortable pants and shirts when I overheard them.

"Did you hear? The mother of the little girl killed over by Bright Futures is pregnant." A very pregnant thirty-something tipped her head back as she downed the rest of her bottled water.

"Oh my God, really? My life would be over if anything ever happened to Robbie," said her nonpregnant friend. "How can she start over like that, when they don't even know who did it."

"I know, I would die." Thirty-something stroked her belly and pasted a frown on. "You're not going to believe what my cousin Charlie told me."

From the opposite side of a rack of tent-size dresses I could hear pieces of the conversation between the two gossip shoppers as they casually discussed my life. I dropped some of the clothes I held but didn't bend down to pick them up. I was afraid I'd miss what they'd say next. It took everything in my power to resist the urge to scream *shut up.* I stood strong when they stopped talking about me and moved on to the investigation. I leaned into the rack, for once thankful I'm small.

"Well, you know Charlie joined the force about six months ago, he worked with that big cop, you know the one I mean. How does someone get that fat? Anyway, everyone thinks that he knows who did it and he's covering up for someone."

I swallowed the bile that had forced itself into the back of my throat. My back hurt from leaning in; sheer will kept my legs from buckling.

"I never thought something like this could happen in Wenonah Falls. Charlie says if they have no proof, there's nothing anybody can do," the pregnant one said.

I carried the clothes I had left in my arms to the register. I threw them down in a heap. "I'll be back. Suddenly, I don't feel well."

I don't know if the gossip shoppers realized who I was or not, but the last things I saw as I flew out of the store were their guilty faces.

When I finished throwing up in the parking lot, I made my way home. I don't remember the drive. All I could think about was putting calls in to Ethan, Pat, and North. I cursed myself for leaving my cell phone on the kitchen counter. It was a damn good thing the red light was blinking on the answering machine, and the first message I played was from Pat. I was sick of being one step ahead of my so-called allies.

"I wonder if you could call me at the office or on my cell. It's not the break we're looking for, but it's very important you call me. Soon."

What the gossip shoppers said had to be true. Pat's voice said so. I was torn between calling her and calling Ethan.

"Ethan, please come home."

"Honey, what's the matter? Is it the baby?"

"No, the baby's fine. I'm fine—no, I'm not. I heard something unbelievable about Caulfield. We need to get Pat over here. Come home."

I started to dial Pat on my cell while I was still talking to Ethan.

"I'll be right there. Call Rosemary to be with you while you wait for me. Promise?"

"Hurry. I'm calling Pat." I felt like I was going to be sick again, so I moved toward the kitchen sink. I hung up so he'd get here faster.

Pat's Saab shot into the driveway and she got out almost before she turned off the ignition. Ethan made it home from the office right behind her. I met them both at the door. The lump was back in my throat, stopping me from telling them what I'd heard.

"Good. You're both here," Pat said. "Let's talk inside."

She took charge like the funeral director did on the day we chose Abby's casket. She said sit. So we sat.

"I have disturbing news. Detective Caulfield is going to be arrested this afternoon."

"He knows who killed Abby and he isn't going to tell us." I got up and started pacing the family room.

Ethan moved to the edge of his couch cushion. "Back up a minute. What are the two of you talking about? Tessa, come sit down."

"I overheard two women talking about it in a store at the mall. He knows, doesn't he?" I asked Pat.

Pat opened her briefcase and pulled out a thick, legal-size stack of paper. "The state grand jury is handing down indictments, charging him with several counts of police misconduct including accepting bribes, conspiracy to commit crimes, and obstruction of justice. The first of the indictments has nothing to do with Abby's case." She put the papers down on the coffee table.

"What about the other charge?" I sat back down and reached for Ethan's hand to ground me. I could no longer feel the floor under my feet.

"It might," she said. "What I know is this, there has to be strong evidence for the bribery and conspiracy charges. With obstruction charges, they don't have to have substantiated suspicion to file that charge. I don't know."

Now Ethan sounded like me. "Pat, for Christ's sake speak English."

She put the papers back in her briefcase and closed it. She leaned in to both of us. "They're thinking he intentionally mis-handled Abby's case. I don't know if that means he knows who did it. Right now, they may or may not have a lot of evidence, they're not saying. It doesn't matter. They can file that charge without proof."

Ethan put his head in his hands. I sat there staring at Pat, her voice getting harder and harder to hear.

"This will allow them to go after him for more information about Abby's accident. They can investigate their suspicions in more detail. I've set up a meeting with North and the three of us, tomorrow. I set it up for here, if you don't mind, because—"

When the phone rang, it startled me. Ethan popped up from the couch. Pat put her hand out to stop him.

"Check the caller ID or better yet leave it to the message machine. I have a feeling you're going to be inundated with media requests for a statement. We need to talk about that. We need more time."

149

I slept in her bed last night, or should I say, I laid there. Sleep didn't come, not that I wanted it to. I didn't toss and turn in fear of a morning filled with hazy thoughts and strong desires for coffee. I laid my growing body against her princess sheets, the ones I haven't washed since she last slept there. I struggled to find her smell, but it no longer lingers between the covers. I thought about our next investigation meeting, only hours away. I clutched her Tootsie Rabbit close to my chest. Then I felt it. Like the quivering wings of a trapped bird, my baby moved. That she chose this place to introduce herself wasn't lost on me.

With Abby, I hadn't known the feeling. The first few times I felt her, I was unaware she was trying to get my attention. It was like walking through a spiderweb, I felt something, but I couldn't see or put my hands on it, no matter how hard I tried.

No, sleep didn't come as I said good-bye to one daughter, once more, while I said hello to the other.

150

I've never minded a polite phone call trying to scoop an interview, but reporters camped out all over my front lawn, that's sinful. I couldn't pass the time on my window seat in the family room. I couldn't sit by the dining room window, the one that overlooks the street. Or watch Caulfield's block-shaped jaw and arrogant walk replayed on the news. So I poured a cup of the coffee Ethan had brewed for Pat and North, sprawled undercover on the family room couch, and waited for them to come.

Ethan found me there, sipping. "Don't say a word," I said. "I'm not getting through this without it."

"Okay, but make it last, I didn't make it for you. To tell you the truth, I didn't make it for them either. I needed something to do."

Ethan's last sentence was punctuated by the doorbell. I wanted it to be Pat and North. It could just as easily have been another reptilian reporter.

I don't know if Pat's taller than North or just more confident. She waltzed into the house with her back straight and head high, even his spiked hair couldn't match her height. "Well, it would've been worse if you'd left the house," she said. "Let's meet in the kitchen."

We all followed her into the kitchen. When Pat directs, everyone follows. Even me. After Ethan poured coffee and we were seated in our usual seats—we'd done this before—she began.

"The status of the Caulfield situation is unchanged from what I told you yesterday."

Pat had one hand draped over the other on the tabletop while she delivered what sounded like lines from a play she'd rehearsed. "He's been arraigned. He pled not guilty to all the charges and was released on his own recognizance."

North, who'd been jingling his pocket change since he came in, tipped his head and leaned closer to me while he looked across the table at Ethan. "How are you guys doing with all this?"

"I go back and forth between furious and devastated," Ethan said. He brushed a dark curl off his forehead.

"Detective, I don't mean to be unkind, but I've already got a therapist. Do you have anything new to tell us? I mean, we've waited weeks for you to either rule in or out those two suspects. Is Caulfield's arrest going to help the case or prove to be one more huge distraction?" Leave it to me to play bad cop to his good cop.

North took an audible breath while Pat wrung her hands. "Tessa, Ethan, we do have information," she said. "I'm afraid it doesn't move the case forward." Her hands stopped moving, and then North took over.

"I know everything seems to be happening at once. None of it seems like the break we're looking for," North said.

"For God's sake, tell us." Ethan put down his coffee cup, sloshing a puddle in Pat's direction. He let go of his frustration, and no one moved to clean it up.

"The teenager we were interested in, Nicco Julian, it turns out his alibi is solid. His car didn't turn up anything, though it was unlikely it would, given his corroborating evidence. I think I told you, I never really thought he was a probable suspect. Neil Ford, he's another story," North said.

He'd stopped jingling his change. The room was still. "Ford's car didn't produce any evidence. No hair, no clothing fibers. No other DNA that would link him to the case. But witnesses do put him in the area around the time of the accident. He has no alibi, and we know he's a repeat DUI offender. I can't rule him out yet. It nags me that his previous arrests were all during the day."

"This is bad news because you have nothing. Do you still think he did it?" The sound of my voice got weaker with each word.

Pat used her hand as a stop sign toward North. "It doesn't matter what he thinks. The police don't have anything linking Ford to Abby's death. They still can't find the missing paint sample or the autopsy photos. Mrs. Dwyer doesn't know anything. Unless Caulfield's willing to fill in the blanks, we don't have Ford."

While Pat was talking, Ethan's jaw dropped. "What, are you Ford's lawyer, too, Pat?"

"Of course not." Her tone softened, and suddenly she looked really young. "I refuse to give you any more false hope. Look, we still have whatever the police can get out of Caulfield. But I won't lie to you, without some revelation from him, I'm not optimistic you're going to get the answers you deserve. Last week, I didn't feel this way. It might be time now to start coming to some acceptance about the possibility. I'm really sorry."

Pat moved her paper napkin over to mop up Ethan's mess. North was frozen like the inner harbor before a thaw. Ethan wiped his eyes with the back of his hand. I pushed back my chair, arced my body out of my seat, and stood.

"You can accept it if you want to—all of you." My voice was controlled, but loud enough for my new lawn ornaments to hear me. "I will never accept it."

Tessa was different today. She wasn't the young mother curled up in my chair, who talked about how much she loved her sweet, funny Abby, or how she longed to love her second daughter, while tears came and went. She wasn't the edgy, fierce Tessa, either, the one who fights her way through her grief, step after faltering step.

No, today I saw an altogether different Tessa. Dressed in an indigo paisley maternity top and jeans, her hair caught up in a knot. She didn't talk about Abby or her baby. She wasn't angry at Ethan or Rosemary or her lawyer or the police. She was steady, composed, and she didn't swear. Tessa was living stone.

"They're done," she said. "Pat and North, they'll continue to go through the motions, I think. They've pretty much said it's over." Her hands were tucked under her thighs and her feet barely touched the floor.

Tessa rarely presented me with subtlety. I sat up straighter in my chair. I'd need to work harder now to uncover her hidden thoughts and secret feelings. Unmistakable emotions were easier for me to explore, at least with clients.

"That surprises me, Tessa. I would've thought the arrest of that detective makes getting more information quite possible. What makes you feel so certain it won't?"

"Detective Caulfield isn't going to offer up anything. I knew from the moment I met him, something was wrong with him. I thought he was incompetent, not dirty." Despite her growing size, she barely shifted in her chair.

I felt the need to push her. Some emotion, even negative, is better than none. "It's possible the stress of all of this is coloring your view of the situation. There's hope, isn't there, that the other detective—Mr. North—the one you trust, will put the pieces together?"

"No, I've lost my confidence in him. And Pat." She looked at her watch and then pierced my eyes with her cold ones. "You know, you really can't trust anyone but yourself. Would you mind if I cut our session short? I've got a few things I need to do." She didn't wait for an answer, she headed for the door.

The shell of Tessa walked past me. Her slight body simultaneously light from the absence of the will to fight and heavy from the weight of hopelessness. I recognized her emptiness. Tessa was me ten years ago, leaning against the wall outside the cheerfully painted pediatric oncologist's office, after receiving the news that there was nothing left to do to save my girl. I'd had the will to fight once upon a time. Then lost it, like Tessa.

The weather teased me that day, lulling me into believing my life was perfect. Harry was teaching Ian how to tie knots. The boat swayed in the surf the way a mother rocks a cradle. The sun was hot on my bare skin, the gentle breeze eased the sting. I pulled my protesting five-year-old up the ladder. She never stopped swimming willingly.

"I'll read you a story while you paint a picture for Daddy.

You've been in the water a long time." I used a thick towel, covered in sea horses, to wrap her wriggling body.

"Did you watch me, Mommy? I can swim like Daddy." She shook her bob of hair, a miniversion of my own, sprinkling the front of my suit with salty water. She giggled and did it again. In a mock wrestle to dry her off, I felt the firm rounded mass in her belly. Protruding from my stick of a girl, I knew immediately it was unnatural. Something that shouldn't be growing inside my child's body.

Three days later in a disinfectant-laced office, Harry and I heard foreign words that would change our lives forever. *Stage three anaplastic nephroblastoma. Wilms' tumor. A common form of childhood kidney cancer. Radiation and chemotherapy, first. To be followed by surgery.*

The robotic white-coated man wrote everything down. He knew we hadn't heard anything after the word *cancer*. Harry swore the doctor said there was no reason to believe she wouldn't beat it. The doctor had never seen our daughter's fire, so we convinced ourselves he had that part of the diagnosis right.

For two years she extended her arm so the dialysis nurses could access her arterio-venous shunt. Each day, we checked its thrill and bruit to be sure it hadn't clotted. She couldn't take another surgery. Her fingers stayed strong, her sketches the only distraction from the pricks and pains of treatment. Treatment not meant for any grown-up, never mind a child. She fought the good fight and we ran the race right alongside her. In the end, she knew she would leave us.

She begged Harry to take her back to the harbor, the place she loved more than any other on earth. I didn't think it was a good idea. There was no room for death on our family boat. Harry fought me and the doctors for permission. The nurses agreed with Harry; this was what she wanted, so this was what she should have. They helped him organize everything to get her comfortable bobbing up and down in Wenonah Harbor. On a steamy August evening, as the sun dipped below the horizon, we lost faith and we lost our daughter. As the ambulance took her away from me, I walked off the pier and haven't stepped onto its wood since.

MONDAY, MARCH 6   **8:00 A.M.**

I suppose serenity can be measured two ways. Harmony and understanding. Or, quiet resolve—no fighting, not even a miniature skirmish. On my birthday, I had the childish fantasy that everyone could get along. In the last week, peace in my family comes in the form of silence.

After Harry and Ian left my party, I arranged my gifts on the coffee table, doing my best to summon the courage to tell Alden about my daughter. In his preoccupation with Harry, he'd missed the significance of Ian asking about his beloved sister. Alden failed to register her name because I haven't said it out loud in ten years. I never told him she existed. The longer I waited, looking for the perfect time to tell him, the more impossible it became to find it.

When I came into the kitchen, he was wiping counters and rearranging dirty dishes. Steaming water and white fluff billowed from the soaking pans that filled the sink. Alden used each task as a reason to avoid me. He got quiet when he harbored resentment toward my other husband. For one split second, I thought it would be easier to let him stay angry with Harry.

"Can you stop cleaning for a minute? There's something I should have told you. I have to tell you now."

I don't know what he imagined, but the fear that filled his eyes and the tension that shaped his mouth told me he knew it would be a defining moment.

"I had a daughter. She died ten years ago, she was seven."

Alden threw the scouring pad he gripped into the sink, splashing sudsy water up onto his shirt. Like a Rorschach image it emerged across his chest. Though drenched, he didn't react to it. He simply stood there, waiting for me to say more.

I told him about her cancer. Her treatment. Her response to her chemo and then her lack of it. The way she bravely hopped into the recliner at dialysis, after hugging her favorite nurse. How she'd squeeze her failing body to one side, making room enough for Ian on the days I couldn't find someone to watch him. The two of them would pass the time watching the same cartoons over and over again. I shared the unqualified hope we had in the beginning and the overpowering despair in the end.

Yet I couldn't really tell him about her, the things that truly defined her. Her talent for sketching the ocean that was beyond her years or her musical giggle that rang off the deck of our boat every time her perfect feet stepped on it. I was afraid to call her vivid color back into my heart or that room. I didn't know if I could handle him hearing my words and still not having the faintest idea of who she was or what it meant to live with her and then without her. So I kept things clinical, accurate. And so did he.

And as if the worse thing he could do was leave me with a mess on my birthday, he left the kitchen and left the house.

Since that night, Alden retreats each evening to his armchair, anchored by a history book and a glass of port. Little if any conversation flows between us.

My only contact with Ian is as a result of my motherly phone calls. Ones where I prod him to tell me about school and homework. I've stopped asking about Lacey.

Then there's Harry. I didn't expect any contact with Harry.

With each relationship silenced, the weekend held no lunch plans or movie dates. No dinners with friends or colleagues of Alden's. No chitchat about spring warmth or false starts for crocuses. I concentrated on writing thank-you notes and catching up on my newspapers.

Drawn to the stories about Tessa's family and the investigation,

I understand why she's shutting down. It's bad enough to lose a daughter, to grapple with unrelenting forces of nature. Day after day, to witness the subtle demise of a once rambunctious child is nothing short of cruel. Yet unlike Tessa, I had the chance to hold my child's disappearing body in my arms and whisper my good-byes. No mother should learn in the span of one phone call or a single knock at the door, that the irresponsible nature of another ended the life of her child.

I was tempted to call Tessa. I wanted to climb out of the fortress I'd made and go talk to her, one mother to another. Instead, I put on the necklace Harry gave me, the one that holds the birthstones of my children. I buried the stones deep under the collar of the soft sweater Ian gave me for my birthday. I sat next to my husband who, like my first one had, spent the weekend holding a drink instead of me.

TUESDAY, MARCH 7 **8:00 A.M.**

It was a school night, but it was my Tuesday to have Ian over for dinner. Alden surprised me, offering to make Ian's favorite meal, spaghetti and meatballs to be served right at the kitchen table. With his unexpected generosity and no more secrets, I prayed we'd get through one night without conflict.

I passed the time waiting for Ian by sorting through cabinets in the studio. Watercolor pans came out of one box and went into another, brushes were moved an inch here or there. I reordered shelves and shifted boxes more than I made any progress packing things up. I couldn't bring myself to do away with this space and these memories. I thought about Tessa not being able to rearrange a single item in Abby's room, and then about what I had done.

Two weeks after I was robbed of my daughter, I dismantled her room. Ian had just started kindergarten. Harry worked short-ened days, taking on the job of picking him up after school, since

I couldn't be trusted to remember the time of day. It started out innocently enough, no one would've been troubled by what I discarded, if only it hadn't launched my cleaning frenzy.

I went to get a simple drink of water. When I opened the cabinet that held our glasses, there were her medicines lined up like soldiers ready for battle. I pulled a trash bag from under the sink and swiped the whole army into it. For an instant I felt a tingle of relief. I moved through the downstairs, gathering her slippers, her books, and her charcoal pencils. The tingle turned to mania and I took the stairs to her room. As I opened the door, I knew what I would do.

Harry and Ian found me hours later. By then it was too late. Her toys were in boxes and her bed stripped of its clothes, the usual bright pink glow of her room diminished by the white paint I whacked and slapped on its walls.

"Mommy, don't," Ian screamed.

"Celia, what have you done?"

Harry moved to take the brush from me, I resisted until I saw Ian hoarding armloads of her things from the boxes, tears pouring down his sweet face.

"She's not coming back," I shouted. "I can't take having her things all around me."

Harry caressed my back with one hand, and with the gentle yet strong fingertips of the other, he lifted my chin. "C, I know it hurts like hell, but this isn't going to help us feel better. Please talk to someone. I promise I'll come with you."

"I don't need you, I don't need anybody. I know how to do this."

Harry and I turned at the same time to see Ian sitting on the floor, his legs crisscrossed, his body rocking. He held her pillow to his face, his eyes were closed.

"This isn't how you do this," Harry said.

"Want some help?" Ian startled me back to the present. When I turned around, he was leaning up against the studio door frame.

Even slouching, he looked more like a man than a boy. His hair dipped down on his forehead. I would've given anything at that moment to sweep it back into place with a loving touch.

"I don't really know what I'm doing. Originally I wanted to pack it all up and give Alden a room of his own. Now I don't think I can."

He came in, taking in the framed mother and daughter artwork as he moved forward. "Remember when you used to let us play in here? You gave us our own stuff. You said we could use anything we wanted, as long as it was on that one shelf."

I opened the cabinet doors all the way and pointed to the shelf, left exactly as I'd organized it for them. "You loved using tracing paper to copy my sketches."

He fingered the crayons and child-friendly scissors. "She used to sneak your paints off the higher shelves. She showed me how to use your special brushes to make different kinds of lines."

"You don't think for one second that I didn't know you two did that?" I tentatively placed a hand on his shoulder. Their shelf and my touch opened him up to me.

"I miss her so much. I hate it that I can't remember her voice. Do you—"

"Good to see you, Ian," Alden said. "Are you two ready for dinner, or do you need a few more minutes?" His timing was in serious need of fine-tuning, but I could tell he was trying to reach out.

Awkwardly we moved down the hall toward dinner. A meal that was unremarkable in almost every way. Alden was uncharacteristically chatty, his efforts to connect with us forced and insincere. Ian pushed the food around his plate in tiny semicircles, the way he does when he has no intention of eating. Then he picked and pulled at a roll. Alden nudged Ian's salad bowl toward his plate, a clear message to eat food, not play with it.

"What do the two of you think about the investigation into that police detective's misconduct?" He tapped Ian's napkin on the table, a gesture that suggested he put it in his lap, and went back to halving a meatball. He looked over to me to gauge my reaction, asking without speaking if this was an acceptable conversation.

"I think it's heartbreaking. Imagine how that poor mother feels, losing her daughter and then getting pulled into all this corruption. All she wants to know is who killed her daughter and left her lying alone near that school."

"It's terrible what happened, but I've met the detective a number of times and he's not as despicable as the papers lead you to believe. Oh, speaking of school—"

Alden put down his fork and knife, food swirled in circles on his plate, too. He walked over to the counter and pulled a medium-size bag marked TRADEWINDS BOOK SHOP from it and handed it to Ian.

"It's a chemistry review book. A colleague of mine highly recommends it as an adjunct to your regular text. I thought you could use some help."

Ian put it down on the corner of the table and starting collecting plates. "I'm done. Aren't you done yet, Mom?" He held my stare, and I knew he wasn't talking about dinner.

"Here let me." I reached out to take the plates. "I'll clear the table and we can play a game of cribbage."

"No, I should go." He grabbed his sweatshirt from the back of his chair. Once he finished fighting to get it over his head, he didn't bother to fix his tousled hair. Without planting his usual good-bye kiss on my cheek, he slammed the back door and was gone, leaving the book hanging off the edge of the table.

"What in the world set him off this time?" Alden mumbled as he headed out of the kitchen, leaving me once again to clean up a mess he'd played a role in making.

156

Wrapped tightly in my robe, I waved to Ethan from the farmer's porch as he pulled out of the driveway, then I headed upstairs to its hiding place. Pulling the list from my underwear drawer, I realized I hadn't looked at it since the day I was duped into thinking North could solve this. I should've known if you want something done—

I dropped my heavy body down on my unmade bed. I read their names along with all the notes I'd made, back when I was certain there was a way to get the answers I needed.

Feeling certain again, I laid the list down and got dressed. Saving my energy for the work to be done, I left my bedroom the way it was and went back down to the kitchen. With my notebook off to one side of the table and the list in front of me, I crossed off the names of the drunks who couldn't have done it.

Red line after red line brought me to Neil Ford. I wouldn't be rash. After all, what were a few more agonizing days of waiting going to do to me? I could do more research online. When I'm ready, I'll pay him a visit. When I do, I'll look into his bloodshot eyes and I'll know. If he isn't the one, I'll go see every person on this list. Sometimes you have to do things yourself.

159—March 12

Abby's friends and their mothers played *I can top that* when it came to birthday parties. Moonwalks, ponies, clowns, and magic shows. Those had certainly been done before. I don't know anyone who's fifth birthday was celebrated in a cemetery.

Ethan, Rosemary, Kevin, and Matthew carried the five balloons, the two cans of Silly String, and a bakery box of chocolate cupcakes. I carried my grief. There were other mourners in various stages of disbelief, staring at grave stones, depositing flowers. But none of them had our finesse. There was an ancient woman carrying blue-stained carnations in one hand, gripping the arm of what had to be her son, though he must have been at least seventy. There was an unmistakable father-and-son team. Both in tears, their only contrasting feature was the one's light and the other's dark hair. Trying to keep my mind on anything and everything except where I was walking, I noticed the father's arm around the boy's shoulder. Their grief was as fresh as a newly dug plot.

They stared at me as I walked past them, probably connecting to my identical emotions. I wondered who they'd come to visit. The boy let out a low moan when he saw Matthew carrying the balloons. I heard the father's undertone say, "It's okay, keep walking."

Then we were there. There was a small bouquet of daisies hiding her birth date. I guessed they were Ethan's doing. He's a frequent flyer to Abby's new home.

"Auntie Tessa, when do I get to send the balloons to Abby?" Matthew asked. He was holding them with two hands, trying hard to hold on until the time was right.

"Let Auntie have a minute to say her prayers, okay, honey?"
Rosemary knew I was the reluctant party guest.

I squatted down, eye level with him. He blocked my view of
her stone. "Mattie, you tell me how it should go. Do you want to
spray the Silly String first or send up the balloons? It's up to you."

And so it went Silly String, cupcakes, and balloons. After the
last balloon disappeared from view, Matthew started to cry. "I forgot to bring her a present."

160

When I woke up this morning, I knew I was ready. Ethan mis-
took my getting up before him as a good thing, a sign my grief
was moving in his direction.

"Morning, honey." He came up behind me and wrapped his
arms around me, his hands landing on my belly.

"Are you talking to me or someone else?" I turned around inside his circle. I smiled and kissed him, a kiss that said more than
good morning.

"Both of you, of course." After a softer kiss, he disentangled
himself and reached for a piece of my pumpernickel. "Are you
willing to share? I'm running a little late. By the way, why are you
up so early? Doctor's appointment?" He straightened his tie and
looked right into my eyes. Ethan always makes eye contact.

I'd told myself I wouldn't lie to him. "I'm doing some research.
I'm working today." I looked down at the lonely piece of toast decorated with rivers of butter.

"Really, I didn't know you were writing a new piece. That's
great. What magazine?" His face practically screamed, *Yeah I get
my wife back—finally.*

"I'm doing a little poking around. I don't have a lot to go on
yet." I was honest, but I wasn't going to tell him my whole plan. I
knew he'd stop me.

"I can't wait to hear more. I'm one hundred percent behind you on this Tessa. You're a wonderful journalist. Freelancing will be perfect right now. Will you tell me more tonight? I've really got to fly." He grabbed his briefcase, then doubled back for a quick peck.

I followed him to the door. "You know, I'd rather wait until I have something more solid to pitch. You don't mind, do you?"

He put down his briefcase, turned, and put both hands on my shoulders. "I'm so happy you've found something to take your mind off things. You have my complete support for whatever you're doing." With another quick kiss and an *I love you,* he was off.

I tossed the shred of guilt I felt out the door as I closed it. He might be mad at first, but when I find out who did it, he will forgive me. He'll be glad. I skipped the rest of the toast and grabbed my stuff. It was time to pay Neil Ford a visit.

161

I tried to guess how many times I must have driven past Clean Closets, the dry cleaner owned by Ford and his family. It had to number in the hundreds. It stood out, tucked between a French bakery and a specialty wine store. I hadn't noticed that irony before. He could drink before, during, and after work; how convenient. I parked my minivan in the only free spot, directly in front of the wine store. I reached between the driver and passenger seats and took out a shopping bag. These were not clothes that held cherished memories or the possibility of a stray hair or even the slightest hint of her. Two of the dresses were brand-new, tags still suspended from their necklines. They would serve their purpose.

I didn't want to waste my chance, so I walked up and down the quaint village street. I noticed right away the bright COME IN, WE'RE OPEN sign dangling from the entrance door. All I could see was an old woman behind the counter organizing the day's starting cash. There were only a few other shoppers walking through the drizzle, but my heartbeat was so loud, I wondered if they could hear it. Nobody seemed to notice that I'd made a third pass in front of the cleaners. With no sight of Neil Ford, I decided to stop at the bakery and wait until I could get my nerves under control.

I sipped a juice, nibbled a croissant, and breathed in through my nose and out my mouth. As I told myself I could do this, he walked right by the bakery window. From newspaper pictures and ones I'd found online, I'd studied his emaciated face and sunken eyes so often I knew him.

I didn't want to ambush him. I would be the picture of stability, steady but unyielding. As I walked from the bakery to the cleaners, the sky opened up and pelted me with rain. Others rushed to get to their destination; I strolled. In only a couple of minutes, I would know. The question was, would I feel any different?

I placed my rolled-up bag of clothes down on the counter in front of the old woman. As she went to open it, I pulled it back toward me. "Can I see Mr. Ford, please? A friend of mine says he's the one I want to talk to."

She gave me a suspicious look and with a brogue as thick as the steam coming from the back of the shop, she called him. "Neilly, there's someone here who needs to speak to you."

He walked out from the back, and before he saw me he threw back the rest of a Coke. When our eyes locked, I dumped out the contents of the bag. Frilly clothes littered the counter.

His deep voice didn't fit his scrawny body; it belonged to a different man. Maybe he'd been a different man once. His eyes registered alarm, like he thought I'd be the customer from hell, bent on making a scene. It wasn't the dread I'd expected to see, the look that would tell me he's guilty.

"I know you," he said. "You're that poor kid's mother." He didn't move and he didn't touch the clothes.

The old woman's face registered recognition. She didn't move or say anything either.

Calm washed over me, and before he could tell me so, I knew he didn't do it.

"Do you want to go somewhere and talk? I didn't do it—so's I don't mind answering any of your questions. I could buy you a drink. Over there." He pointed in the direction of the bakery.

"Why should I believe you?" I wanted to test him, to be sure.

"The police don't. They say you were near her school that morning, you don't have an alibi, and you've got a serious drinking problem. Convince me." It was just the three of us in the shop and time was standing still, along with the rest of us.

"I admit I'm an alky. I'm off the wagon more than I'm on it. After my last arrest a year ago, my wife and kid left me. I love my girl more than anything in the world, lady. I'm telling you the truth. I didn't kill yours. I may still drink, but I don't drive. Ask her." He pointed again, this time to the woman.

Her wrinkles softened, as if the steam from the shop had relaxed them. "He's got his troubles, he does. But he didn't hurt your little one. I'd know," she said.

Though I believed her, when she reached her hand out to cover mine, I pulled away from her touch, shoving the dresses back in my shopping bag.

The next thing I knew, I was back in my kitchen, replaying it over again in my mind to be sure.

I'm sure.

THURSDAY, MARCH 16 9:00 A.M.

Ian's guidance counselor and I played phone tag for three days until I finally managed to reach her. She spoke barely above a whisper, and I wondered how she survived the powerful personalities of the teenagers she worked to serve.

"Thank you for returning my call, Mrs. Reed. I wanted to share Ian's current grades with you. He really hasn't been able to get anything up over a C since we last spoke." I could picture her through the phone, her face accented with glasses too dark and sharp angled for even a grandmother to wear.

"I stand corrected. He's getting an A in English." She said it seriously, as if his one good grade would be enough to redeem him.

"You know he's been working with the tutor you recommended. Do his teachers say anything about his effort? If he's really trying and these are his grades, well then, I suppose we have one set of problems. If he's not doing the work, it's another, isn't it?" I was sorting out the difference as I spoke.

"If you like, I can call a team meeting to get all of his teachers around the table, but I have to tell you, they say he's going through the motions." She paused. "Have you and Ian's father settled on the matter of counseling and maybe medication?"

We hadn't; we needed to now. This had gone on long enough. When I hung up with Miss Lapin, I called Harry.

"I agree, face-to-face would be best. No, you don't have to meet me at my office, it's too far to walk and I know you have a short lunch break. Harry, I insist. I'll meet you at your house."

It made no difference where we met. We agreed we had to talk. I postponed a client, giving me some wiggle room to pick up sandwiches and get over to Harry's. When I turned onto his street I didn't see him walking; a pang of guilt surprised me. Even though the Boatworks is only a couple of blocks away, I should have offered to pick him up.

Thinking maybe he was already there, I walked up the front path and peered in through the side glass that frames the front door. Though I didn't see him milling about, I knocked anyway. Not expecting him to answer and knowing Harry never locks the door, I tried the handle. He wouldn't mind me getting the sandwiches on plates and pouring us something to drink.

I let myself in and headed straight for the clutter. I couldn't help noticing the mess. Newspapers, soda cans, and half-opened mail distinguished Harry's side of the living room. A stack of DVDs, not in their cases, a lonely iPod, and Ian's hooded sweatshirt marked his. I resisted midtidy, the memory of the day I'd cleaned Ian's room pinged my brain like the flick of a finger on my head. Maybe I shouldn't have let myself in. This was their home, not mine. Then I remembered Ian's journal.

Could I steal a peek? I'd already crossed one threshold. I could slip into his room and read a page. It could help me to help him. He'd never know.

I glanced out the front window, down the street. No Harry. I laid the bag of sandwiches down on the end table, next to Harry's

chair, and ducked down the hall to Ian's room. I was distracted by
the same disarray I'd seen the last time I'd been in it. Knowing
my time was limited, I went right for Ian's underwear drawer. I
dug under balls of socks, belts curled like snakes, and underwear
tossed this way and that. It wasn't there.

I opened the next drawer and the next. No journal. I walked
toward the desk and Ian's laptop. I could turn it on, but I couldn't
read an e-mail or view his MySpace page because I still hadn't
pinned him down to give me his passwords. Cursing my lack of
limits, I saw a fast-moving shadow run behind the shade covering Ian's window. Unmistakably, Harry.

I dashed back down the hall, grabbed the sandwich bag, and
slowed my pace toward the kitchen.

"Jesus, Celia. You scared the shit out of me. What are you doing in here?" Harry's eyes darted from the back door to the door
to the garage, wondering where I might have come from. He tried
to catch his rapid breathing.

"It wasn't until after I was inside that I realized perhaps I'd
overstepped my boundaries. Forgive me?" I took my time with
lunch and thought the best way to cover my own panting was to
keep talking. "Do you remember when you finally agreed to lock
up the house and you bought that horrid fake stone you could
hide the key inside?"

"Yeah, I remember. It wasn't classy enough for Miss Fancy-
pants."

When he laughed, I knew I wouldn't be found out. Over lunch,
all I could think about was where Ian might have put his journal.

FRIDAY, MARCH 17 9:00 A.M.

The office is chilly. I've got my sweater wrapped tight, and
though it kills me to do it this time of year, I've turned the heat up

a few degrees. Three days from its official start date and spring hasn't fully sprung.

I pulled out the seven folders I'll need for the day. Laying them out in order of their scheduled arrival, I turn them so no one can read my clients' names. Confidentiality is a privilege everyone should enjoy.

Harry opened up to me yesterday. Without a power struggle, he agreed that it's time Ian see a counselor. When he meets me here today, after my last session, we'll tackle putting together a list of possibles from a referral list I keep here. Harry jumped at the chance to make the first contact with a psychiatrist, showing me he's really on board. I think I should be the one to do it, counselor to counselor. But God forbid I do anything to squelch Harry. He's agreed Ian should get help, and I'm not going to annoy him. If I nitpick over who makes the appointment, he might change his mind. After my session with Tessa, Harry and I will deal with Ian's depression head-on.

164

I almost told Celia. I hadn't thought I would, but when I was sitting in that chair looking at her kind face, I almost told her.

I tucked my legs under me, although it's getting harder and harder to get into my therapy position these days. "I'm a little better. I figured out that I really need to distance myself from this Caulfield thing. I don't have any control there."

She went into her spiel about what I had control over and what I didn't. Hell, I knew exactly what I didn't have control over. I didn't need her to tell me. Something about her softens me. I can cry real easily at Celia's. Even though I didn't cry today, I felt something bubble up. Whatever it was, it almost made me spill my plan.

I was about to tell her, when we heard arguing coming from her waiting room. At first we ignored it. The sound got louder, like a train pulling into a station. I wasn't surprised Celia took charge by going out to check on what was going on. I was stunned when she scolded whoever was out there like they were her children. She placed herself between the office and the waiting room, cutting her body in two with the door.

"Shhh. Stop it this instant." She kept her head turned toward the waiting room for longer than necessary. When she came back and took her chair, one hand gripped the arm of her chair, the other held tight to her necklace.

"Forgive the interruption. Where were we? Oh, yes. You've had a bit of a revelation? Tell me more."

In the time it took for her to check on the squabble, I had second thoughts about telling her about my dead end with Neil Ford and what I planned to do next. She pretended to be interested in what I'd been about to say. I knew she was still out in the waiting room.

I told her I'd decided to work and let her think what she wanted to. The rest of the session, I went through the motions. I had to admit, I was distracted by whoever had been fighting in the waiting room, too. I knew one of them was a man; even through Celia's office door you could make out a low voice.

When my session was over, I left the office and couldn't help but look at the two men sitting in opposite chairs with their arms firmly crossed in front of their bodies. These human bookends were quiet now, their anger toward each other still palpable. As I walked past them, I was struck by two things. One was that I couldn't see them as a couple. I pitied Celia trying to get to the bottom of their issues. The second was that one of them looked familiar.

167

I was up and out the door by nine. By the time I got two blocks from Sea Street, I realized I'd forgotten my notebook with the list inside and I needed it to confirm the number of his house. I knew it was 78, but I couldn't take the risk I was wrong, so I went back home to get it. As I pulled onto my street, I saw Rosemary power walking toward the house. Her teal tie-front cami showed through her cream-colored athletic jacket. She waved when she saw me.

"What are you doing out so early?" She chased her breath.

I got out of my van, searching for a good excuse. "I had to drop some bills at the post office. They needed to go out first thing." I lied.

"Since when does Ethan let you get hold of the checkbook?" She laughed and started walking toward the porch, poking a rip in my jean jacket.

"He lets me mail them." Leave it to Rosemary to find the hole in my excuse and my jacket.

"Can I skip the rest of my walk? I'd rather come in and talk to you. I shouldn't have gone the long way, I'm so out of shape."

"Liar. You haven't been out of shape a day in your life."

I couldn't rush her off, but I'd hoped she had other things to do before she needed to pick up Matthew. I only had the morning to do it. We sat in the family room, drinking rewarmed coffee, talking about everything and nothing. We hadn't done this without kids since that first week when Abby and Matthew started Bright Futures.

On their first day being dropped off together, Abby took her younger cousin's hand and led him into school like she'd been going there forever. She kissed him on the cheek as she left him at the doorway to the young threes classroom and she skipped down the hall to her own. I couldn't believe Rosemary still brought Mattie there.

"You seem better. Are you really okay or just sick of talking about everything?" She cradled her mug in her hands, as if the purpose of the drink was to warm them, not to jump-start her morning.

"Yeah, I'm better I guess. For a long time, I didn't want to feel better. I hate that if I'm doing better people think it means I can go on without her. I don't want to live without her. But what choice do I have?" My hand smoothed out the wrinkle of fabric that ran diagonally across my baby.

"I don't want to get all spiritual on you, Tessa, but don't you think the decision to move on has been made for you?" She pulled a coaster toward her, put her mug down, and reached over to place her delicate fingers on my stomach.

I put my hand over hers. "I'm afraid to believe that. If I do, then I have to believe there was a reason Abby was taken from me. I can't think of a single good reason for that." I sat forward and shoved a throw pillow behind my back.

"The fact that someone hit Abby by accident and was too much of a coward to take responsibility—well, that's all about the underbelly of human nature. You don't think that was God's choice, do you?"

If anyone except maybe Ethan tried to walk on this thin ice with me, I would've blown. "Rosemary, maybe someday I can debate the divine intervention versus free will thing with you. Right now, there's nothing that works to justify why some drunk should be getting away with murder." My tone said this line of questioning was over.

"I'm sorry. I'm just saying, this baby will help. I didn't mean to make you mad. It's just that, well, never mind." She picked up her mug and stared into it.

"What? You know I hate when you do that." I sighed loud enough to guilt her into telling me what she'd been about to say.

"I don't mean to be selfish. I miss you. We use to be able to talk about anything. I could ask you a question, and even if I ticked you off, we both knew we were fine. Now, I don't really talk to you because I'm afraid you won't be okay." She pulled a small pack of tissues from the pocket of her pristine jacket and used one to dab her eyes. She hates when her mascara runs. "I miss Abby so much, I can't lose you, too." She sniffed and tossed the tissue pack on the coffee table.

"Come on, Rosemary. I know I've been hard to be with, but we're fine. Go ahead, ask me anything and I promise not to lose it.

Go ahead." I grabbed another tissue out of her pack and wafted it toward her as playfully as I could.

"Really, anything." I meant it and I didn't.

"You're always talking about how some drunk did it. I wonder why you're so stuck on that. I mean, does it help to think that, even though there are millions of other possibilities?" She held her breath and waited. She wasn't trying to upset me. She really wanted to know.

"Right now, it helps."

She looked at her watch. "Oh shoot, I've got to go get Mattie. Will you drive me to my house, so I can get my car? I won't make it in time if I walk."

I got up and reached for my keys. "I'd offer to go get him for you, but I can't."

"I wouldn't think of asking you. If you drive me to my house, I'll have plenty of time." She reached out and pulled me in. For a bony woman, she gave a great hug.

On the ride, Rosemary noticed my tank was on E. When we got to her house she pulled a folded twenty out of her pocket. "Here take this, you need to get gas. I'd hate to have you run out on the ride home."

There wasn't any way to tell her I wanted it empty. It was part of my plan.

171

It felt like a conspiracy. First, Rosemary dropped by, putting a stop to my visit on Monday. Then Ethan stayed home from work today with a dual diagnosis of head cold and hypochondria. With every ounce of energy, he hoisted his body up in bed to accept the cup of soup and *kill your flu* concoction I'd brought him. His puppy dog look told me he noticed that the only soup I could find was Abby's chicken and stars.

Even with him bed-bound, I didn't dare go out. Patience not being a virtue I own, it drove me crazy to wait. I knew I'd feel safer once he was parked back at work, a solid fifteen minutes from downtown. I used my time to keep searching online for more information about the others on the list. I spent the most time planning my visit to 78 Sea Street. To the home of Harry Hayes. I'd cut over to Center Street through Sea Street only twice that I could remember, both times on my way to playdates. It was a nice neighborhood dotted with modest ranches and simple Capes, minutes walking distance to the harbor. I couldn't find his picture on the Web or any information about his family. For all I knew he lived with a wife and kids. That's why I needed an empty gas tank.

Lost in my imaginary trip down Sea Street, I startled when the phone rang. I snatched it up, not wanting it to wake Ethan, in case he'd finally fallen asleep.

"Hello, may I speak to Mrs. Ethan Gray, please?" The caller's voice had a Katharine Hepburn crackle to it. I recognized immediately who it was.

"Mrs. Dwyer, hello. It's Tessa."

"Oh, I hope I'm not interrupting anything." She talked so slowly it was hard to decide whether it was because she had all day or Parkinson's.

"Not at all." I chose to keep my end short so she'd have all the time she needed to tell me why she'd called.

"Forgive me, I should've called to tell you this sooner, but I haven't been well. Doctor's visits. Medications. It's terrible to get old." She paused to catch her breath.

I wanted to climb through the phone, instead I jumped to conclusions. She remembered something.

"Never mind that," she said. "I'm calling because I wanted to tell you, you're welcome to have all the cards and letters I've collected. I've saved every last one."

I dropped my body hard into the kitchen chair. She wasn't

remembering anything now and she never would. I remembered Abby's roadside tribute. I'd only been there once, the day I'd gone there to ask Mrs. Dwyer if she knew anything. Of course, it couldn't stay there forever.

"I do apologize for not calling sooner. Might be now's a better time to read them."

Now my voice was the one crackling. "Yes, thank you."

"I pray every day that God gives you the strength to handle your loss. I lost my third child when I was eight months along. My only boy. I've got wonderful children, but I still miss my Georgie." She sighed, and I knew she was remembering the promise of her child.

I caressed mine. "I'm five months pregnant."

"Oh, dear, I didn't know. I hope I haven't frightened you with my story."

"No, I'm glad you told me. Sometimes it's a little too easy for me to take this baby for granted. I miss Abby so much."

"From one mother to another, you'll never stop missing your girl. You can live on and love more children though. You'll see." Her voice was getting softer, as if she'd worn out what was left of it.

"Mrs. Dwyer? Would you mind if my husband picked up the cards when he's feeling better? He's got the flu, and I can't drive down your street. Not yet."

"I completely understand. Give him my well wishes, won't you? Have him call me before he comes. All those darn appointments, I spend most of my time at the doctor's office."

When I hung up the phone, I looked up to see a weary Ethan in mismatched pajamas staggering into the kitchen.

"Who was that? Is everything okay?" He blew his noisy nose into a wad of tissues, drowning out my answer.

Alden hates pansies. I've always loved their bright gold and rich purple petals, especially after a cold winter. He said he's bothered by their little faces looking back at him. What troubles me is that Ian lied to me.

Yesterday, I made the first of my usual spring trips to Four Seasons Nursery. Lugging a bag of Flower Booster and two ceramic window boxes, I bumped into Ian's boss from landscaping.

"Michael, how are you? Getting ready for a busy spring?" I parked the window boxes at my feet; it's always worth stopping to make pleasant conversation with your child's supervisor.

"Yes, we are. We've been booking new clients since right after Christmas, and we've had enough small jobs through the low season to keep us out of trouble. Do you think there's any way we could twist Ian's arm and get him to come back to work for us? He's the best kid we've ever had on the crew." Michael bent down, picked up the containers, took the bag of fertilizer out of my arms, and carried everything to the register.

Suddenly I felt capable of twisting more than Ian's arm. "I have every intention of talking to him about it. I'll have to find out what's going on." I left my sentence hanging like one of the ferns in the greenhouse, not knowing what else to say. Ian had lied to me.

Back in the fall, when I'd asked him why he'd stopped working, he'd said Michael let people go until spring because it wasn't busy enough.

I paid for my things and resisted the urge to drive right over to Harry's; I knew discussing this in the heat of the moment wouldn't do any of us any good. Of course I'd have to tell Harry. This was a perfect example of why Ian needed to go to counseling. I wondered whether he'd called yet for an appointment.

Back home in my kitchen, I cooled down with a cup of hot tea and a few deep breaths. I lifted the phone to call them. I'd be firm. I needed to come over to talk.

Alden came into the kitchen with a book under his arm. "Are you all right? You look a bit pale." I knew his concern was sincere; right then his care was unwelcome.

"I'm fine. I need some privacy to make a call. Would you mind giving me a few minutes?" I knew before I asked that my request would move him farther from me than the library. I could be angry with Ian, I was his mother. I didn't need to hear Alden say anything negative about my son.

I tried calling them over and over. The first time I left a message. By the fifth try, I'd hear the beginning of Harry's outgoing message and hang up. I could have gone over there, but every other time I'd done that my spontaneity started an argument. This time, I wouldn't let anything Alden said or I did take the focus off what's really going on.

Why haven't I heard from them? I can't tell if the turning of my stomach and the tightness in my throat are linked to my anger or my worry. Where are they?

5:00 P.M.

Harry finally called. It was around one, and I had my hand on the phone when it rang. I'd been about to call school, thinking if Ian was there then all must be well. Harry tried to buy time by pushing me off.

"I'm coming over after my last client. You can't close me out. He's my son, too, and I've held my tongue long enough." I was glad the waiting room was empty, when I realized I was barking into the phone.

"Relax, C. We've been right here. We had the phone turned down, and you know I'm not good at checking messages. There's no conspiracy to ignore you." He kept his voice low and calm. That's exactly what I thought they had.

"Have you scheduled an appointment with one of the counselors yet?" I uncrossed my fingers when he said no.

"I haven't had a spare minute. Things have been really crazy around here. I'll put in a couple calls tomorrow, promise," he said. "He's okay, C. Really."

I'd fallen for similar reassurances before. He wasn't going to call. He'd offered to take charge, with no intention of digging Ian out of the depression that had swallowed him. Harry had never been good at unearthing a person from the depths of depression. Not himself. Not me.

"He isn't okay, Harry. Why won't you admit it? Can't you see what all our fighting has done to him? His guidance counselor says he's just taking up space in school. When he goes. And now he's lying to me." I was shouting.

"He's not the only one who's lied."

"My relationship with Alden is none of your business, it's complicated. You've hardly earned the right to judge me. Forget it, I'll make the calls. I'll take him to the appointment. I should've known I'd have to do this myself." I hung the phone up so hard, I almost broke it. I wouldn't let Harry surrender our child to this. If he wouldn't protect Ian, I would.

TUESDAY, MARCH 28   9:00 A.M.

When I entered the office this morning, the red light was blinking. My mind filled with selfish hopes that my answering machine held the messages of clients with mild illnesses, clingy children, or forgetful babysitters. I didn't feel up to dealing with needy strangers. An hour without someone needing me to sort something out would be such a relief.

Last night started with a war of words with Ian and Harry, and ended with bad blood between Alden and me. When I arrived at Harry and Ian's around six, Ian sat in the middle of the couch with a blank expression on his face. He looked like he was either waiting for me or too lethargic to move; I couldn't tell. Harry was busy moving clutter off the couch so I could sit down.

"Want tea or something?" Harry tried to pretend it was a run-of-the-mill visit.

I didn't acknowledge Harry, instead, I kept my attention on Ian. His jeans were ripped and his long-sleeve T-shirt tattered. It was hard to know if his look was intentional or the result of apathy. On the ride over, I'd decided to leave my anger in the car and meet Ian in a compassionate place.

"Let me start off by saying I'm sorry you're feeling so down lately. Let's promise to be honest with each other. Have you been lying to me about something?" I reached out to him. He pulled his arm away from me, as if my hand were a live wire.

Ian looked at Harry, as though asking for permission to speak. Harry stood behind me, I couldn't see what directive he gave.

"Stop it, you two. Don't you think I know you're keeping something from me? Ian, Michael told me he didn't let you go from work. You quit. Why didn't you tell me you didn't want to

work there? What did you expect me to say?" My tone was childish. I was pleading with him like he'd skipped my turn in a game.

"Dad, please let me tell her." Ian might have continued, if
Harry hadn't taken over.

He sat on the arm of the couch and gripped Ian's arm. "You're
absolutely right. She's going to find out sooner or later. We
botched things up real good, didn't we, huh?" He looked at Ian
and then me. "Ian dropped out of school."

My jaw dropped, I was stunned.

"Now take it easy, after I hung up with you this afternoon, I
put a call into one of the shrinks on your list. I'm all over this
thing. Okay?" His eyes locked onto mine as if he could use them
to pin me to my cushion.

I was up and I was pacing. "I am so sick of you using the word
okay. He's not okay. Ian, how could you have dropped out? I don't
even know if you can, you're not sixteen. More to the point, why
would you want to?"

Harry was about to speak for Ian again.

"Harry, stop it. I want Ian to tell me. First you lied, now you've
dropped out? I can only imagine what else you're keeping from
me. You have got to get some professional help."

I asked him to speak then didn't let him. I fell back onto the
couch. I no longer had the energy to contain my thoughts or actions.

He started to cry. "You're right, I need help. I can't keep everything inside anymore." Like a much smaller boy, he wiped the
tears with the back of his hand.

Harry put his arm around him and Ian buried his face in his
shoulder. I could feel the tie between them. Harry, in his own ex-
tremely inept way, was taking care of Ian.

"Look, C, you're right. I see it now. I should have done things
differently. I'll get him to a doctor. He's out of school for now.
That doesn't mean he can't go back when he's feeling better. He'll

be okay. We'll get through this." Harry lifted Ian's chin and looked into his eyes.

There was that damn word again. It was hard to believe he'd be okay, he looked so lost. I needed to do something, so I started tidying the living room. Stacking newspapers and magazines. Folding clothes and collecting glasses. I didn't care whether Harry wanted me cleaning up his mess or not.

I brought the dishes into the kitchen. As soon as I filled the sink, Harry went around locking doors. After locking the one to the garage, he slipped the key into his pocket.

"When you leave, head out the front. You'll be happy to know, I've started locking up for the night the minute I remember." He put his arm around me, and even though moments ago I was furious with him, his familiar arm, with its strong heat running down the length of my back, steadied me. "See, I can change," he said.

I kissed Ian good-bye, told Harry we'd talk, and drove home to enter a different kind of uncomfortable quiet.

Alden was observing our nightly ritual. I thought maybe he hadn't noticed I wasn't there to join him. Then two words cut the quiet, telling me he knew I was there.

"Hello, Celia." He didn't ask me if I was okay. Or where I'd been. He didn't reprimand me for the lateness of the hour or for worrying him. I didn't offer to explain.

I climbed the stairs, snatched my robe from the bottom of my bed, and debated which door to open. I chose Ian's room. Without turning on the light—a mother knows her child's room in the darkness—I pulled down the covers and climbed into his bed. Resting my head down on his pillow, I wondered how many more nights I could manage to stay awake in the dark.

176

No one could have stopped me today, though a few certainly tried. I had his number and street committed to memory, no need for my notebook. My cell phone was turned off and buried deep inside my messenger bag. My hand had turned the doorknob when I heard it. Though I wasn't prepared to accept another detour, by the fourth ring I picked up the home phone. If it was Ethan and he couldn't get me here or on my cell, I feared he'd come looking for me. No need to worry, it was Pat.

"Hi, Tessa, I was getting ready to leave a message." The rhythm of her words was out of sync. Maybe she really didn't expect me to answer or maybe something was wrong.

"I'm here. What's the matter? You don't sound like yourself." I needed to cut to the chase. I had someplace to be.

"I don't know, do you want to tell me what you've been doing lately? We could meet for coffee. Thing is, I won't be able to keep it a secret from Ethan." Pat wasn't talking about the forbidden coffee.

"I'm a little busy. If you have something to say, why don't you say it?" I was done with her. I'd gotten to like her, but she hadn't done what she'd promised.

"Tessa, Jack and I know you went to see Neil Ford. Look, I'm going to be blunt. That wasn't a very smart move." She had more to say, but I cut her off.

"There haven't been many smart moves on anyone's part. Agreed? Yeah, I went to see him because I needed to know." I grabbed a breath. "He didn't do it."

"I had the same gut feeling after I saw the police interview video. His story rings true. That's not the point."

"I get it. If he had anything to do with it, I jeopardized the in-vestigation. Except, you and I both know there isn't one. Any-thing else? I have to go."

"I want you to know I'll keep driving the police for answers. I just don't want you getting your hopes up." Her tone slipped into her off-duty voice, the Pat I could've been friends with.

"You do that." I hung up and headed out. Time to do my own driving.

My next potential obstacle came in blue and white. I'd come out of an intersection and taken a right. I was two streets from his when a siren went off. I could see out of my rearview mirror a police cruiser coming toward me. Why would Pat send them after me? She couldn't know where I was going. When it flew past me, I stayed off to the side of the road to get my heart seated back into my chest. I put down my window to let a blast of cool air in, while I let out the crazy thoughts that had popped into my head.

I convinced myself that checking out his house wasn't crimi-nal. He probably wouldn't even be there. I let a string of cars go before I pulled back onto the road. In fewer than three minutes, I was on Sea Street. The house numbers went down in predictable odd-even order. I slowed as I drove by 78. In a five-second glance,

I noticed the house was an ordinary ranch. It likely had five rooms in all, not enough space for a big family. There wasn't a car in the driveway, but there was a garage.

Driving at a crawl, I made the van buck twice before I pulled over and turned it off. If anyone looked out a window, my story would fit what I did next. I waited in my seat and counted to twenty, I could do this. Getting out, I put my car keys in the breast pocket of my jean jacket and slung my messenger bag across my widening girth. I started walking toward his house. Looking up and down the street, it seemed a lonely neighborhood by morning. The bikes discarded carelessly on front lawns, the multicolored plastic playhouses and swing sets in backyards said this neighborhood was teeming with kids in the afternoon.

Walking up the front path, I rehearsed my scripted lines over and over in my head. If I had to say them, I wanted them to sound natural. I pressed the doorbell and waited. My baby kicked me hard, her first attempt at warning me to leave. I heard nothing from inside. I looked back behind me then rang the bell again. Seeing no one on the street, I peeked in through one of the glass panels that framed the door. The house was certainly lived in, the room I faced, small and cluttered.

I could've left then, I hadn't found anything suspicious. The street was quiet, no one would know if I slipped around back and took another look in a different window. One more window, I told myself, and then I would leave. Approaching the garage, I was tempted to look in. Cursing my height, I stood on the tips of my toes, and still I couldn't see in one of the windows that ran the length of the garage door. Walking away from the street toward Harry Hayes's backyard, I was rewarded with a windowed door that gave me a better view of his garage. I could see a midsize sedan parked there. Its color was either midnight blue or deep burgundy, the light coming in through the garage door windows not enough for me to guess. My body pulsated now, part heartbeat part baby kicking. I didn't even think about it, I tried the door. It was locked, but that didn't matter, I already knew what I was going to do.

There wasn't anyone home, I told myself. I'd seen no one on the street. I bent down and picked up a rock, tapping it lightly at first and then progressively harder on the lower left windowpane. I realized breaking the glass was the harder way to do it. Digging into my bag, I found my wallet and slipped out my debit card as easily as if I were buying clothes on impulse. I slid it in between the door and the casing. Jiggling the doorknob while I forced the card this way and that, I prayed the button would give way from the strike plate. In all these months, my first conversation with God was to unlock this door so I could come face-to-face with a car.

I was in. It was too easy. Or so I thought. I circled the car from behind. It was burgundy and clean, not new, not old. The hood was cold to the touch and the car unremarkable in every way, until I saw the new front headlight on the passenger side.

I put my messenger bag down on the workbench to take a closer look. The click clack of a door handle opening made me step away from the door I'd just broken through and I bumped against the workbench, sending hammers and screwdrivers crashing to the floor.

It wasn't that doorway that filled with a tall, familiar boy; it was the door between the garage and the house. He looked sleepy and scared, and he didn't speak at first.

"I can explain. I ran out of gas in front of your house. I knocked and rang the bell and no one answered. Oh, God. This looks so bad. I left my cell phone at home and I thought maybe you'd have a gas can lying around." I paused. "I would've left a note. Really."

"We don't have any. Gas, I mean." His voice wavered like puberty was waiting for him inside. He had to be in his early teens. "Do you want to use my phone?"

"That would be great." I made a circular motion over my baby for two reasons. She could make him feel bad enough to let me get a look inside and I was trying to calm her down. In the last few minutes, it was as if she'd decided to kick her way out of this mess.

Looking down at my basketball-shaped stomach, he said, "Okay." The veins in his skinny neck were throbbing. He opened the door to the kitchen, and once we were inside he closed it, leaning his scrawny body against it. His relief mingled with body language that said he was barring me from going back that way.

A new headlight and a nervous boy. He was the boy I'd seen in the cemetery. I started to get light-headed. Without asking, I pulled out a chair, plopped into it, and put my head between my knees.

"Are you okay, Mrs. Gray? You're not having the baby are you?" He fired his questions at the back of my head.

"How do you know my name? Why is there a new headlight on that car?" My questions were muffled; still, I knew he heard me.

"Everybody in town knows you. My dad fixed the headlight 'cause it burned out." Now it was his turn to deliver scripted lines. I didn't believe a single word.

I lifted my head and crossed my arms over my stomach. "I need some juice or something, I'm dizzy." I kept asking questions while he moved away from the door and toward the refrigerator. "Is your dad Harry Hayes? Who are you?"

"Yeah, but he didn't do anything." He paused. "I'm Ian." He wouldn't give me eye contact but he handed me some juice.

I drank it down in one motion, my hand shook as I set the glass down on the kitchen table. I used both hands to push off from the chair, not knowing how I would make it to the van. He was back in front of the door to the garage. "I've got to get out of here. Which door are you going to let me out?" I screamed at the boy.

He pointed to a back door that would dump me in the back-yard. I moved toward it while staring at him.

"I thought you didn't have any gas," he said.

I stopped and gave him a threatening look. "I have enough to get to the police station."

I had car keys, but no messenger bag, which meant no cell phone. I don't remember the drive home. Once there, my feet flew over the pavement and I was in the house. The message light on the phone was blinking the number three. I had no desire to listen. The first call I made was to North. I wasn't going to call some random police officer, there'd be too much to explain.

"You have to come over here. Please. I have to talk to you."

"I take it you got my message." North's tone was apologetic. "I want to catch up with you, too, but it isn't an emergency. Can I come by later this afternoon?"

I didn't know what message he was talking about. I only knew he wasn't going to come unless I told him. "What I have to tell you can't wait. I found out who did it."

I called Ethan next. I didn't filter out what I'd done, and he was furious. With a sharp tone and the threat of hanging up, I told him his anger could wait. "I need you to come home now. We need the police to get over there before they get rid of the car."

Arriving within seconds of each other, they ran up the drive-way like three little ducks, Ethan, North, and Pat. I wondered who'd called her.

With the door still open and without hellos, I launched into what I'd found on Sea Street. "There's a car in his garage, with touched-up paint on the front quarter panel and a new headlight on the passenger side. I know that proves nothing to you. Then there's the boy."

Everyone took seats in the family room. North had taken out his flip pad and looked all official.

"Tessa, I won't even get started on the trouble you could be in for breaking and entering. You can't pick random houses and check them out. People get into accidents and replace headlights." He closed the book.

"Okay, I know it sounds like I'm losing it. There was a teenage boy at home. He was at the cemetery on Abby's birthday. When I saw him there, he and his father were crying." I kept spitting out my evidence.

"He knew my name and I could tell he's covering up for his father."

"Honey, slow down." Ethan put his hand on my back and started rubbing it. I jerked my shoulders away from his touch. He didn't believe me either.

"Wait a minute everyone," Pat said. "Jack, what can you do for the Grays? Tessa is well aware that she shouldn't have done things this way, but it sounds to me like you should check it out. I think you can come up with a creative reason to get over there, don't you?" She placed her hand on his arm below the rolled-up sleeve of his shirt. Pat was calling in a favor.

I chose not to mention that he could go over there to get my messenger bag, the one I'd left on Harry Hayes's workbench.

North let Pat's hand linger on his arm then let it drop off as he flipped open his notepad again. "It's a slippery slope. If I go over, checking in on what happened today, I could get Tessa a criminal charge. I could start by seeing if there's something else that can get me over there. Does that work?" North asked. "What's the address?"

Wednesday, March 29   5:00 p.m.

Distracted, I listened to clients, waiting all afternoon for word. When Harry finally called me, his news wasn't about Ian's doctor visit.

I called the Boatworks at twelve, just as we'd agreed. I'd been firm; if Harry hadn't had any luck getting an appointment by the time we spoke, I would take over getting Ian an emergency psych visit. I knew I'd be embarrassed things had gotten so out of hand, but I knew a few colleagues who owed me favors and wouldn't judge.

Harry's boss, always the salt of the earth, picked up. "He left here around ten," Lewis said. "Told me he needed to take Ian to the doctor. Sure hope it's something minor."

It was something major, I wanted to tell kind Lewis. I was annoyed Harry didn't have the decency to call to tell me, though I was happy he'd finally gotten Ian an appointment. So I waited, taking my time tidying up after clients, holding off leaving for home. I didn't want to miss Harry's call and I wanted even less to go home and try to explain everything to Alden. I sensed before I even picked up the next call, it was Harry.

"How is he? What did the doctor say?" I shot my questions at him.

Harry's tone was easier than it should be under the circumstances. "Ian's fine."

"You know, I've been kicking myself all day. I should've been the one to take him. I could've canceled clients. Can I talk to him?" I wasn't going to hold my feelings back anymore.

"He's sleeping. I had a stray sleeping pill kicking around. Kid's had a rough day, C." Harry spoke quietly into the phone. He didn't know you can't wake a person who's taken an Ambien.

"I'm not comfortable with that, Harry. You should never give your medications to someone else. Didn't the doctor give Ian any prescriptions?" I tried not to sound worried. I didn't want to shut him off.

"Celia." He stopped me with my name. He only called me that when things were serious. "I'm going to tell you all about it tomorrow, okay? Today was rough on the kid—and me. Let me off the hook on making your day tough, too. For tonight?" His voice was stronger now, though I could hear the resignation flow over him.

"I'm disappointed you don't want to tell me about it." I softened my tone. "Are you still angry with me about my stand on counseling?"

"I understand why you want Ian to go. I guess I still don't know why you wouldn't go for yourself, with me. For us."

I didn't have the answer to this thing we'd fought about for ten years. This thing that drove us apart and started him drinking.

"You still there?" he asked. "Look, we'll talk tomorrow. I'll tell you everything, I promise. Maybe you can take the day off. We'll meet."

"I've got a couple of early clients I should see. I could cancel the rest. How's ten-thirty at my office?"

"I'll wait on the bench right inside the gate of the park. C, there's one more thing. Something I've waited way too long to say." There was a catch in his voice, though Harry isn't one to cry.

"I should've tried harder to work things out with you. Force you to talk to me about her," he said. "I wish I could say I stood up and acted more like a man than a drunk. I want you to know I've changed. I'll stand up now."

There was a split-second gap between one sentence and the next. "Celia, I love you. I love you and Ian more than you can ever know."

The line went quiet, though I knew he was still there.

"I don't know what to say," I said. Sniffing, I ripped a tissue from the full box, forever perched on the edge of my desk.

"Nothing *to* say. I just wanted you to know. I'll see you in the morning. Good night."

It wasn't a good night. I still love him, but my other husband's waiting at home in my library.

177

I felt like I was under house arrest. Ethan and I wandered around the house waiting for our update from North. I had the distinct impression Ethan was following me. When I went into the office, he'd pop in there.

"You don't mind me working in here, too, do you?"

When I was in the bathroom, more than once he called in, "Are you okay in there, honey?"

I didn't mind when he tracked me down in Abby's room. I'd stretched out on her bed, sorting through the cards and letters he'd picked up from Mrs. Dwyer. Everything took so long I thought I'd go crazy waiting to hear from North. I needed something to do.

He stood on the threshold of her doorway, wistfully he looked at the clouds on her walls. Her dolls and her books.

"Want me to help you with that? I could make a big pot of coffee and we could spread everything out on the kitchen table."

Apparently Tessa on caffeine was better than Tessa on Prozac. His false cheeriness didn't irritate, since I owed him one for not yelling at me about snooping. Once he'd heard the story of my visit to Neil Ford's and then to Harry Hayes's house, he seemed frightened of me. He treated me like he thought I might break. Everything about the way he looked reminded me of the first time he'd held Abby.

"Sure we can go through the cards together. I think it would be better if we talked, though."

He took measured steps toward Abby's rocking chair. His reluctance to be in her room forced him to move slowly, as if a strong wind kept him from his destination. I put out my hand to stop him. "Oh, I still want that coffee."

He laughed.

"What? You're the one who offered."

More comfortable back in the kitchen, he didn't count my cups. I didn't refuse his questions. I told him about the list Melanie made for me back in December. How I'd abandoned my research when North looked confident and capable and Pat assured me she'd find answers. I tried to find the words to tell him how much I needed to know the truth about what happened to Abby.

Halfway through the conversation, I started to cry. The first tears I'd willingly shed in his company were contagious.

He held me and stroked our growing child. "I'm so sorry you couldn't tell me all of this. I'm glad you're telling me now." He laced a hand through mine while his other one mopped his wet face with a paper napkin.

"I don't blame you, you needed to move forward. I just couldn't. Hell, I still don't know if I can. Part of me isn't sorry I didn't tell you. If I didn't do it, we might not know now." I looked deep into his slate eyes. I needed to know he believed what I believed. Harry Hayes killed Abby.

"About that. Promise me you won't get mad. I want to believe you. Still I'm going to need a lot more, and so are the police." I could see our talk had made him less worried about me, he held back nothing now. "Tessa, I'm afraid of what might happen to you if this doesn't lead where you want it to."

Our one-to-one was broken by two loud raps on the door. We both went to get it and I prayed it was North with good news. Ethan opened the door to North and Pat.

"Are you two always together?" I asked. They exchanged a look that told me the answer was yes. "Never mind. Did you go over there?"

Pat led the way to the kitchen. "Let's sit."

North started. "I have some news, and some of it isn't good. Tessa, I'll be honest, you're going to have to trust me and be patient. I know I'm asking a lot." He wasn't going to baby me. North had hit his detective stride. I liked him more for it. Sitting up straighter in my chair, I reached over to take Ethan's hand.

"She's going to be fine. Go ahead." Ethan squeezed mine, and for the first time, I thought maybe we could get through this, if we did it together.

"Start with the bad news."

"We can't go over there and confront him, not yet anyway. I know you're worried about him getting rid of the car. He hasn't done it yet for whatever reason and now would be a very stupid time to do it. By now the boy has probably told him you were there and you saw it." North's hands were folded on top of the table; his former nuns would be proud. "What Chief O'Brien and I are going to do is bring him in for a chat, and I've got officers circling his neighborhood around the clock."

"The police can bring anyone in for questioning." Pat threw in her lawyerly two cents. "They don't need any evidence or cause. Once he's in, even with a lawyer in tow, Jack will have a better sense of where we go from here."

"I assume that's the bad news because this is going to take a while, and you need me to stay under control." No one said anything, so I continued with the ultimate question. All four of us knew whatever way this was answered, it had the power to save me or put me under. "What happens if you can't prove he did it?"

Ethan turned my face with a gentle hand under my chin. "Let's let it play out one song at a time."

"All right, I'll try." I turned back to North. "What's the other news?"

"This is what my message was about yesterday," he said. "With everything that happened, well, I thought it should wait."

I'd forgotten about the messages. Ethan read my mind and answered. "He said he wanted to talk. The other ones were Rosemary and a telemarketer."

North continued. "We found the autopsy photos and the paint sample. Caulfield didn't have anything to do with them being misplaced. In fact, he came clean about accepting small bribes, but he swears under oath he did nothing to undermine Abby's investigation. Turns out he really is more lazy than crooked. I'm embarrassed to say the misplaced evidence had to do with someone on our end being very disorganized."

"Where were they?" Ethan asked.

"Right around the time the photos went missing, there was a domestic case that opened up. As much as we can figure, at one point Abby's evidence and the woman's were on the same detective's desk, and both were placed in the woman's case folder. It wasn't until yesterday when her case got reopened that my buddy found the missing photos of Abby." He paused, and I sensed that wasn't the end to the bad news.

"This next part is hard to tell you." He was the gentle North wind blowing again.

"Go ahead." Pat prodded him. She knew we were about as desensitized as we could get.

"The two photos were close-ups of clear tire marks that ran diagonally across Abby's left arm. I know that sounds terrible—it is terrible. The upside is that the tire marks and the paint sample can be used to narrow down possible vehicles." He clasped his hands together again. "This evidence will rule in or out that car you saw. You've got to give me time to get him in. All right?"

It was horrible. Abby's little arm tattooed by a tire. I hope she hadn't felt the pain of its impression. Still I hadn't felt this good in a long time, because soon Harry Hayes would be the one feeling the pain of what he'd done to her.

"I can wait now."

SATURDAY, APRIL 1   11 A.M.

Forty-eight hours ago, Harry unraveled the ties to my life before.

As I got ready to leave the office, I looked out my window and saw him sitting inside the gate to Verity Park, as he promised he would. It took me only a few minutes to walk to him. I was eager to hear what he had to say.

"So tell me all about it. Does Ian like Dr. Hall?" I took a seat on the bench and accepted the Styrofoam cup Harry offered me. I knew the minute I saw him he didn't come with news of an appointment he and Ian had with a psychiatrist. There had been no such visit.

"Celia, I need you to be the strong woman you are." He put his cup down and turned to face me. "You're probably going to hate me by the end of this. Try to listen." Harry's face was clean-shaven and pleading. He wore nicer-than-work clothes. His look had my attention.

I twisted my body fully toward him, clutching my cup.

"You didn't take Ian to the doctor."

"Don't worry, he's going to be fine once I'm out of the picture."
He would have continued talking, but I sighed.

Here we go again, I thought. Excuses, delay tactics. Why was he
against counseling now, when I as much as admitted I should've
gone with him? Was he trying to get back at me for all the times I
said I wouldn't go?

"This is really hard to do without a drink." He picked up his
cup and thinking better of it, put it back on the ground. "I'm going away. I'm trying to do the responsible thing here." He looked
away, not to admire the manicured gardens or to listen to the
seagulls screech overhead.

"Why? Where will you go? Oh God, you're not taking Ian, you
can't take my child. Harry, you're scaring me."

He took my free hand and stared down at my wedding ring.

"I've done a horrible thing. Back in the fall, I got drunk as
usual, and I hit the little Gray girl."

I dropped my cup, and tea gushed over the red bricks. Harry
kicked the cup away from my feet. I pulled my hand from his,
dropping both hands limp on my lap.

"Harry, no." Disbelief crawled up one side of me and down the
other. He was mouthing a jumble of words without meaning.
Then with clarity I heard *I hit the girl,* and I knew he'd done it.
Harry had done a lot of lousy things to me, but he'd never lied.

I didn't move a muscle, my body frozen despite the heat from
the sun. Harry got up off the bench, he began pacing. Standing
above me in silhouette, he kept talking.

"I spent the night before the accident at the yacht club bar.
Late into the night, Luke refused me. I went to the car and pulled
out a bottle of Cutty I kept tucked under the seat. The rest of the
night is a blur."

Sitting back down, he plowed ahead with his story, still not looking at me. The whole time he spoke, I shook my head, humming, no, no.

"I must've passed out. I woke up hours later by the side of the road, somewhere between the club and home. Even when I came to, I was pretty drunk. I didn't think twice, I drove home." He stopped. Then he looked me right in my eyes.

"I never saw her, C. Honest." Tears took turns running down both sides of his face, he made no move to wipe them.

"You killed her." When I spoke those three unbelievable words, my tone was malicious. Harry picked at a pull in the fabric of his pants. I reached over and gripped his thigh. His eyes told me my disgust of him hurt more than my hand pinching his leg.

"I did it," he whispered. "I let one damn drink lead to another. I did a lousy job handling losing our girl. I put you and Ian through hell, and then I lost you. I know you'll never forgive me. But you've got to know I wasn't a drunk because I didn't care, I was one because I did. I know this is horrible, but it's the last mistake I'll ever make. This is where I come clean. Right now, after you, I'm going to the police. To confess."

Ian's face flashed in my mind. "Ian knows. Is that why he's a mess, because you made him cover up for you? My sweet boy has been keeping your unforgivable secret." The pieces of our jigsaw family suddenly came together completely.

"He's known since the beginning," Harry said. "He dealt with me when I came home drunk. He cleaned the car and helped me repair the damage. Look, we've got to leave him out of this; he's a kid. I've already screwed up my life. I'll confess, then you and he can get on with yours."

He'd thought it all out, though he'd certainly waited long enough. I wondered if he'd be taking responsibility at all if Ian weren't crumbling under all of this.

"I can't believe you involved our son in this. What kind of father are you?"

Then I thought about Tessa. Knowing what happened to Abby might have lifted her weight. Knowing my family was involved would drop the load back down.

"Why, Harry? How many times did I beg you not to drink and drive?" My voice was raised, but I couldn't lift my body.

"I'm sober now, and I'm going to do the right thing." He plunged through the ocean of my thoughts, the ones flowing in every direction.

"C, go to Ian. He needs you. It's killing him that I'll be going to jail."

He stood and took my arm, pulling me up to stand.

"I meant what I said last night. I love you." He took my head in his hands and kissed me. When it dawned on me what he was doing, I pulled back from his hold. "No matter how you feel about me now, I always will." He didn't wait for me to say anything. He started walking.

My mind went to Ian. I had to get to him. The full measure of this shouldn't hit either of us alone.

I dashed back into my office. With one arm I swept everything off my desk into my bag: wallet, glasses, journal. I grabbed my car keys and ran. On the drive over, I called him. He didn't pick up, I didn't leave a message. I had images of him sitting petrified on the couch or lying motionless on his bed, his depression deeper and darker than ever. He'd need me to pull him free from this place he was locked into.

Harry's story, etched into my mind, made me drive cautiously. Needing to get to Ian made me drive fast. I was annoyed when a Big Sister's Clothing Drive van blocked Harry's driveway. I parked on the street and ran up the front walk. The door wasn't locked. Harry hadn't changed that much.

Ian wasn't in the living room. I noticed immediately the house had been cleaned. The towers of newspapers were gone from the corners of the living room, and Harry's books were stacked neatly on shelves.

I headed to Ian's room, calling, not shouting his name. I didn't want to startle him. He wasn't there.

Walking toward the kitchen, I felt my panic rise. He couldn't be at school, he'd quit. Where was he? As I passed the front window, I noticed the Big Sister's van was gone, though I could still hear its engine running. I saw an open note lying on top of the spic-and-span kitchen table. One hand grabbed the note as I flew with the other hand outstretched toward the door to the garage. I knew where Ian was. The door was locked, the key no longer sitting in the knob. I ran out the door to the backyard.

My head arrived at the side door almost before my feet did. It was locked, too. I could see my Ian slumped over the wheel of Harry's car. The car that kills children. I picked up a rock and slammed it with all the force I had through the lower left windowpane. Shoving my hand through shards of glass, I opened the door. I slapped the garage door opener button and ran to the driver's-side door.

I didn't feel for a pulse. I wouldn't let him be dead. Coughing, I tugged him and yanked him, screaming his name over and over. Louder and louder. His limp body and long legs made pulling him free take forever. It couldn't have been long because the garage door had just made it to the top when I dragged him into the driveway. Fresh air. He needed fresh air, I told myself. Though I knew he wasn't breathing.

I placed lips over lips and sent my love for him deep into his chest. Breathe, my baby, breathe I chanted, silently. I don't know how long I forced air into his toxic lungs, but paramedics later peeled me off of him.

I don't know who called them for me. It could have been any

one of the three young mothers who'd gathered at the end of Harry's driveway. I'll never forget the one who dared to comfort me.

"It'll be okay," she said. "They're professionals, they know what they're doing." She reached over to pull down my skirt, in my gymnastics it had ridden up my thighs.

I smoothed out my skirt with my bleeding hand and felt Ian's note. I must have put it in my pocket. I heard the gurney snap open and upright as they loaded his lifeless body into the ambulance. I didn't need to read the note to know what Ian had done.

I've known for forty-eight hours and I don't feel the tiniest bit different. Harry Hayes confessed. The day after I confronted his son, the bastard walked into the police station and told Jack North he did it. He'd waited until I'd backed him into a corner, and only then did he tell the truth. His lies almost destroyed me and they almost destroyed his own son.

Pat was the one to tell us. I sat in my window seat, staring at the crocuses that were popping their little heads out of the ground. The purple and gold flowers Abby had planted, the ones she never got to see. Ethan was sleeping under the morning edition of the *Globe*. Pat waved as she walked up toward the porch door, she didn't smile. North asked her to come. He didn't want us to hear it from some reporter.

All these months I waited, needing to know. Now I do. Harry Hayes passed out on the side of the road early in the morning of October 5, and when he came to, still drunk, he headed home. On the way there, he hit and killed Abby. He was too drunk to know he did it or too cowardly to stop and help her. My vote goes to coward.

What's worse, he'd made his own son keep his horrific secret for almost six months. That secret nearly killed his child, too. After Hayes went to the police, his son tried to kill himself in the very garage I'd met him in, in the very car that is the vehicle of all this pain. The poor kid had been made to choose between doing the right thing and being loyal to his father. What kind of father puts his son in that position?

Pat says he's in bad shape. Carbon monoxide poisoning ruined his kidneys, and he's still on a breathing machine. I've been praying for him and his mother all weekend. They don't deserve to pay for the sins of Harry Hayes. Then again, neither did Abby. Or Ethan and our baby. Or me.

181

Ethan took it upon himself to call Dr. Hilliard, asking him to set up another ultrasound. They agreed that with all the stress of the last week, another look at the baby was a good idea. Days ago, his meddling would have infuriated me. After everything we've been through, for once I didn't mind him taking charge.

"I'm taking the rest of this week off." Ethan rolled up on one elbow toward me in bed. The sun peeked through the sheers that draped our windows. "In a way, I feel like she died all over again." He wiped his tears on a corner of our sheets.

"I feel like that, too. I almost slept in her bed last night." I turned toward him and kissed his forehead.

"I'm glad you stayed with me," he said. "I needed you last night." Then he told me about the ultrasound; he made no apologies. I was glad he wasn't tiptoeing around me anymore.

We breezed into the hospital and climbed the escalator to

Radiology. I was in and out in record time. Our daughter was active and growing; she was fine. The rest of our visit to the hospital was anything but. Walking out of Radiology, I saw Celia coming out of the Intensive Care Unit.

Her service had canceled our Friday session without explanation, maybe her being here was the reason why. When she turned, I saw she recognized me. Her look didn't say she was glad to see me. She walked toward me anyway. I'd never seen Celia look so shaken.

"Hello, Tessa." Her voice was flat as she stretched her hand out. "You must be Ethan." She didn't add *I've heard so much about you.* In her business, that's not necessarily a good thing. She didn't add her relationship to me. Another taboo, since she couldn't be sure I'd want Ethan to know.

"Ethan, this is Celia." I reached a hand out to support her elbow as she leaned against the pale gray wall. I wanted to know why she was there. I wasn't sure it was my place to ask. Celia hated prying. But then since when do I follow the rules?

"Are you okay?" I asked.

"Actually, no. No, I'm not okay." A pathetic look crossed her face for an instant, then went back to vacant. "I wonder if I could talk to the two of you. There's a visitors' lounge that might be free."

We followed her as she rounded the corner. Once inside, she closed the door and took a seat. I felt like I'd walked into her satellite therapy office.

"I don't know where to begin or how." She took a deep breath, and looked from one of us to the other. "Tessa, Ethan. My son is very ill." She paused. Tipping her head down to find a pack of tissues, tears bounced off the plastic patient belongings bag she'd been holding, they landed on her pants.

"What can I do to help you?" Right then, I would've done anything to help Celia after all she'd done for me. She didn't let me finish. It was as if she didn't say it right then, she'd never be able to tell us the rest.

"I know you've heard that Harry Hayes confessed to hitting Abby." She choked out the last of it. "Harry's my ex-husband. Ian is my son."

Her words hit me like an arrow dipped in poison. Searing pain. Fresh anger. Like a wounded animal, I fled. She kept talking. I didn't stay to hear what more she said. Ethan was right behind me.

182

From the beginning, I've struggled with wanting to live. I've never wanted to die. I understand depression as black as midnight. I've known days that have no light. Sure, I'd thought about it, it would have been my way to see her again. I never actually imagined doing it. At first, because of Ethan. Then because of my baby.

Her son, Ian, did. Celia's child, the boy I'd met, he crossed the chasm between thinking about it and doing it. When I found out he was Harry Hayes's son, it was easy to fall back to compassion. For Ian. Not Hayes, never for Harry Hayes. The pain of what his father had done was too much for him to live with. Finding out he was Celia's son, I couldn't process one more thing. Not one more terrible thing.

Sitting in my kitchen, I went over every session I'd ever had with Celia to see if there were any clues. Did she know what Hayes had done or did she find out like I did? All I kept remembering was her face, her kind face, the one that hid little from me. She cried with me during some of my worst moments. She even held me once. She couldn't have known. She's a mother; Celia would have told me.

There was nothing left for me to do. No lists to check. No people to investigate. No meetings with police. It was done.

Ethan went out to get groceries. I couldn't handle being out, picking up frozen stares and fresh pity. I took the afternoon to sort through the rest of the letters Mrs. Dwyer had saved for us. Letters from her teachers. Drawings from her friends. There were only a few I'd yet to read.

Then there it was. It had been there the whole time. The paper it was written on the texture of parchment, the victim of spring rain. The words were few, the meaning and the author clear. With the handwriting of a child, he wrote that he'd killed her, and that he was sorry.

I read it over three times, the words pounding in my head. I struggled to stand. I needed to tell North. When I got to the porch door, I nearly screamed because he was standing there about to knock. He was holding my messenger bag, the one I'd left at Hayes's.

Still holding the note, I waved it at him. My other hand protected my child. "The boy, Ian. He's the one who killed her."

He stepped into the family room and handed me my bag. He closed the door without turning away from me. "I know," he said. "That's what I came here to tell you."

APRIL 4

The rhythm that pulsed from Ian's heart monitor slowed along with his breathing, telling me he was falling asleep. I'd dimmed the fluorescent overbed light and drew the shades. Harry nodded to the security guard who sat in the hallway, and closed the door to the hospital room. Ian lay still. Curled on his side, one armed rested along the length of him, the other was tucked under his pillow. Harry and I took our seats next to each other; neither one of us wanted to be the first to leave this place.

I'd been so furious with Harry, so devastated when I'd thought he'd killed her. Then I'd learned of his misguided, foolish attempt to protect Ian, and I loved him all over again, like I had in the beginning. What he'd done was wrong, but the depth of his love for Ian tied me back up to him like our family was tied to that boat.

Harry took my hand in his and without looking away from Ian he whispered, "It was hard as hell, but it was the right thing to do."

It had only been hours ago—though it could have been days—that we called the detective and told him the real story. Tomorrow Detective North would take Ian's confession. Tonight I needed to reread Ian's letter one more time. I pulled it from my bag and rested my head on Harry's shoulder; we read it silently, in shadow.

Dear Mom,

I hear it happen and I see it happen. Because I was there. It's time for me to straighten out this mess I've made. I killed Abby, Mom. I did it. And I can't stand how horrible I feel knowing I did.

I feel worse seeing that kid's mother coming apart bit by bit. She came here and touched the car that killed her kid. She looked right into my eyes and told me she knew Dad did it. Now Dad's going to the police to tell them he did. I can't let Dad fix this for me. I won't lie about it anymore.

She needs to know the truth. It's one thing to hear stories about her freaking out all over town, it's another to see her losing it in person. And she's having another kid. She has a right to know.

I stayed at Dad's the night before the accident. He came home really late, sometime around four. I helped him take off his shoes and pants and I heaved him up on his bed. I couldn't get back to sleep so I started getting ready for school. When I was in the shower, I got this crazy idea, this childish stupid idea. I would get rid of Dad's car. He couldn't get arrested again if he didn't have a car. I'd heard about this kid from Corcoran Village who steals cars. He takes them apart and sells parts for pot. If I left right then, I could get Dad's car there. Of all days, Dad staggered out of bed when his alarm went off. How do drunks do that? Drink all night, sleep for two hours, and then go to work? I thought my plan was ruined, but Dad decided he felt more like shit than usual. He asked me to call in for him before I went to school.

On the way to school, I thought I could still do it. I know it sounds sick but I thought I could finally take charge and do something good for this screwed-up family. I thought I could keep Dad out of trouble. It turns out I made an even bigger mess than he's ever made, didn't I?

I figured I'd show up at school, sneak out, and go back home. You remember how it was after Dad had a rough night, he'd be out for a while. I planned on making it look like the car was stolen. I convinced myself that I could drive the car over to the Village and then walk back to school. I know it seems insane now. At the time it seemed like a good way to keep Dad off the street. I didn't want him to hurt anybody.

By now you know it didn't happen that way. I did check in at school, but I started to get nervous. I stayed for two periods, the whole time I was talking myself into doing this ridiculous thing. I talked myself into it. Can you believe I didn't spend my time talking myself out of it? I went home and made it look like a robbery. Dad was still out cold. I took the car over the back roads to Corcoran Village.

On that street with the kid's school, I hit that little girl. I didn't even see her, Mom. She was so small. One minute things were fine. I reached down to grab my CD case and when I looked up she was there. Before that, the street was empty, no cars, no kids. I didn't think I was going too fast, but all of a sudden, I saw her. I couldn't find the brake and then it was too late. I hit her. There was a thud and she fell onto the street. I kept going. When I looked over, she was lying there like she was sleeping. I kept on going. I kept looking in the rearview mirror. I kept waiting for her to get up. I stopped at the end of the street. I didn't hear anything. No people, no cars. I panicked. I swear if I was really me at the time, I would have stopped to help her. But I wasn't me. I don't know who I was, but I wasn't me.

I drove away. I circled back over Spring Rose Lane to go back home. I knew then that the whole idea was unbelievably stupid. On Spring Rose, I could tell that someone found her because I heard a lady screaming. I told myself she'd be fine. I blocked it out and focused on getting home. I cleaned the car off with some of that heavy-duty stuff Dad keeps in the garage. I saw the scratch on the side of the car and the broken headlight, still I told myself I couldn't have hit her that hard. I put the house back the way it was before I left. I figured no one had to know what an idiot I was, because she'd be fine. But she wasn't fine, was she? She's dead and I'm the one who killed her.

I killed a little girl. Somebody else's sister.

Mom, do you remember when I was little, I'd ask you what you did for work? You'd say the same thing every time. You'd say, "Sometimes life is harder for people than it should be. These people need help to get through things. I'm the person who helps them."

Well, Mom, life's always been harder for me than it is for other people. But this time it's my fault. I know you tried to help me. Only some things can't be fixed. You can't fix it. Dad can't fix it either. I'm not strong. I'm not dependable. I'm a monster. No one can help me. Who kills a kid and then hides in his room, one minute hoping no one will ever know and the next minute wanting to scream so everyone in the world will find out? Dad tried to protect me. Don't be mad at him, he already feels bad enough. He said none of it would have happened if it weren't for him.

I'm tired of holding this in. So tired, it's killing me. That day Mrs. Gray came here, I wanted to tell her. I know she deserves to know. I knew she thought it was Dad and I let her think it. Can't you see what a horrible person I am?

Mom, can you help me set this right? Please tell Mrs. Gray what happened. Tell her I didn't mean to do it. Tell her I'm sorry. I would tell her myself, but remember I'm weak. Things will be easier for her when she knows.

I can only think of one other way to make things better—for

everyone. For Mrs. Gray, and Dad, and you. Things will be better if
I'm gone. Please tell her I'm sorry. Tell her I am so sorry.
   I love you, Ian

It had been ten years since I let my tears run free. I'd kept them
well hidden in a secret corner of me. As soon as one found its way
out, the others dashed right out after it. No matter how many times
my eyes scanned those pages, the words hurt me like they did the
first time I'd read them, though the minute it registered what Ian
had done, there was only one thing to do. On this Harry and I
agreed. We would hand the letter over to be entered into evidence
against our son.

APRIL 5

Alden placed the last box of books in the passenger seat of his
Lexus, closed the door, and walked back up the brick steps to me.

"That's the last of it." His tone was matter-of-fact, as if he'd finished packing for an overdue getaway weekend. He kicked two
stray stones from the brick walkway. When he got to me, he
reached for my hands.

"I'm sorry things didn't work out in my favor. I'm truly glad
Ian will be okay. I know you need him here."

I squeezed his hands. "I'm sorry about so many things, Alden."
I swallowed the lump in my throat. "Someday perhaps you'll forgive me." My eyes filled, and he pulled a handkerchief from his
blazer pocket.

"I already have." He handed it to me and smiled. "Wish me
luck with the job?"

A boxy medical supply truck pulled up, the driver checked a
piece of paper against the number next to my front door. I waved
to let him know he'd found the right place. Alden took my wave
as his cue to leave.

In short order, the oxygen tank was set up in the family room. The directions were simple, and the supplier quick to move on to his next stop. With that, I was ready to head to the hospital, ready for Ian to come home.

Harry was waiting for me when I stepped out of the elevator and into the lobby of the dialysis unit. He offered a kiss on the cheek and I accepted it. "I can't wait to spring him from here. You ready?" We were right on time for the first of our two scheduled meetings.

"Everything's set at home. He'll do better there." I clutched my purse, stuffing all my anxiety into it.

"The meeting with the police, that's not going to be easy, is it? What if there's a trial? Harry, can he handle this?"

Harry took hold of my shoulders. With one hand, his gentle yet strong fingertips lifted my chin. "He's alive and he's going to be okay. We're a family, one that plans on sticking together this time."

Hand in hand we walked into the conference room for our first meeting. This one was with a team of doctors and nurses— none from before—who assured us Ian's kidneys were on the mend. Dialysis once a week for another few weeks. Oxygen as needed. Twice a week visits to Dr. Hall for therapy. Prescriptions and follow-up doctors' visits scrawled out on little cards. I could do all of this. Soon I would leave this unit, never to return. Ian would get better.

As Ian's nurse handed me the final discharge instructions, the police detective walked past us and headed into Ian's room.

Six months to the day Abby Gray died at the hands of our son, Detective North took Ian's confession and possession of the letter, all while he lay in a hospital bed surrounded by his mother, his father, and his lawyer.

With Harry's hand on one shoulder and mine on the other, Ian did what the three of us had agreed as a family he'd do. Our immovable position had been made clear to his lawyer, in advance. Ian told his story, exactly as he'd written it in his note.

Detective North glanced up when Ian finally stopped speaking. He stopped taking his detailed notes. "You know you won't be taken into custody. You're being released into your mother's care." He pointed to Ian's lawyer. "Mr. Collins will keep you posted from here on in on the arraignment and sentencing."

Ian's face was the only thing about his damaged body that looked strong. He waved my hand aside as I used a tissue to dab the single tear that crept down his cheek.

"When do you think all that will be?" His voice was older yet weak.

Detective North took the tissue from me and handed it to Ian. He spoke directly to him, treating him like an adult. "The arraignment will be any day now. You won't need to be there for that, given your medical condition. There won't be a trial, since you've confessed. The sentencing will likely be in a month or so. Mr. Collins can give you a better estimate than I can. Given your age, I think you're looking at anything from probation to five years." He turned to Harry, his clipboard poised, his demeanor official.

"You're probably looking at a year, since both of you have made statements about your driving that night with a suspended license, and for your recent false confession. My advice to you, Mr. Hayes, is to get your own lawyer, a good one."

"I've already made some calls," I said. Harry mouthed the words *it will be okay* as I patted Ian's hand.

Ian took my hand in his own and with a feeble effort, squeezed it. He looked at me, then Harry; his eyes came to rest on Detective North.

"The sentence—it doesn't really matter. There's only one way to set this right for the Grays and for my family. I need to start paying for what I've done. I'm ready."

As Summer Was

Just Beginning

Thursday, June 22

Mirielle Caroline Gray was born at 7:20 A.M. on the first day of summer. Eight weeks early, nothing could stop her from making her grand entrance. Dr. Hilliard tried to slow her arrival when I went into premature labor, but Mirielle had already made up her mind. She'd waited long enough to join our family. Weighing in at four pounds eight ounces, she was big for a preemie. I was weak after delivery, but everyone marveled at her strength. I could've told them she'd be tough; she hadn't stopped kicking me from the moment she'd made her presence known.

It's hard not to contrast her dark looks and fiery personality with Abby's light angelic one. Ethan and I didn't hide our observations; we chose to include Abby in this miraculous day. After knowing Mirielle for only a few hours, we agreed. She'd be her own person, never lost in Abby's shadow.

Ethan and I sat with her, talking in low tones, reassuring her we were there without overstimulating her little body and soul. Her skin was pale and thinned over her scrawny bones, but there was nothing fragile about the way she moved her legs and arms. She kept fighting her way out of her napkinlike blanket and her tissue-size diaper. When finally they let me hold her to try feeding, she latched onto my breast without coaxing. Ethan and I were connected hand-to-hand; Mirielle and I heart-to-heart.

When Ethan and I could no longer sit upright, two nurses insisted we go back to my room to get some sleep. The soft-spoken one told us Mirielle would need her parents healthy and strong for her extended hospital stay.

When we got back to the room, Rosemary was there, smoothing out my bedsheets and lining up the vases of flowers that had already started arriving.

"This gorgeous one's from Pat and Jack," she said. "This droopy peony, Matthew plucked out of my garden as I was leaving to come here." She smiled as she looked at it, as if it were Matthew himself. "Do they know how long she'll need to stay?"

I didn't hear Ethan answer, I'd already started falling asleep. I remember thinking no matter how long she stayed, when they sent me home with Mirielle, they'd be sending me home with hope.

Friday, July 21

It had to be ninety degrees. She didn't need to wear much, and still dressing Mirielle took forever. I'd already abandoned any attempt at a dress and moved right on to the navy blue and red sailor set. Her zippy little legs fought getting confined in any clothing at all. Then she demanded a feeding. Mirielle was a force to be reckoned with. As I fed her, I said a little prayer she'd show her happy, easy side at group today.

At first, it had to be hard for the mothers in my child-loss support group to see me pregnant; I'd joined when I was six months and fully round. I hadn't meant to cause them pain each week as they gathered in the fellowship room of the stately church in Corcoran Village. I didn't want to be the one to remind them I had the hope of new life when they gathered together to talk about how life as they knew it was over. We all wanted to loosen the grip our children had on our hearts, at least for an hour a week.

Clearly sessions with Celia were no longer an option. I still needed a place to bring my grief; I knew I would never stop missing Abby. Dr. Hilliard put me in touch with Mary, the support group's social worker. She'd assured me she was comfortable helping the women work through their feelings about my pregnancy. Months later, I was surprised when the group sent me flowers to celebrate Mirielle's arrival, along with an open invitation to bring her to group whenever I felt up to it.

I'd imagined countless places I might see her again. I never thought I would see Celia inside that church. I walked in, and as my eyes adjusted to the dim light of the vestibule from the bright sunshine outside, there she was, standing hesitantly outside the doorway to the meeting room. I stopped, my feet frozen to the steamy mosaic tiles. With my overstuffed baby bag over my shoulder and Mirielle in my arms, I stared at Celia from behind. She stood stuck in her place, too. This had once been a safe place for Mirielle and me. Celia must've sensed me there. She turned to face me, and her eyes dropped to my bundle. She was dressed in a casual sundress; even her hair was different, the humidity waving its tips.

"Congratulations, Tessa." She looked from Mirielle to me. The light cotton bundle I clutched moved this way and that.

"Is Mary not here today?" I asked. I appreciated the role Celia played in letting me have the truth, but I didn't know if I could stay if she was running group. With her in charge, I certainly couldn't tell the group what I came here to say. I couldn't say out loud that it helped a little, to know a scared kid killed Abby by accident, instead of thinking my precious daughter was lost to me because of the actions of an irrepressible drunk.

"Mary is here today," Celia said. "I'm not here as a professional."

She glanced toward the meeting room and then back to me. "I'm here as a mother."

"Celia, your son? I heard he was doing better." We both knew of our unending connection to each other. She'd been filled in on me and my baby, and I'd been filled in on her and her child. A boy. One I'd never once wished the kind of harm I'd wished upon his father.

She looked down as she switched her handbag from one arm to the other. "Ian's actually doing pretty well—physically."

Then like the old Celia, the one who knew what I was thinking, sometimes long before I did, she looked into my eyes and told me what she was doing standing there.

"I didn't come to lead the group or talk about Ian and how terrible he feels about what happened. I lost my daughter ten years ago. Her name was Summer. Instead of fighting my way through the pain of losing her like you did, I let the sea of pain drag my family under." She started to reach out to touch Mirielle's cap-covered head and then rethought it, not certain I would let anyone from her family touch another one of my children.

"I imagine you hate every one of us for the part we played in Abby's death. I don't expect you to care about what we did or didn't do with our feelings for Summer. I didn't face her death then, but I need to face it now." Celia moved two steps closer to me, as she moved away from the meeting room and toward the door to the street.

"I can find a different place to do it."

I didn't speak. I didn't think it through. I was done analyzing every thought and feeling, every single thing I'd done for the last ten months. I looked at Mirielle's face for strength. I simply reached down, took Celia's hand, and we walked into the meeting together.

acknowledgments

All my gratitude begins and ends with my husband and best friend, Tom Griffin. He has believed in this story and my ability to tell it since the day I put the first words down on the page. My circle of support is wider and richer because of my wonderful children. I am deeply grateful to Caitlin and Stephen Griffin for generously offering me the time I needed to write this novel, but more important for the unconditional love they offer me every day. It is the depth of my love for them that has enabled me to imagine this story.

The ripple effect continues with a circle of remarkable people who have supported my writing. A true and genuine blessing in my life is my writers' group. From the moment I arrived at the first meeting, nervously clutching the first ten pages of this novel, I have been indebted to Lisa Marnell, Amy MacKinnon, and Hannah Roveto. As women and as writers, they astonish me.

I'd like to thank the rich community of writers that make up Grub Street in Boston. I've met so many writers I admire and learned so much about living a literary life since becoming connected to this nurturing group of talented people.

Sincere appreciation belongs to my impressive editor, Hilary Teeman. From the beginning, she grasped the importance of this redemptive story about truth and healing. Her deft editorial touch and strong leadership have been indispensable. I'd also like to extend thanks to my amazing team at St. Martin's Press, which includes Shelly Peron, Michael Storrings, Sarah Goldstein, Rachel Ekstrom, Lisa Senz, George Witte, and Sally Richardson. I've been warmly accepted and my book enthusiastically championed every step of the way.

As always, enormous recognition must go to my extraordinary agent, Elisabeth Weed. She is forever there to offer the precious gifts of honesty and perspective. For her commitment to challenging me to become a better writer ever-present, Elisabeth is in a class by herself. Every writer should be so fortunate to have her representation.

And to the parents who've shared their grief stories with me: This story of hope is for you.